SAVING GRACE

SAVING GRACE

R. W. JONES

St. Martin's Press
New York

Library of Congress Cataloging in Publication Data
Jones, R. W. (Roger William), 1941-
    Saving Grace.

    I. Title.
PR6060.0576S38 1986   823'.914   86-1862
ISBN 0-312-69986-7

First published in Great Britain by Michael Joseph Ltd.

10 9 8 7 6 5 4 3 2

*For my mother and father, with love
and gratitude; and for Jill, again.*

SAVING GRACE

Prologue

A taut and slender shadow at the hinge of the curtain, the woman watched, uneasy. Window-gazing cheapened her; she was by nature neither voyeur nor spy. A tiny movement, a deprecatory tilt of the head. Don't be absurd, she chided herself. There is no shame in waiting for Caroline.

Drizzle diffused the streetlights and blurred the glass like tears. The bus drifted into view, massive and cheerful, its wheels hissing and spewing spray. Civilisation, she thought in relief, is only indifference to the elements; Caroline will be warm and dry. A sigh of air-brakes, the chug of an idle engine. Around the shelter, a mushrooming of umbrellas, a flurry of motion, indistinct figures rising and descending. A couple trudged away, muffled and stolid. A tall man lifted his collar and thrust his briefcase into the rain. The bus shuddered and rolled past, its slogan loud in the sodium glare; the Sunshine Breakfast. Her faint, ironic smile widened in anticipation. In a moment Caroline would appear, raincoat flapping, pigtail aloft, white-clad ankles flashing above the puddles. She would storm the hallway breathless and aglow, full of weekend pleasure and the antics of her schoolmate's household. But she didn't. The shelter stood deserted, an empty island in the flowing street. Later, Grace Yardley would recall the feeling exactly, a first flicker of anxiety quickly controlled and dismissed. She turned away, made herself tea, and resumed her vigil.

'Pound to a mouldy leek, City stuff 'em Wednesday. Playin brilliant, they are.'

Sunday night at the nick, confinement, rain and the pubs shut; just like mid-Wales. Jolted out of nostalgia, Evans eyed

1

the speaker narrowly. Beddoes wore his barrer-boy look; sharp, provocative, faintly predatory. Come out and play, invited the dark intelligent eyes, I'm bored. Cued by exaggerated cockney, Evans slipped comfortably into his own idiom.

'Gamblin on the Sabbath? For shame, mun! Where's your decency, then?'

'Sanctimonious Welsh git!'

'Oho, big words, is it. Bin watchin Beeb Two by mistake, have we?'

'Hobserver actually, ole boy. News of the Screws sold out.'

'There's a pity. Blighted your whole weekend, I bet.'

Beddoes cackled gleefully.

'Gotcha! Now 'oo's gamblin on Sunday? C'mon then, 'ow about City?'

'Soccer,' said Evans with vast contempt. 'Common as dirt. Long-haired ponces kissing and cuddling and sleeping in their vests. Call that *sport*?'

'La-di-da,' sang Beddoes. 'Shampers and bonomee at Twickers, what. 'Ow d'you get in, I ask meself, an uppity Celtic peasant?'

'Not me, boyo. *Good show, cheps, and O do pull finga, Quins.* Chinless fairyland!'

''Ard bein a forriner, innit.'

'Football, now,' continued Evans, aloof and bardic, 'is a phenomenon peculiar to the Valleys.'

'Peculiar's right, mate. Poison dwarfs singin, miners wrestlin in the mud. Bleedin ball's not even *round*!'

The exotic insults flowed and Evans let them. It passed the time.

The telephone checked Beddoes in full flow.

'Stone me, somebody loves us.' He gave his name, listened, reached for his notebook. Something in his manner alerted Evans; no-side, time to be policemen again. Beddoes set the receiver down and faced him, calm and sober.

'Short straw for you, Blodwyn. Seems you gotta runaway.'

Chief Justice Sir George Stanmore was elderly and running to fat. So far, Nigel Buxton had observed no hint of the incisive brain which lurked behind the CJ's bucolic facade. Still revelling in recently bestowed silk, Nigel had endured soggy sprouts and memoirs, comforted only by the elegance of the setting. The Lady Wife, to whom milud deferred frequently, accepted tribute as her due and peered down her nose at the newly elevated.

Nigel's dinner companion, chosen for more obvious talents, revealed an unexpected social grace. Gushing over period furniture, bone china and moderate silverware, she slowly thawed her hostess. Then, training false eyelashes and an eminently natural cleavage on the judge, she proceeded to shameless flattery. Nigel left his mind in neutral and coasted along on pleasantries.

'Judicial chaos,' confided Stanmore, to a prim nod from his spouse and a flashing smile from Theresa. 'Gaols overflowing, whippersnappers on the benches, Wets in the Home Office. Enforcement castrated by the media – pardon, my dear – where will it end, I ask myself? Can't have law without order, what? Like religion without sin.'

Under his sly gaze, Theresa tittered. Lovely verb, Nigel thought; and the old man chortled at his own wit.

At last, Theresa was enjoined to powder her nose. A ghostly retainer delivered decanters, and Nigel composed himself for ordeal by Madeira.

In drier style, Stanmore conducted a rapid tour of the judicial hierarchy; who was climbing, who had stuck, who had begun the slow but irreversible decline.

'Don't do this for everyone, m'boy. Not all acolytes are called, y'know.'

'I'm mindful of the privilege, sir.'

'You've done well, young Buxton. Some memorable triumphs, damsels in distress, and so on. Solid research, a sound turn of phrase, a shrewd touch with the jury.'

'You flatter me, sir.'

The sharp old eyes narrowed, a touch of frost on the geniality. 'I never do that, Buxton. Don't be coy.' He quaffed port and shoved the decanter across. Subdued light made ruby shards of the crystal.

'Time to steady down, m'boy, take up the slack. More law

3

and less histrionics, d'you see. Too much dazzle upsets the establishment. Blinds 'em to real achievement.'

Nigel weighed this advice cautiously.

'I don't honestly see myself as dazzling, Sir George. Just bumble along from one brief to the next.'

'Hmph. Bumble, you say? Curious word. Ever thought of marrying?'

Half a mellow mouthful went down the wrong way, causing Nigel some discreet spluttering. Solemn and apparently unaware, Stanmore ran on blandly.

'This young lady tonight, for instance. Charming, decorative and – hm – compliant, no doubt, but surely no part of your long-term plans?'

'Ah, I haven't really given it much thought, sir.'

'You should, m'boy, indeed you should. Steadies a man wonderfully, marriage, gives him a bit of depth, d'you see. The Valentino image sits ill on men of our vocation, fiction johnnies notwithstanding. Shall we join the ladies?'

Stunned and deflated, Nigel tagged along. It was years since he'd experienced a wigging ...

... And somewhere amid the rainswept warrens of dockland, a man conveyed a grisly cargo. For him, the freezing wind and desolate alleys were friends; unique in this foul night, he sought darkness and solitude. The upward dashboard glow played on hollow cheeks and darting eyes. His breath came short and tight, and he cleared the misted screen with impatient, spastic swipes. His mind adrift and vacant, he felt no remorse, only the instinctual terror of the hunted animal.

As the epilogue faded from twenty million screens, he bore the heavy shroud along a mouldering wharf. Bending in the silent dark, his neck exposed, he cringed against the sudden light of discovery. Waiting, petrified, he heard only the whisper of the waiting river. A grunt of effort, a spreading bulge on the pimpled, odorous water, an explosive sigh of release. Stumbling and lurching, hunched and drenched and sweating, he ran for the car. Inside, breathless, he coaxed the engine to life. His mouth gaped in soundless relief, and his hand writhed stickily in his lap ...

Chapter One

You're barmy, boyo, Evans told himself for the fourth time in less than a mile. Local people, local turf, let Beddoes drive in the rain. That's what sergeants are for, even bright ones; not swilling tea and calling hospitals. A layer of gunge smeared the windscreen and he stabbed the washer button irritably. Nothing happened. Ararat in the streets and the reservoir dry. Bloody typical.

Moodily, he foresaw the nature of his reception. The father, sullen and embarrassed; what did we do to deserve this, she's in for a hiding when she gets home. A distraught mother; she's our baby, you will find her won't you? Haggard faces, stilted gestures, halting replies. Didn't show that on *The Sweeney*, did they. So why had he come? Duty and boredom make masochists of us all, he thought, and wagged his head at the pomposity.

He parked and cased the locality through bleared glass. Gracious semis and cosseted lawns. Tidy, even in the wet. 'Dunroamin' for retired professionals, halfway house for the climbers, seclusion for the modestly successful. Who'd turn their backs on this: why do kids do anything? He sighed and launched himself across the slick pavement.

She opened the door at once, a slender silhouette against the hall light. She'd been waiting, of course. During ritual foot-wiping, coat-shedding and introductions, he studied the back-drop. Regency paper, fitted carpet, Scandinavian furniture and no telly. A parlour, then. Probably she called it the lounge. Accepting a chair and refusing a drink, he settled himself deliberately and opened his notebook. Subtly projected calm, he knew, could be as infectious as terror.

She paced as she talked, blind to his covert assessment. Early thirties, he guessed, pale and brunette. Her suit was classically tailored, her hair smooth and lustrous; she took good care of herself. No hint yet of deterioration, the surrender of appearances to anxiety. Fine bones, slim hips, elegant legs. In another time and place he might have found her very fetching.

The story unfolded. Caroline was a sunny, well-adjusted child, clever at school, level-headed and responsible. She'd spent the weekend with friends, nothing unusual, a regular exchange. It was frightening, inexplicable. She'd *never* been late, she had no reason. Evans had heard it all before. Runaways.

As she spoke, Evans sensed a distance and a reserve, an air of rigid containment. It was as though every word must be forced, reluctant confessions to an importunate priest. Grace Yardley, he realised, was a very private person. And something else, something in her movements and the way she held herself; something scarcely perceived and not yet defined.

She faltered only once when telling of the lonely wait. The third bus had come and gone; she'd phoned the Woods.

'Caroline was fine, but she'd left early.' Evans, alerted, looked up quickly. She'd turned away, head bowed, shoulders drooping. 'She wanted to reach the market before it closed. To buy a present for me. If only she hadn't!'

Her posture invited the comfort of familiar arms. The illusion of completeness vanished. Evans, appalled at his own denseness, asked the obvious questions.

'Where's your husband, Mrs Yardley? Does he know about this?'

Visibly steadying herself, she faced him, her eyes bright, her hands tightly clasped.

'It's *Miss* Yardley, Inspector. I'm not married. Caroline was a love-child. Illegitimate, if you prefer.'

Coming hard upon the first, this revelation left him groping, raising the darkest of suspicions in his mind. He wished he'd looked more closely at the clothing in the hall. Had Miss Yardley left the house today? Clearly misinterpreting his silence, she spoke quite sharply.

'Shocked, Inspector? You shouldn't be. One-parent families are considered chic, I'm told. This is, after all, an age of

6

promiscuity.' A brief, negligent wave of the hand encompassing the whole room. 'Caroline never lacked for comfort; or love.'

He caught his balance, aware of a gulf of understanding he couldn't bridge. Her tense, not her status, had confounded him. A slip of the tongue, or something more sinister?

'Forgive me, ma'am. I'm sure she doesn't. A surprise, that's all. Sorry.' She gave him a quizzical, almost pitying glance. Men are not indispensable. She had a point, no question.

'Sit down ma'am, please. We've a way to go yet.'

She obeyed, unwilling and uncomfortable on the very edge of the sofa. Her slim ringless fingers twisted in her lap.

'Caroline went to a mixed school. Lots of friends, you said. Angela, Jean, Debbie, right?'

'Yes.' Faintly defiant, sensing his drift and building barriers.

'Not a boy on the horizon anywhere, then?'

'Of course not!'

'Not of course, Miss Yardley. Oh, you do your best, no doubt. Protection and shelter, love and care. It's not enough, see. We can't escape, it's all around us every day. In the cinemas, on the telly, shouting from the bookstalls and the hoardings. Even in school, older ones talk. You said it yourself; a promiscuous age. There's no anchor these days, is there? No religion, no morality, not even convention. In public, I mean. Anything goes. Kids get curious, we have to accept it. They're natural experimenters. Gymslips and ankle-socks or not.'

She rounded on him, very angry.

'For heaven's sake, man, she's only fourteen!'

He couldn't help himself, it slipped out without volition or intent.

'So was Juliet, they say.'

He regretted it at once, recognising his own cynicism and the anguish in her face. Awkwardly, he fumbled for a concession.

'P'raps we could have some tea now.'

She wasn't long about it. She placed the cup beside him and her perfume lingered. For a second time he was conscious of her femininity, the litheness of her carriage, the challenge she

7

wore like armour. And suddenly, he knew. A deeply suppressed, perhaps unwitting sensuality, an instinctive awareness of her own body. Easy, boyo. Been a bachelor too long. She's uptight and skittish, you're dreaming.

Sipping tea, her hands only a little unsteady, she declared the truce.

'What will you do?'

It was unnatural, really. Eerie. Sitting like a statue in this rich and comfortable room, her daughter God knows where, she could ask the question calmly, almost diffidently. Yet he sensed the pent-up misery, the deep bewilderment and pain, and he told her as gently as he could. Cinemas, dance halls, youth clubs; doctors, hospitals, other police stations. Routine. He wanted a photograph and she took one from her handbag. Again the reluctance, as if she were surrendering part of her life. Which, of course, she was. He saw a pretty pigtailed child, blue-eyed and impish.

'Just the job. We'll get this circulated. Maybe someone saw her.'

'Oh.' A soft sound of acute distress and his heart went out to her.

'It *is* an intrusion, fair play. Still, we have to move fast. Time's a factor, see. The quicker the coverage the better the hope.' Her face told him he was whistling in the wind and he hurried on. 'I'll call the station with the description. Thing is, what will you do? You shouldn't be here alone.' She seemed taken aback at his concern, her guard momentarily lowered.

Quietly and without self-pity, she said, 'My parents are dead. I value a few close friends and try not to impose.'

'Our girls are good, you know. Trained, see.'

She drew back, her eyebrows high and eloquent.

'A policewoman, a stranger? Really, I couldn't; thank you.'

'Call your doctor then. Get something to sleep.' He paused, gauging her emotions, awed by her control, 'It will be a hard night for you.' He went to phone Beddoes.

When he returned she was prowling again. Grace, he thought fleetingly, very apt. She chose words, a statement of position.

'My parents were rather – provincial – Inspector. They

8

found Caroline, their only grandchild, something of a social embarrassment. Or perhaps it was me. Anyway, they gave very little and too late. I brought her up alone. I'll wait for her the same way.'

Madness, though he had to admire it. She was watching him now, the long-contained defiance open.

'One more thing, Inspector. Whatever you believe, Caroline is not joy-riding and neither has she shacked up with some boy. I'm her mother and I know.'

Rising to leave, he kept his response to himself. I hope to God you're wrong.

She'd never had police to the house and at first he had dismayed her. His height and bulk seemed alien and vaguely menacing; at odds with the scale of her home. The freckled face, pale eyes and carroty hair repelled her; she didn't care for the Welsh. Despite her distraction, she'd seen him pricing her carpets, read the small envy in his gaze. Civility had cost her an enormous effort.

In the event, he'd proved gentle and perceptive. A massively reassuring presence, an unselfconscious voice, a man devoid of pretence. Then, even as she warmed to him, the usual reaction to Caroline's parentage. She hadn't expected it of him, such prejudice. Chauvinism, the Non-conformist narrowness, or merely some reflection on his own private life? She dismissed the trivial mystery impatiently, she hadn't time for other people's troubles.

In one way, he'd been prophetic. Silence echoed around her, fear and loneliness invaded her mind. The shored-up horrors of the evening broke loose and surged against her self-control. She found herself once more at the curtain, her whole being focused on the desolate shelter. Reason mocked her. If Caroline returned, it would not be by bus; and she abandoned reason to faith. Despite the warmth at her back, she was shivering violently.

Her eyes are haunted grey, Evans decided. Haunted by what? *Caroline was a love-child*. Was? Hell, there might be a drunken sailor in the bedroom and a dismembered corpse in the loft.

9

That he could think it measured how little she'd revealed and how much he had to learn. A very composed lady. Damn, I shouldn't've left her alone. Those as can't bend must break.

How did a single woman keep a house like that? Must be worth sixty grand. A legacy, maybe, the last penance of 'provincial' parents. What about maintenance? No shortage of cash there, bach. Patrimony, then. She'd taken a fall with a high-rolling Catholic years ago and lived on conscience money. How about this: a babysitter twice a week while she gets cosy with the moguls. Plenty of blokes fancy the ice-maiden touch – Huw Evans for one. The trouble with chapel is the glitter it paints on sin. Give over, boyo, guesswork's for punters. It's the girl you're after.

He shifted gears and wiped condensation from the screen. Where do you look for a runaway fourteen-year-old girl at nine on a wet Sunday night? A question he could answer at last. You don't. Not physically anyway. You seek her in the people she knows. Once you discover the company she keeps, it's only elimination. Subconsciously he'd accepted this, was already edging towards a known destination. Edging, because he could summon little enthusiasm. He'd had enough aggro for one day.

A taxi, travelling much too fast, cut him up and was gone before he could take the number. Mad bugger. Then he pictured her, tense and solitary, waiting at the window for a bus which would never arrive. She had a right and he had a duty; that bloody word again.

The Woods restored him. A concerned, taciturn father, a homely and comfortable wife, a hint of the down-to-earth North in their voices. Through them he saw the Yardley females more rationally. Caroline, though shy on the surface, was bubbly and impulsive underneath. Open-handed and girlish, young for her age. Grace, they thought, was simply grand. Quiet, stylish, well-off but nice. No airs, no attitudes, not a bit uppity, though she had every cause, mind. Lived for Caroline, tried not to smother her, took a turn as hostess to the girls and no nonsense.

Debbie Woods had walked Caroline to the market. 'To see her away, like,' Mrs Woods explained, garrulous with worry.

10

'The big one, you know, near the docks. Some nice bargains to be had there, I will say. The lass bought a lovely vase, our Debbie says. Been saving her pocket-money, she had. A pretty thing, our Debbie says, fine, like you could almost see through. A nice pattern, violets they were, and it looked old. The lass couldn't wait to be home for her mum's surprise. Oh, it's an awful bother. She'll be *all right*, won't she?'

The room was a shambles. Scrapbooks and heart throbs, gonks and jig-saws, Sindy and Action Man. The childish debris of a rainy weekend. Beware of the kids. Which brought him to his central purpose and quite unexpected resistance.

'Debbie's in her bed,' Frank Woods said firmly. 'Bin there an hour or more. Wake her now, you'll get nowt. You're polis and a stranger, she'd be out of her wits. We'll break it in the morning, gently like, and keep her from school. Come around nine.'

Unassailable logic. You can't pull rank on common sense. Better to preserve the amenities, set up the ballyhoo and get started on the report. At the door, Frank Woods muttered, 'Good luck, Inspector. 'Appen you'll nail the bastard.'

Evans stared at him in consternation.

'Here now, steady on, sir. Early days yet.'

'Mebbe. Listen, that little girl'd never give her mother the worry. Wherever she is, she didn't go on her own accord. Don't fret, I'll say nowt to the women. It's bloody wicked.'

More driving in the rain, more introspection. Thus far, the vote for Caroline seemed unanimous, which brought him no comfort whatever. If the Woods' judgement and a mother's intuition could be trusted ... But he couldn't tell, yet. One precocious teenager had already come to mind and now he remembered another. Lolita. Stranger things have happened; though not many.

Grace Yardley continued to puzzle and elude him. Still waters if ever he'd seen them. In domestic affairs, the Woods' opinion carried weight. Securely married and family-oriented, they would not lightly give the nod to an unwed mother – if they knew her as such. Still, they were essentially charitable folk, taking others at face value. Caroline was cherished, which put her mother beyond reproach. Should Miss Yardley

11

Senior emerge as the Harlot of Maida Vale, they would simply refuse to believe it. At this point, Evans owned no such certainty.

Beddoes had left a note, a hasty ballpoint scrawl: 'Hospitals and outstations informed, also our noble foot brigade. Piccy urgently needed. All response negative (10 p.m.). Tea's cold and so am I. See you at Sparrers. P.S. City for the cup.' Evans tore it to confetti over the wastebin. Daft, insensitive young sod. He sighed. Fair play; for all Roy Beddoes knew, it was a straightforward runaway. But somehow, as he hauled out the typewriter, he doubted it.

Rain sluicing the gutter bulged over an obstruction, a fine jagged shard. Slowly the pressure built. The shard shifted, drifted, held. In time, it neared a gurgling drain-cover. A car crawled past and the backwash foamed. The shard rose, swirled madly, and vanished. In that instant, the streetlight fixed it sharply; small mauve flowers on white porcelain.

Chapter Two

Though he couldn't hear the rain, Nigel Buxton knew it was there; somewhere behind brocade curtains and double glazing, it leaned and dripped stealthily. There is no finer place on a night like this, he thought, than bed with a spectacularly naked young woman. Sipping Beaujolais, he drawled an appropriate line.

'A jug of wine, a crust of bread and thee.'

'Thou,' murmured Theresa drowsily.

'*Tee aitch ee*,' he countered, 'get it?'

'Oh. Personalised poetry. How clever.'

'Beauty and the brain.'

'You got the quote wrong in three places.'

'I do so love a literate houri.'

'Do you?'

She stirred and shifted, stretching her long legs as unself-consciously as a cat. For the moment he was content to watch, his enjoyment purely visual, as soft shadows played on her body. Not for the first time, he wondered how someone so perfect could bear his own flawed physique. Tall, lean and passably handsome, he relied on an erect bearing and expensive tailors to disguise incipient flabbiness.

Relaxed and exposed on the duvet, he was conscious of an unseemly paunch and spindly shanks. Experience comforted him. As long as a willing bloodflow stood the test, she wouldn't complain. Wealth and a vigorous libido were sufficient aphrodisiac.

Theresa propped herself against a pillow and drained her glass. Her breasts were remarkable – only the faintest of concessions to gravity. She caught his eye and smiled.

'Enjoying the scenery?'

13

'Very much.'

'You're a disgraceful old letch.'

'Careful. Not so much of the old. You didn't seem to mind milud's breathy leer.'

'What am I supposed to do, confess my passion for senile voyeurs?'

'It is Sunday and Theresa's a good Catholic name.'

'You're not dressed for it.'

'Use your imagination.'

She set the glass aside and he divined a cooler atmosphere. 'Remember, you asked for it.'

She bowed her head and closed her eyes in mock contrition. 'Oh, Father. I have lain with a man who is not my husband. I have sinned and enjoyed it. But my heart is heavy, for I am becoming involved and I am afraid. What should I do, Father?' She gazed at him, straight and level. 'There.'

'Oh dear. Wrong profession, my child. The problem is strictly medical. Post-coital melancholia and female complications. Lie down, relax, it will pass. Just keep taking the pills.'

'Stop it, Nigel. I'm serious for once.'

He released her and sat up, miffed.

'What brought this on, old thing?' And, in a flash of insight, demanded, 'What poison did the dragon lay down?'

'You're quick, Nigel, I'll say that for you. She was hateful. Bombazine and disapproval, pure Victoriana.' She assumed a prissy face and a severe voice. 'Law, Miss Da Silva, is a very *strict* calling. Its practitioners must be *wholly* beyond reproach. A single man is suspect, d'you see; what people don't know they will invent. So difficult for those with ambition, my dear. Mr Buxton is such a promising young man. A pity if his career were – impeded, you understand.'

'Cow,' Nigel muttered, and Theresa nodded.

'At least.' A beat, a mustering of resolve; then, 'You're a womaniser, aren't you, Nigel?'

It was not a new charge and he had his rebuttal ready.

'A womaniser regards sex as a field of conquest; a scalp collector. For him, women are objects, not individuals. Does that sound like me?'

She would permit no concession.

14

'What are you, then?'

'I really don't care for inquisitions, old thing. *Ve* ask der questions!'

'Don't wriggle Nigel. You're not in court now.'

'You could've fooled me.'

'I'm waiting.'

'You missed your vocation. You'd make a formidable barrister.'

'I just did. And I'm still waiting.'

'No stay of execution?'

'Not even an adjournment.' For an aspiring actress, Nigel allowed, she was really rather bright.

'Very well. This time, *you* asked for it. Women fascinate me, Theresa. Their faces, their bodies, the way they move. God help me, even their minds enslave me. If you want me to be serious you mustn't snigger.'

'Sorry.'

'Forsaking all others seems awfully final. I couldn't guarantee it, would hate to swear it. Oddly enough, I set some store by oaths. Know thyself, all right? Would you believe I once fell in love three times in a single day? Naturally polygamous, I'm afraid.'

'I hope you never have to face a jury with that one.'

He grinned ruefully. 'Me too.' Seeing her expression, he added quietly, 'Look, Theresa, I never made any promises, did I?'

She sighed, a delightful sight.

'You're honest, if nothing else.'

'Listen, old thing, it's a conspiracy. The Stanmore Commission on Judicial Morality. The old goat gave me the same line. Hypocritical swine!' She raised her eyebrows, curious in spite of herself.

'Rest at ease, my lovely. I have a tale to tell.'

'A diversion, you mean.'

'May I proceed, milud?'

'You're going to anyway.'

'Thank you. Stanmore's father was landed gentry, estates in Cornwall, the feudal syndrome. Rumour hath it George was raised in the shade of *droit de seigneur*. A regular nature boy, a

15

milkmaid's delight. The serfs, one must assume, tolerated it. They hadn't much choice. There are sophisticated women, you know, who crave the masterful approach, and young Georgie sowed wild oats in some very rich soil. Literally shagged his way to the top, if you'll excuse the indelicacy.'

'O you do talk naice.'

'A tool of the trade. The story has substance, but it's not the whole truth. When Stanmore lifts his sights above the crotch, he's nobody's fool. To a large degree, he prospered on merit. But old habits die hard, and George's eye continued to wander. Things came to a head in farcical style. He was hearing a rape case and the defendant's lawyer was a statuesque and sporty blonde. When the jury retired she was summoned to his chambers. It appears the bell sounded at a singularly inopportune moment; they hadn't even time to dress. He delivered sentence red-faced, breathless and bare-assed beneath the robes. The press attributed it to wrathful indignation at a foul crime; the Bar knew better. For years he was known as Courthouse Interruptus.'

She had moved closer and her laughter produced seductive contact of breast and thigh; and a predictable reaction.

'My,' she murmered huskily. 'What have we here?'

'Don't you want the end of it?'

'I want it all."

Later, she asked sleepily, 'What *was* the end of it?'

'He married the dragon, went straight, and rose to his current lofty perch.'

'Well, then.'

'Sorry. The defence rests.'

Evans slept badly, woke early and reached the station before the cleaners left. No messages. For a while he toyed with the report while instinct and reason warred. In the end he called her.

She must've been waiting; she answered at the first ring. 'Yes?'

'It's me, Evans. Nothing from this side. Sorry.'

Amazing the depth of feeling she could bring to a single sound. He imagined her, bowed and hopeless, and tried for a

16

commonplace tone, a semblance of normality. It was easier from a distance.

'I saw the Woods, found a reference point. We'll have someone at the market by now. Debbie was in bed. I'm off there any minute. After, I'll go to school, talk to her friends, see.' A long pause. 'Are you still there?'

She sounded lost and strained. 'Please, before then, I have to talk to you.'

'They're keeping Debbie home. They're expecting me.'

'No, not the Woods, it's about school. Please.' Her voice shook in wholly uncharacteristic supplication.

'All right. I'll come. After Debbie.'

Frank Woods had left and Debbie faced him nervously. He sat down, made himself small, took her tactfully through the litany; and achieved nothing fresh. No, no boyfriend. A fifth former had eyes for her. Debbie thought him 'super' but Caroline had laughed and called him soppy. Evans took note of what she was wearing and the name of the market stall. Delicately, against stiff resistance, he extracted the name of the soppy boy and told her, 'Now, lovely, you think hard then. If you remember anything, anything at all unusual, you tell your mum and she'll tell me, OK?'

She nodded solemnly, gazing up at him. Her eyes were damp and wary. 'Has something nasty happened? She was my best friend.'

Again the slip of tense.

Prudently, Mrs Woods intervened. 'Here now, our Debbie, no time for old gossip. You're late already.'

And Evans had to be content with another good character reference.

As before, Grace Yardley was waiting – what else would she do? He actually saw the curtains flicker as he drew up. Though pale and drawn, she looked immaculate as ever. Another model suit, a hint of make-up, every hair in place. Bandbox. For a wild moment, he imagined the effort might be for him; then sanity prevailed. She would do as much for any visitor.

They exchanged the barest of courtesies, and she cried; 'I don't want you to go to school!'

17

'Oh? and why would that be, ma'am?'

She set herself to persuade; again he saw how appealing she might be.

'You're going to ask questions, make innuendoes. You know what people are like, what they'll say, teachers, children, everyone. *There's no smoke without fire.* She has to go back there, don't you understand? She'll be someone different, to look at slyly and wonder and giggle. I won't allow it.'

Yesterday she had consigned her daughter to the past; already she was concerned for the future. He'd seen this before, too, among the tough ones. Sometime last night, he reckoned, she'd touched bottom, rebelled, and fought her way back into some sort of light. An act of faith. Well, he knew a bit about that himself. He had a logical counter, of course. If Caroline returned, the whole world would be changed, not just school. He kept his peace; this step she must take herself. Instead, he clung to practicality, the lore of his trade.

'It's a question of sources, see. Nothing's taken for granted, even a mother's word. No offence, mind. I need to know how others saw her. There's no better place to start.'

'It's not how she's seen but what she is!'

'Maybe I'm not saying it right. There's such a thing as negative evidence.' He felt her disbelief like a living force and sought to deflect it. 'Are you a wealthy person, ma'am?'

'I – What on earth . . .?' Her grey eyes widened as comprehension dawned. 'You think she's been kidnapped?'

'It's possible.'

'Very well. The house is mine. I have a reasonable salary. I'd give everything tomorrow, but no one would become a millionaire.'

'See what I mean? Negative evidence.'

She shot him a glance of cold reproach. 'Please don't play games, Inspector.'

'I wouldn't presume, believe me.'

'Proving your points, then. Call it what you will. You'll go to the school anyway, I gather.' She'd left him no choice, demanded the truth no matter how stark.

'All right, Miss Yardley, I'll say it plain. First we have to find Caroline; after, you can worry about the homecoming.' It

18

was as though he had struck her, exposed the vulnerable feminine core.

'Oh! But of course. Please excuse me. I'm a little – overwrought.' As close as she could bring herself to revealing her agony and he let up at once.

'It's routine, really. Low-key, very discreet, mind.'

'I suppose you must have to do this often.' He sensed the effort this cost her and heard the unspoken plea.

'More often than I'd care to. It's the sensible way, see, the reasoned approach.' She waited, but he said no more, not giving her false hopes. She'd enough to carry already.

From her parents she'd absorbed an attitude to policemen. Their presence in a house spelt social disaster. Evans, to his credit, had disabused her. Such genteel ethics hampered the search for her daughter. She felt drained and unsteady, her beliefs crumbling, her resources stretched beyond their limit. The present was too much with her and she took refuge in the past ...

She grew up a solitary, cosseted and pretty child. At an early age she discovered a gift for numbers which blossomed into real mathematical talent. This curious inheritance thrust her into almost exclusively male territory; she became a tomboy. The pose lasted through adolescence and into her late teens. By this time she'd outgrown her peers both physically and intellectually, but her emotional and sexual awakening still lay ahead.

The chance discovery of computer science opened new horizons to her. In the face of desperate parental opposition, she declined a university place and joined the fledgling computer industry. She inhabited a man's world, dressing severely, making few concessions to femininity and losing herself in the intricacies of programming. Thus, as she later realised, when Mr Wrong finally appeared, she was more than ripe for him.

Tony Adams was thirty and divorced, a softwear salesman with a Jaguar and a reputation. Assured and sophisticated, he'd cut a swathe through the company's female workforce. Grace's colleagues called him the Sec's Dream.

19

Meeting him casually, she'd found him conceited and over-familiar.

It began in mundane circumstances, as she walked to her car one day. His approach was uncharacteristically tentative.

'Miss Yardley, may I speak to you a moment?'

'Oh. Actually, I'm in rather a hurry.'

'It won't take long.'

She hesitated, trapped by natural politeness; and was lost. He gave her a lopsided and engaging grin.

'I've been chatting to your colleagues. Made an ass of myself, I'm afraid. You see, I find you very attractive. They told me you were aloof and cold and allergic to men. Wait! Please don't be angry!'

She felt the blush and spoke icily.

'Mr Adams, my colleagues' opinions mean nothing to me. Neither do yours, for that matter.'

'Don't blame you. But you see I made a bet. A tenner you'd come to dinner and the ballet. I have tickets for Wednesday, *Swan Lake*. Look, it's strictly above board. I'm sure you'd enjoy it.'

He'd been clever, ballet was her only passion. Even so, resenting the presumption, she was prepared to spite herself.

'I have no desire to help you gamble, Mr Adams.'

'Fair enough, the bet's off. But come anyway. I'll gladly give up a tenner for the privilege of your company.' He stood before her humble and handsome, the very image of a model suitor. She wavered and he grasped his opportunity.

'Don't decide now, I'll ring you tomorrow. Please think about it carefully.'

He smiled and turned away; she would have to shout to deny him. And of course, she went.

For the first time she took trouble over her appearance, and won his frank admiration.

'My God,' he told her, 'I was right. You're stunning!' Later she was glad she'd bothered.

His knowledge of the dance surprised and impressed her, and he behaved impeccably. In a theatre bar bursting with glamour and *décolletage*, he gave her his whole attention. His eyes never left her, and she blossomed under his effortless

20

charm. It was an evening of delight, a taste of the purely female pleasure she had so long avoided.

At her gate in the small hours, she asked, 'Will you collect your bet?'

'Of course not. I'll say they were right and pay up with a smile. It's our secret.'

'Thank you. And for a really lovely time.' A moment's indecision, should she allow herself to be kissed?

He took her hands and squeezed them warmly. 'My pleasure. We must do it again soon.' And was gone.

In the weeks that followed, Tony Adams showed her a new world. She marvelled at her own body, at the pleasure it brought her, at the effect it had on him. Expertly and gently, step by careful step, he led her deeper into sensual experience; until, one summer evening, she lay abandoned to him on the wide back seat, trembling uncontrollably. Lifting his mouth from her breast he murmured, 'You've never made love properly, have you?

'You know it.'

'It shouldn't be like this. Come back to the flat.'

She tensed, trapping his hand between her thighs. 'Our secret?'

'Of course.'

At the flat, he gave her coffee, played her music, let her make the pace. Then, in fading light, he undressed her and showed her the hunger she provoked.

'I was only half right about you,' he whispered. 'You're magnificent.'

And she believed him.

It lasted six months. Half a year in which she lived two wholly separate lives. To parents, acquaintances and colleagues she remained sober and conscientious, the dutiful daughter, dedicated worker and unawakened virgin. So far as she knew, Tony kept his word. She encountered no curious glances and overheard no gossip. Sometimes at night she would stand before the mirror and wonder at herself. Her eyes, her body, her movements were all subtly changed; she was amazed no one else had noticed.

Alone with Tony, the transformation was immediate and

complete. She became a creature of blind passion, wanton and insatiable. She couldn't have enough of him, or he of her. Going to him, she wore casual clothes and no underwear, the faster to be naked. The mirrors in his flat showed another Grace, and she gloried in their reflections. In this way, she learned those small, private movements which gave him most pleasure. Occasionally, in a pub or a theatre, she would rehearse them, fully dressed, and bask in the heat of his glance. She never for a moment doubted she was in love, and knew he felt the same. So, when he told her he'd been offered better money and would be moving away, she simply couldn't believe it.

'Don't worry, love, I'll write,' he said, and, too distraught even to argue, she let him go.

That weekend she drove into the country and walked for hours. With genuine amazement, she realised she hardly knew him. The relationship had been wholly physical, a violent meeting of bodies which left no time for other intimacies. In this one way she would miss him poignantly, would remember him kindly. In leaving, he had wounded her pride, but had given her much and taken little. She returned subdued but whole, pleased at her own good sense and maturity.

Three weeks later she knew she was pregnant.

This time the heart-search probed deeper and took longer. She'd already dismissed him as a man; eventually, she rejected him as a husband. Would she bear his child? She didn't know. Even her sheltered upbringing had permitted discussion of abortion – on moral and abstract levels, of course. It struck her as a messy, sordid and probably painful process; anyway, she'd been taught to accept the consequences of her own actions. And she'd always loved children. Finally, she faced the sternest test of all, and told her parents.

It almost killed her mother. There were long, shapeless, tearful arguments and bitter recriminations. Who was he, why had she never brought him home? How could she be so selfish? Who would support the child? Why should such a rogue escape scot-free? Their convention compelled them to stand by her and they did; but without sympathy or conviction. An expression of duty, not love. Through it all she remained outwardly calm and utterly certain. Never once, then or later, did she reveal his name, nor anything about him. To the end, that would be 'our secret'.

Perhaps they really did try to welcome Caroline; if so, they failed. They could not conceal the shame and embarrassment with which they spoke the child's name. It was this she could never forgive, the visitation of her own sin upon an innocent. The sheer mindless injustice lent her strength through the years of struggle. Without it, she could not have managed alone ...

Dully, she realised the wheel had turned full circle. For the first time in fourteen years, she was dependent on an outsider, a man. Forfeiting independence of mind and spirit, she must allow publicity and police routine to attempt what she, a mother, couldn't. And hope that, like her own mother, she had been excluded from her daughter's most secret life.

Chapter Three

When he returned, Beddoes was there, bright-eyed and dapper.

''Eard you really were in at sparrers. What's up, couldn't you sleep?'

Evans, disinclined to banter, answered shortly, 'Matter of fact, I couldn't.'

'Oho, 'oo's the lucky girl then?'

Smart as a whip, Beddoes, but at times, wearing.

'Out of your league, boyo. Real class, – all on her own, something you wouldn't recognise if it hit you in the eye. I doubt if she feels lucky. Her teenage daughter never came home last night. Another thing. You want to be careful what you write.'

'Your eyes only, wasn't it. What'm I supposed to use, microdots?'

'Just watch it. Use what little common you've got.'

'Sure, sure. So what's with the runaway?'

'School kid, the innocent type. She's still AWOL.'

Beddoes shrugged easily. 'Rich bitch, spoiled brat, 'appens all the time. She'll roll in lunchtime smug an' purrin. Life's great mystery solved and the bit between 'er legs. You're behind the times, uncle. They start early these days.'

'Duw, boyo, I hope you'll never be a father.'

'I take every precaution mate, believe me. Spermicidal jelly's best.'

'Prefer raspberry, I do,' Evans murmured, and the tension dissolved in laughter.

A uniform brought them tea. When he'd gone, Evans asked, 'Any sightings?'

'Usual cranks. Reported at a nightclub with Ronnie Biggs,

someone saw her on a broomstick in Dorset. You know.'

'Aye. Hospitals?'

'Teenagers is off, luv. 'Ere, come on then. Give us a clue.'

Roy Beddoes was young for his rank, had been assigned to Evans to learn the ropes. A likely lad, a natural; sharp, good-humoured and streetwise. He had patience and the listener's gift; women found him irresistible. Evans had high hopes of him; mostly, they got on well.

They'd played this game often – a pooling of abilities. Beddoes's raw intelligence and his own long experience made a formidable combination. Baldly, Evans laid out the facts. Beddoes sniffed, his supercilious face.

'It's a doddle, innit. I mean either she's alive or dead.'

'Darro, there's a brain!'

'Give over. Thinkin aloud.'

'Well at least that shouldn't take long.'

'If she's dead, we wait for the body or till 'e does it again, right?'

'Cheerful bugger, you. You ought to meet the mum. She doesn't think so.'

'OK, so she's alive. Gives us three options, broadly.' Beddoes was concentrating now, eyes intent, cockney under control. 'One, like I said, Gosh superboy, so that's how they make babies, let's do it again. Two, she's gone walkabout. Doting mum, lap of luxury and she's bored. Overdose of security, see. No impact. Gone to be a pop star or nurse refugees in Matabeleland. Don't look like that. It 'appens.'

'Tried for *Opportunity Knocks*, 'ave you?'

'Three, she's been nabbed. Deposit 'alf a million in Venezuela, collect her at midnight near Stonehenge. And don't tell the filth.' Beddoes, favouring the exotic, had nevertheless covered basic possibilities. Working to familiar routine, Evans demolished them.

'She's fourteen and never been kissed. Young for her age. Her mother doesn't *dote*. She hasn't a passport or a guitar. Kidnapping's out. You should listen; I said comfortable, not loaded.'

Beddoes smiled, quite unruffled. 'Right. It's all eyewash. Just testin, grandad.'

25

'Steady on.'

'Sauce for the goose, mate. You bin connin me, tryin a snow job. You slipped it over lovely, never even saw your lips move. Missed it yourself first time round, didn't yer?'

'Dunno what you're on about.'

''Ark at it! And you chapel, too.'

'Stop clucking and lay your egg.'

'There's a feller somewhere broodin, right? Not knowin what became of 'is little accident in the night. Middle-aged now or older, like you. Maybe 'e never planted again, maybe the second crop went sour. It got too much for 'im, 'e's lyin in bed wonderin. Is she thin or fat, 'as she got my nose? 'E had to *know*, see. Go on, tell me, I'm wrong.'

Evans nodded slowly. He'd caught it last evening in her home and she'd thrown him off the scent. Ever since, the phantom figure of Caroline's father had beckoned him.

'You're not bad, boyo. We'll make a copper of you yet.'

'Don't applaud, just throw money.'

'Credit where it's due, fair play. So what's next, genius?'

Beddoes stood up and stretched.

'Shershay lee papa,' he said.

All very well for Beddoes to talk, Evans grumbled to himself, on the road again; but where to start? The girl was fourteen, the father could be anywhere. What had been the craze then? Mods and rockers, Beatlemania, skinheads? No idea, have to check the back-numbers. Waste of time, bach. She wasn't the type for motor-bikes and casual groping. So what had happened? Your friendly Mr Softee gone hard, stop me and buy one? An earnest student, love is free, pay later? A clinical experiment with the boy next door? *Slow down, you're movin' too fast*, warned a hit from his own era; but he was in a groove, and echoes from his youth lured him away ...

Huw Evans grew up before promiscuity surfaced in the Valleys. It had been there, of course, but underground, dark and difficult and secret as the coal. Girls preened and giggled, boys leered and yearned, but no one *did* anything. All gas and no go. X films in Cardiff, the glimpse of nipple which put a strain on the Y-fronts, wet dreams of Bardot in the raw. When would he be old enough to get a share? There *were* fast pieces, everyone knew them. Sharp-faced beauties in tight jumpers and uplift bras, hard-eyed, wide-mouthed, legs your hungry gaze could climb like ladders. Common, his Mam had called them, and she'd been right. But duw, he'd fancied them in his time, had longed for manhood at their hands and bellies. In the end, he waited, like most of his peers; in fear of grubby underwear, disease, and the wrath of his Methodist God.

Eirwen's Dad poured steel and sung first tenor, her Mum made the best Welshcakes in the village. A fresh-faced pony-tailed roly-poly kid two years behind him in school. Then one spring her features matured, the puppy-fat melted and he fell, once and for good. Twenty years old, a trainee copper, playing front row and soft on a girl. It wasn't easy. Off the field and in her presence, co-ordination deserted him. He felt oafish and graceless, a shire horse pursuing an Arab filly. Miraculously, she welcomed his gawky attentions.

Walking out. Best suit and new dress to chapel Sundays, no high heels, mind. Summer strolls on the mountain, holding hands, but shyly. Dances in Ponty, home by eleven though. A decorous courtship, despite growing awareness of each other's minds and bodies. Eirwen's Dad, whom he could've crushed with one hand, tyrannised him cheerfully; Mrs Morgan forbad him washing up, never mind his protests.

'You sit by here, Huw bach. We'll be needing those dishes *next* week.'

They married in winter – recruits don't get leave at holiday time – and honeymooned in a draughty off-season resort hotel. The food was tacky, the service halting and the company moribund. Dark wallpaper and dying plants. Daytimes, muffled against the gales, they romped along deserted sands and laughed like children. At night, by fitful gas-fire glow, she showed him an erotic beauty he could never have imagined; a warmth and sweetness which banished sex symbols and easy girls from his fantasies for ever. Because it was close and real and for him alone. This is how it should be, he thought, in comfort and in private and with all our hearts; and blessed the strictness of his upbringing. Sometimes, as she spoke her love

27

and strained against him, he was grateful for darkness. Then, as now, he thought it unmanly to weep.

He was posted to Aberystwyth, a neat semi-detached overlooking the bay. The sea's nearness pleased them, its magic held them still. It was a peaceful town. Drugs had yet to infiltrate British campuses and the Cardi farmers were too mean for serious drinking. Real crime was almost unknown. Evans rode herd on the students and Eirwen learned Welsh. The idyll continued. Together, they pitied the frenetic cattle-market atmosphere of weekly college dances.

At first they hadn't wanted children. Now they did and nothing happened. Imperceptibly, her marvellous warmth dwindled. She became restrained and reserved, talking of sin and a divine plan. Always staunch chapel, she moved ever nearer to God, and her newfound Welsh sisters applauded. Evans, by no means agnostic himself, took a more pragmatic line. There are tests, new drugs, not to worry, cariad, give it time. Yet he himself fretted. Police work fascinated him and he wasn't doing any. Just a sheepdog, really, keeping the students penned.

One day, alone, he scaled the slate hill beyond the prom. With the sun and wind in his face and a placid sea below, he thought things through. Privately, he'd had the tests, knew himself to be potent. He would not accept barrenness in Eirwen; such love and femininity could not be in vain. Yet she was in retreat, moving steadily from reality into ritual and mysticism. He had to rescue her.

Behind him, gorse bloomed and gulls mewed. There was beauty in him and around him, a deep feeling for land and life. Yet he, too, must leave, for his vocation demanded an encounter with crime. So, from the very purest of motives, he requested transfer to the Smoke.

Deprived of her coven, apprehensive of and unused to city ways, Eirwen turned to him more ardently and frequently. They enjoyed a brief and blazing second honeymoon, this time in a cramped suburban police flat. And still it didn't take. Patiently, valiantly, Evans pressed for specialist advice; stubbornly, Eirwen resisted.

The flats were home to young police couples. Inevitably,

28

Eirwen dwelt among heavy bellies and gurgling infants. The women were altogether more worldly, given to fashionable cleavage and *double entendre*. Eirwen, isolated, estranged and embittered, rejected their well-meant overtures. Innuendo, crime, fashion and gynaecology left her equally cold. The cycle began again.

They talked less and argued more. Eirwen resented the irregular hours and incipient dangers of his work, the absence of familiar voices and the calm Christian air of chapel. Evans, deeply absorbed in his work and often physically exhausted, lost patience. He remembered the final clash almost word for word. His mother had died recently and his emotions were still raw.

They'd been out celebrating a friend's anniversary, a good restaurant. Four couples, all police, two of the women pregnant. As usual, Eirwen had been reserved; unusually, she'd taken a lot of wine. Back home, she undressed and he reached for her; she turned on him like a startled cat.

'Don't touch me! Leave me be!'

'Hey, what's up then?'

'What's up indeed. Sluts, they are, sneering, foul-mouthed little snobs!'

'Aw, come on, luv. They're not so bad.'

'Aye, take their part, go on, same as always. Dresses slit to the navel and lewd talk. Is that what you fancy, then? Pity you didn't marry one, isn't it? Could have all the kids you like!'

'Cariad, cariad, you don't know what you're saying. Leave it now, girl.'

'It can't be left, Huw. Every day I'm hearing it, see a specialist, have tests. What about you then? Sauce for the goose, boy.'

An unguarded moment, a quite unwarranted attack and the words spilled out, no time for thought.

'Me? I've *had* the tests, girl, I'm all right, see.'

The shock stopped her dead and pain took her like fever.

'When?' she whispered, her eyes wide and wild. 'You never told me.'

He tried to embrace her, the old clumsiness flaring in the heat of crisis. She stood, stiff and unyielding, in his arms.

29

'Why have you hidden things from me?'

'If you try too hard you get tense, doctors say, and it doesn't work.'

'Doctors!'

'Give 'em a chance, luv. There's nothing wrong with us, I know it!' She pushed him away, her face set and pinched.

'Don't start. I've told you a thousand times, you know how I feel. It's not something for test-tubes and thermometers and little bottles of pills. It's not for us to decide.'

'Oh aye. Man proposes, God disposes, eh? For Christ's sake, girl, d'you want children or not?'

'Don't blaspheme, Huw. You know I hate it. I told you, leave me alone.'

'Eirwen, what is it?'

Her lips came together in a tight line. She looked older and colder and very angry.

'I want my man home nights. I want people around me to talk to. I want mountains and grass and clean air. I want to go home!'

He tried again to comfort her and she would have none of it. She cried herself to sleep.

She didn't go at once, which made things worse. She was with him yet apart. Something he'd cherished was slipping irretrievably away, and he could do nothing to save it. He threw himself into work, he must've been a bit crazy. One day the Superintendent sent for him.

'Ease up, Evans, you're getting reckless.' He made some flippant comment and the Super chewed him out. 'I don't give a damn for you, laddie, you can go to hell any way you like. You're putting good men in danger, I've no use for tearaways. Now take a grip or you'll be back on the beat.'

Twice she came to him in the night, abandoning herself with a ferocity which awed him. Much later, he pieced it together and realised she had, after all, read the manuals and tried to catch him at the best time; and once again failed. He arrived home one evening shattered after a particularly gruesome road accident to find an empty house and a terse note: 'It's finished, Huw. I can't take any more. You can have a divorce any time but don't follow me and don't ask me to come back. Sorry.'

He was to learn that most suicides left an apology, as if an expression of regret could somehow erase pain. Such a short, useless word, sorry.

Work saved him. He brought to it a tenacity, a dogged and persistent logic, which earned the wonder of his contemporaries and the growing approval of his superiors. Within a year of her departure, he'd risen to sergeant and been assigned to CID.

The final humiliation came at his father's funeral. On a slate-grey Welsh afternoon rich with hymns and beerfumes, she'd approached demurely, a new husband on her arm and a pram in front of her.

'Mysterious ways, Huw,' she'd murmured slyly. 'Keeping well, are you?'

Since then, his faith in man and God had steadily diminished . . .

In which case, what did he say to a woman who once long ago had fallen and now grieved for a missing daughter? We're kindred souls, having both known loss, and time's a wondrous healer? Say nothing, bach, that's the best. It's knowledge she needs, not comfort.

For once he had to stand on the porch and brave the wind. At last she appeared, groomed and trim, only the brightness of her eyes betraying her.

'Please come in, Inspector. Any news?'

Her greeting and her smile were as fragile and false as December sunshine.

''Fraid not, ma'am.'

She fussed over him, insisted on making tea. The room was spotless, gleaming; dumb witness to her compulsion for activity.

Reminiscences had depressed him, her absurd display of courage grated. He could find no small talk, no inclination to dissemble. Without preliminary, he demanded, 'Miss Yardley, who was Caroline's father?'

A slight check, the smallest hitch in the smoothness of her movements. She poured tea steadily, controlled as a duchess.

'I don't see how it can possibly help.'

Brusquely he outlined the Beddoes theory. She watched him tightly, attentive but calm.

'You can't be serious.'

'Indeed I am. It makes as much sense as anything.'

Having preserved her secret this long, Grace Yardley did not intend to disclose it now. The enquiry, made so crudely, seemed little more than prurient curiosity. Her faith in Evans, always a delicate plant, withered rapidly.

Frigidly, she said, 'I assure you the idea is ridiculous.'

'You'd best let me judge for myself.'

She nodded, smiling grimly.

'Very well. When he went away he didn't even know I was pregnant.'

The disappointment on his face gave her satisfaction; swiftly forgotten. Simultaneously, she understood how much hope he'd lodged in the question; and how, by her answer, she'd destroyed it. Quietly, shakily, in realisation and recompense, she murmured, 'I never told anyone, not even my parents. Believe me, his name is meaningless.' She saw that he believed her and had closed off one more possibility.

He paced the chilly midday streets, a man alone yet unremarked among the crowd; slight and insignificant, sharp-featured and neat in regulation suiting. Yet a sense of his own uniqueness buoyed him, adding an unobtrusive lilt to his step. The part of him which had once stood aghast no longer functioned. Only a warm glow of achievement remained, creeping like a small animal around his groin. He'd done it again and enjoyed it, and had not been caught. How would they react, these feeble, ordinary fools, if only they knew? He smiled faintly to himself and walked on, whistling.

Chapter Four

Two world conflicts had decimated the Buxton family. Nigel's father, the sole male survivor of his generation, denied combat by diabetes and asthma, had a clever and clandestine war in a Kensington garret. The strain ruined his health and kept him from the neglected estates. He married late and died young, leaving a middle-aged widow, a proud name, and a modest trust for his son's education.

Nigel's mother, Shires born and blue-blooded, cared nothing for economy and finished her life in the style to which she'd become accustomed. Nigel spent happy hours in her company, not having the heart to disillusion her. By the time she died, a socialist government had pared the inheritance to the bone; barely enough remained to see him through law school and Lincoln's Inn.

From his earliest days, Nigel felt the burden of history upon him; that which is lost must be restored. This set him apart from his contemporaries at the Bar, most of whom were wealthy and all of whom were better off than him. Pride made him prickly; a Buxton didn't cadge. One or two debs, liking his looks and sensing his drive, dallied awhile; but he was too poor and too busy, and they soon left him for more marriageable stock.

The days with Mother and her coterie had given him a taste for female company. Clubs and clubmen bored him. He would rather spend one night with a girl of his choice than five at some all-male bar - would rather do it than talk about it. Few of his colleagues became cronies; it was a matter of pride that women who'd once been his lovers usually remained his friends.

He *had* been honest with Theresa, and initially at least, Stanmore had read her right. Decorative and compliant, the latest in a long line of pleasing but casual diversions. He frequently regaled bedmates with risqué tales such as Courthouse Interruptus; glimpses behind the façade for the uninitiated, part of his stock-in-trade. But in the past few weeks, Theresa had inveigled him to talk of *cases*, and that had never happened before.

The Stanmore conspiracy had plagued his mind of late. Trite and Victorian though she may be, the old cow had a point. Lawyers, if they embraced ambition, *were* obliged to conform, and Nigel was nothing if not an ambitious man. In a profession characterised by longevity, one had to chart one's course early. At forty-four, he'd reached a watershed. A remark of Theresa's came back to him; an unwelcome echo.

'It's super now, Nigel. You're attractive, successful and in your prime. Give it a few years and you'll just be another dirty old man.'

In some dismay, he realised he was skirting serious thoughts of matrimony, with Theresa leading the field. Come, m'boy, he reproached himself, aping the Stanmore delivery, one doesn't marry one's mistress. Find a plain and preferably wealthy woman and join us in the fold. The judiciary has no vacancies for philanderers. There is none more devout than a converted sinner, thought Nigel ironically. Wants to spoil everyone else's fun as well.

He *was* content. He cast a benevolent eye over the room – the embossed Chinese carpet, the outmoded but comfortable leather suite, the well-stocked bar and the space-age stereo. Personal indulgences all, and no less satisfying for that, but doubtless dispensable to female taste. Theresa and Stanmore, in their diverse ways, were nudging him in a direction he was reluctant to travel, and he resented it. At the same time, he felt a premonition of change, the approach of a crisis in his life which he could neither foresee nor avoid.

The hell with it, he thought, putting on Rachmaninov's Second and sprawling in his chair. The music soothed him, steering his imagination towards a rather delectable red-head he'd seen in a colleague's chambers.

Ernie Potts lay in darkness, covers to his chin. He'd been

planning this for months, ever since Max Morris sank an extra pint in the Dog and Duck and got chatty. Max was the oracle of the river, a man who took specimen fish where others only drowned worms. Slight, stooped, taciturn and seventy, he'd stalked the embankment for half a century, an angling artist, a law unto himself.

On rare occasions, he would expound, 'Nothin to it, mate. Think fish. If I was a biggun, where'd I lie to get most grub for least effort? Watch the water, see 'ow it moves. First light and last light's best, any kid'll tell you. After that, it's just knowin 'ow to wait.'

Philosophy sometimes, methodology never. He didn't brag, told of his conquests matter-of-factly. 'Float twitched and laid flat. Flick o'the wrist and bingo. Give me a good scrap, ole grampa tench.'

Till that night at the Dog and Duck. Ernie was late, got snarled on a log and spent half an hour teasing it rather than lose previous gear. Max was already on his third, staring sightless at the darts-players, a strange light in his clear old eyes. Presently, unprompted, he spoke.

'There's an eddy by the old wharf. 'Ad it pegged for years, natural fer a biggun. Groundbait down a week, 'eavy tackle on, ready for anything, right. Took a coupla perch, too young to know better, then it went flat.' He paused, swallowed beer brushed the back of his hand over his moustache. 'I could feel 'im there, Ern, a real biggun, know what I mean?'

Ernie, who didn't, nodded.

'Tried everythin. Slow trottin, bouncin on the bottom, whippin it through a coupla times. Getting dark, but 'e wuz there, see, and it narked me. Even tried ledgerin.' He sniffed in self-disgust. 'Bloody dredgin, I call it. Sling an' 'ope. Not a nibble. Laughin at me, 'e wuz.'

He glanced around, lowered his voice.

'Pile 'o dung in the cul-de-sac. Bin there years. Rag'n'bone men, still a few 'orses about. Best red worms I ever seen. Killers. Teased one on, lively like, lobbed 'im into the eddy.' He sat silent, gazing into his glass. Ernie, rapt, waited. 'Gettin dark, see, I said that, din I. Peepers ent what they used to be. Never saw the float go, din believe it, really. Anyow, I struck.

35

Solid, dead. Sod it, thinks I, I've bottomed. Then 'e moved. Only a bit, but you can't mistake it. Tightened, give 'im a bit of butt.' He paused again, blinked, shook his head. ''E just went 'ome, Ernie. Slow an' easy like a bleedin bull. Couldn't turn 'im, couldn't 'old 'im, couldn't even 'urry 'im. Rod doubled an' when the line ran out it broke. Thirty-pound line. 'E just went 'ome, is all.'

Ernie hadn't touched his beer. Now he took a long swallow and asked his single question. 'What was it then?'

'Barbel,' said Max, with utter conviction. 'Nuffin else that big. Bleedin grandaddy. I 'ad 'im, Ernie, an 'e went 'ome anyway. Jesus.'

So, at six on a raw October morning, Ernie Potts chivvied his old bones out of bed, dressed warm, sank a hunter's breakfast and caught the first bus to the docks. In the steam of his own breath, his fingers freezing, he tackled up and walked two hundred yards to the wharf. He staked his pitch, moving cat-footed though his toes were numb, and then went worming in horse manure. Away from the bank, he could afford to flap his arms and stamp his feet and make a terse, obscene reply to the milkman who advised him, 'Gawn back ter bed, yer daft ole git!'

In the palest of dawns, as the town silhouette scarred the skyline, he hooked a bloodworm and watched it wriggle. Satisfied, he cast. The float cocked and glided, ghostly and hypnotic, into the eddy. Almost at once it dipped and he struck. Live but feeble resistance; he reeled in a five-inch bleak. Cheeky little bastard. He fiddled with a fresh worm, the cold a bitter enemy. Three more sprats were beached and released as the grey morning crept in. Then came a lull. The float danced boldly, a breeze bit at his ears. And, for the first time in his life, he sensed it; some deep lurking presence. Soon.

The float checked and slid slowly under. Instantly, the cold a memory, he reacted. A solid weight, a dragging pull. He pumped the rod and made no impression. Line eased out, tight and heavy. Twenty yards, thirty, without a hint of life at the other end. Just steady inexorable pressure. He set himself, jammed his thumb on the reel, and held. The line snapped, a sharp, final crack in the frigid air. Down stream the water roiled. Slack in disappointment, he craned for a glimpse of the great fish. A pale glimmer, surely not that big! The whiteness rose and wallowed, vast and bloated. It took him a second to understand; then his breakfast came up.

The nick at half-nine in the morning. Today, even institutional paint and functional furniture looked cosy after the bleakness outside. Evans, tired and dull, picked at a report, his mind drifting to Grace Yardley. For three weeks he'd watched over her in helpless admiration, unable to stay away. Her pallor had worsened, her cheeks had thinned, there were violet bruises beneath her eyes; yet her faith never wavered. Her grooming remained perfect, her composure absolute. He'd long since given the girl up, himself, stopped inventing reasons for her absence. One way or another, he counted her lost, and had tried to hint as much. Grace Yardley seemed immune. Her optimism went beyond all reason. He was more than ever drawn to her.

Beddoes bustled in, perky with the cold.

'Still seein the bird reglar? Keepin you up late, is she? You look knackered, mate.'

Evans, holding his temper, muttered, 'She's on her own, see. It isn't natural, the way she's behaving. Someone's got to look out for her.'

'Yeah,' said Beddoes knowingly. 'Good ole Christian charity. Not a lot of it about these days. Don't even fancy 'er a bit, do you?'

'Told you once, remember? Not our class.'

'Come off it. Waiting for 'er to crumble, arncher, so's you can pick up the pieces.'

'Know what, boyo? Your mouth'll get you into bad trouble some day. One more crack like that ...'

'Even so, you'd best go easy. It's the car, see. Lots of uniforms know it. Bit of chat goin the rounds.' Beddoes was looking decidedly shifty.

'Passin the time, are you, or is there something *particular* on your tiny mind?'

Beddoes grinned weakly.

'Matter of fact there is. 'Is nibs stopped me in the corridor. Came the heavy. Wants words with you. Your earliest convenience, he said; means yesterday. I'd get up there if I was you.'

'Thanks,' Evans said dryly, 'thanks very much.'

'Tipped you, didn't I?'

'Aye.'

Superintendent Gerald Smythe was short for a copper, small-boned and sinewy. In his mid-fifties, he had hard blue eyes, a spotless reputation and a taste for military discipline. Very conscious of rank, he kept himself aloof from the lower echelons. A summons of this nature could only mean a bollocking. Evans knocked and entered.

The Super sat at his desk, intent on a file. Without looking up, he barked, 'Sit, Evans. With you in a minute.' In fact, five long and comfortless minutes passed before he spoke again, having set the paperwork aside and given Evans a thorough scrutiny. 'This missing girl, Inspector.'

'Yessir.'

'No leads?'

'Nothing so far, sir.'

'Spending time with the mother, I hear.'

'My own time, sir.'

'Mm. Something fishy, you reckon?'

'Not at all. She has no one, won't call on anyone. Bad time for her, fair play.'

'No doubt. Attractive?'

Evans trod carefully. 'Some might say so.'

'Some do, Inspector, indeed they do. Changed your vocation, perhaps?'

'Not with you, sir.'

'You're not a priest, man!' There was another loaded silence.

Diffidently, Evans murmured, 'I told you, it's my own time I'm spending.'

'None of my business, eh?'

'I didn't say so, sir.'

'Really? I rather thought you did. You're right, of course. Your personal life is up to you. Little warning then. Don't get

38

too close. We don't want emotions getting in the road. If you're involved, now's the time to tell me.'

'There's nothing like that, sir.'

The Super sighed, adopted a man-to-man tone. 'All right Evans, no more sparring. Whatever the facts, appearances matter. No telling how things will break, and I'll brook no hint of unprofessional relations. I'll finish, d'you mind? It's very simple, keep the case and your distance or I'll assign someone else. Am I plain enough for you?'

'I'm not too happy with that, sir. Only trying to – '

'Your happiness, Inspector, is of little concern, in the circumstances. Dammit, man, you know perfectly well what I mean. You're not some calfstruck recruit!'

'No, sir.'

'Very good. Then we understand each other. Carry on.'

Evans stood up. As he reached the door, Smythe continued, 'Oh, Inspector, don't go and kick the dog, will you.'

'Pardon?'

'Beddoes works for me too. He didn't like it either.'

Evans trudged downstairs, badly unsettled. Beddoes greeted him warily. 'Nasty?'

''Bout what you'd expect. You should know, mind.'

'Yeah. Really laid into me. Had to tell 'im.'

'Course you did.'

Beddoes licked his lips, refusing to meet Evans's eye. 'Hate to do this, mate. Your day's about to get a whole lot worse.' He passed a slip of paper. 'Came over the blower while you were on high.'

Evans read slowly, not really taking it in. The clinical terms were familiar enough; this time, they filled him with revulsion. Female adolescent corpse, advanced putrefaction due to immersion. Death by strangulation, probably by ligature. Evidence of forceful and repeated rape, possibly before death occurred. Identification checked with missing persons and confirmed by dental records. Name of victim, Caroline Yardley, age fourteen.

'Jesi mawr,' he breathed. 'Has she been told?'

'Sat on it, didn't I.'

'Aye. Well, I'd best be off then.'

39

Beddoes looked alarmed.

''Ere, 'ang about! What about 'is nibs?'

Evans rose deliberately, locked his desk and shrugged into his overcoat. Looking Beddoes straight in the eye, he said quietly, 'Fuck him.'

From long experience, he knew a blow like this couldn't be softened. At six the news would be out, by breakfast tomorrow the nation would be savouring the grisly details. Grace Yardley had to know it now and she had to know it all. Too late, he recognised the trap which both Beddoes and Smythe had predicted and tried to spare him.

Like every copper, he lived on nodding terms with tragedy. In the past, he could keep it factual, leave survivors in someone else's care, walk away sadder but essentially unscarred. Not this time. Smythe was right, he *was* involved, deeply and personally. And hopelessly, he now accepted. For, to her dying day, she would remember him as the one who brought tidings of rape and murder.

Briefly he was tempted. He'd explained already – WPCs specially briefed for the task. Tell her Beddoes had taken the decision, turn up later bringing condolences and a shoulder to cry on. It won't wash, bach, no good pretending you hadn't heard. No way to shirk the responsibility. He drove without thought, his mind bare of everything except a kind of rage.

She opened the door to him, somehow especially frail and beautiful, her eyes still bright with hope. She read him at once, as he'd known she would. She stood dumb and rooted, a hand raised as if to ward him off.

'No,' she said quite reasonably. 'I don't believe you. You must have made some mistake.'

'You'd better let me in,' he said.

'Oh. Yes. Forgive me.'

He followed a pace behind into the now familiar room, ready for anything. She paused with her back to him, arms across her body, head hanging.

'I simply can't believe it.' A statement as true and as poignant as any he'd ever heard. He hesitated, then took her by the shoulders and turned her to face him. She moved

40

lightly, unresisting. It was the first time he'd ever touched her, and she seemed as cool and brittle as porcelain.

'Look at me please, ma'am.' Slowly, she raised blank eyes. Still holding her, he said, 'I promise if there was any possibility of Caroline being alive, I wouldn't be here like this.' Her gaze met his for a long moment, wide and agonised and trusting. It was as though something departed her then; she seemed to diminish in his hands.

'All right,' she mumbled. 'Let me go. I'm all right.'

'Do you believe me?'

A word, short and final, half sigh, half whisper. 'Yes.'

He released her then, his instincts vindicated. He'd been right to come; paltry satisfaction in a vile day.

'I'll make tea,' she said, and he let her, understanding the need for action, any action, at a time such as this. She returned, halting and chalky, unable to control her trembling.

'You'll tell me about it, won't you? Was it an accident? I want to see her. O God.' The cup and saucer rattled; he took it from her and set it down.

'I'll tell you everything. Before I start, there's something you must do for me.'

'Whatever I can.'

'I asked you once for a picture. Now I want them all.'

'All?'

'Albums, scrapbooks, anything you have of Caroline.'

Again the wordless, dependent gaze. She drifted away and came back, placing a pile of Kodak envelopes in his lap.

It didn't take long to find. Not a particularly good photograph, slightly blurred with movement too fast for the camera to freeze. Caroline aged about ten, he guessed, swinging in a park. A leafy hazy green background, her legs flung forward, head back and pigtail askew, a smile of pure joy. The very essence of the child; the thing she must cling to in her agony.

'Hold this, Miss Yardley. Look at it while I talk.'

At last the fear was upon her, and her voice broke. 'Is it – as bad as that?'

'Aye. I'm sorry, but it is.'

He told her then, kindly and briefly, sparing her whatever he could; which was little enough. She listened, totally still,

41

her lips slightly parted, the tears falling unnoticed and unheeded.

'My God,' she whispered when he'd finished. 'Who would do such a thing? Why, for God's sake?'

He couldn't answer, didn't even try. When she folded over in total grief, when the picture slipped from her blind and nerveless fingers, he let it lie. He sat silent while the sobs convulsed her and she keened like a wounded kitten. Dear God, he thought, and once I suspected her.

After many minutes, she fell still. Slowly, with an effort awful to watch, she pushed herself upright. Again he held out the picture.

'You oughtn't to see her, Miss Yardley. Here's Caroline. What she is and what she was. Nothing and no one can ever take it away. She was a little girl, bright and beautiful and innocent. Always remember.'

She took the coloured scrap, held it like a precious stone. 'Yes, I'll remember.'

Slowly, painfully, he forced her to talk. He heard of childhood illness, trouble with algebra, a passion for gerbils and a two-fisted backhand. He drank uncounted cups of tea. Outside, the day lingered and faded. By nightfall, she'd entered a stage of calm – the release of exhaustion rather than peace.

'Now,' he told her, 'you must call someone.'

A brief rally, a shadow of the old obduracy; but he wore her down easily, won consent for the family doctor.

He came quite soon, a brisk, elderly, acerbic man bristling with outrage. Evans met him in the hallway, filled the gaps in his knowledge, and waited while he ministered to her. At the top of the stairs she turned, her face white and ethereal, the picture clasped to her breast.

'Inspector Evans?'

'Ma'am?'

'Thank you. For what you tried to do.'

The doctor came down ten minutes later, still very angry.

'Out like a light. Don't worry, I'll make arrangements. She'll not be alone.'

'Good.'

'Little Caroline,' he growled. 'I damn near brought her up.

Lovely child. What – what lunatic was responsible? How can we call ourselves civilised, eh, and creatures like him on the streets?'

Evans shrugged, beyond caring.

'You'll catch him, will you?'

'Maybe.'

'Then what?'

'I'll tell you,' Evans said, with a bitterness of his own. 'We'll pull him in, he'll confess. They always do, in the end. The shrinks'll get together and say he's not responsible, see. Needing care and attention. Only the best, mind. Send her away, doc. The media'll flog this for a week, and if we get him they'll rake it over, just for luck. Keep her out of it.'

'Teach your grandmother to suck eggs, young man. You've done your bit and I'll do mine. And don't call me doc.'

'Aye. Sorry.' He received a quizzical sidelong stare.

'Grace said a few things about you, Inspector. You should be more careful.'

'Meaning what?'

'Your humanity's showing.'

'Occupational disease.'

The doctor snorted.

'In a policeman, it could prove terminal.'

Chapter Five

Anticlimax, a return to routine as flat and bitter as stale beer. He heard from her a week later, a short handwritten note posted in Eastbourne. Italic and a hint of perfume which had Beddoes drooling.

'It's peaceful here, time to walk and think. The doctor says I can stop the pills soon. The people at work have been very considerate. Take as long as you need, they said. I've had the picture enlarged and framed and I do as you advised. I don't read papers. But it still makes no sense, I suppose it never will. I hope you catch him. Yours sincerely.' The signature was neat and legible.

I hope you catch him. Me too, girl. Smythe, aloof and detached, flogged the public approach: Have you seen this child? But it was six weeks ago, a foul Sunday night, and who could tell one school kid from another? There *were* responses. Weirdos, religious fanatics, compulsive confessors and psychic dabblers; and some just plain lonely, seeking attention. Patiently, Evans interviewed them all, nailed the inconsistencies, the fantasies and the outright lies, cautioned them and let them go. And burned the paperwork.

Then he combed the files for known sex artists, pulled them in and sweated them. Left to himself, he might have been very rough indeed. They weren't his flavour of the month anyway; he'd never come to terms with real perversity, and anger drove him relentlessly. He kept Beddoes handy to hold him on the rails, to save him from excess, to restrain him when they sauntered out, grinning.

Together they quartered the map; the market, the docks, the Embankment. Five million suspects, ten thousand boltholes, and no reasons. They had only the vaguest idea when she'd

44

been killed and no clue as to where. A sad cold trail leading nowhere. Time and the river had done their work well. In the end, he bought the gospel according to Beddoes – a nutter loose, unknowable unless he struck again. Case dormant, file in abeyance, nothing to report. He couldn't bring himself to answer her.

He felt as he had during his divorce, useless and ineffectual, slipping into decline. Work, the faithful anodyne, lost it's appeal. Drab little cases, pathetic individuals, a daily catalogue of unrelieved squalour. Maybe Eirwen had it right. Retreat to the Valleys, where bingo, the workman's hall and the rugby club offered at least a measure of human warmth and companionship. Back home, even childless, they might've made it work.

Fair play, Beddoes did his best. Gave up a few dates, passed time on the dart board, even took him to the soccer. A reversal of roles, the leader led. Evans should've been affronted but couldn't summon the necessary pride. His nerve of morality numbed, his Non-conformist conscience sleeping, he made up foursomes. Beddoes's birds were free spirits; generous. Twice he woke to unfamiliar bodies in his bed, his mind awash with sweat and striving and the harsh moans of animal satisfaction. Empty, meaningless couplings begun in alcoholic haze and ended in studied politeness. He was drinking too much, caring too little, having a good time. Oh, aye, lovely.

At least once a day, and more at night, though she had given him not the slightest cause, he thought of Grace Yardley.

Since his accession to silk, Nigel's professional activities had veered from the sensational. He hadn't planned it so, he had plenty of work; but not the kind which made headlines. This, plus his continuing attachment to Theresa, had clearly won housemarks with the Stanmores. The latest invitation included both names and admitted them to a more select party. The guestlist read like a current events programme: Lord Eaglesfield, Liberal peer; Reggie Marsden, junior Cabinet minister; Clive Hampstead, candid television interviewer; and Paul Jarvis, a theatre critic of notoriety. And wives, of course, some of whom were noteworthy in their own right.

A gracious if somewhat elaborate meal, spiced with witty conversation. The men, word-merchants all, duelled skilfully but without heat. The ladies, an elegant audience, applauded their favourites decorously. A rich setting, chandeliers and silverware, black ties and diamonds. The sort of occasion which gave Nigel much satisfaction. Back where he belonged, at last. The debris had been cleared; Mrs Stanmore, an equine, angular and commanding figure, herded the ladies out. 'So that our lords may wallow in their beastly port, my dears.'

Even in this company, Theresa's beauty stood unrivalled. Nigel watched in proprietary smugness as she followed her hostess gracefully.

He'd met Theresa during one of his rare jaunts to the theatre. She came from Kenya, where her community had acted as clerks and accountants to the colonials, and stayed when India annexed their nation, Goa. She was stagestruck, having worked a while in Nairobi's only professional theatre, now deceased. She preferred older men, she said ingenuously; young Goans in Nairobi tended to run wild. She made it sound like an upmarket *West Side Story.* Her father had given her two years to make the grade, and a generous allowance.

'I'm Catholic,' she told him, demure but twinkling, 'in my mind but not my body.'

He had taken her at her word and into his life.

Across the table, the interviewer and the critic gossiped about the season's Lion of Stratford, a Scottish queer, apparently. Stanmore and the two parliamentarians bewailed the state of British industry. Nigel, conscious of his place below the salt, pulled himself together and paid court. The decanter moved briskly. Lord Eaglesfield, looking like a humorous bloodhound, remarked, 'Our lady at the helm makin warlike noises, what. The Boadicea touch. Hangin this time, I'm told. Wants us back in the Dark Ages, eh George?'

'Now, William,' continued his host, 'let's not be mischievous. *Sub judice,* d'you mind?'

Hampstead the interviewer, polished but ferrety, lifted a pointed and inquisitive nose. 'Come, milud, don't spoil the sport. We laymen are seldom privy to genuinely informed opinion. Off the record, of course.'

46

'Flattery, my dear man, will get you precisely nowhere.'

The junior minister set his glass down carefully. A fleshy handsome man known for straight talk and firm action. 'The public, bless its little nylon socks, gets what it deserves. Personally, I'm for sterner measures.'

The critic, Jarvis, shook his silver locks and pursed his thin lips. 'Heaven forbid. I certainly would.'

'C'mon, George,' urged the peer, 'don't keep us danglin; capital punishment, for or agin?'

Stanmore made a gesture of mock weariness.

'You may rehearse the hoary arguments if you wish, gentlemen. I pass.'

'Well, I'm agin,' said Lord Eaglesfield firmly. 'Sheer barbarity.'

'Murder, sir, is a barbaric crime,' retorted Marsden. 'Seems to me we should concern ourselves with victims, not psychopaths.'

'Fifteen all,' murmured Nigel, and won an approving glance from the judge.

'I agree with Lord Eaglesfield,' said Hampstead. 'A retrograde and pointless step. Criminologists are unanimous, the statistics prove it. Hanging's no deterrent.'

'Statistics?' echoed Jarvis, his eyes bright with malice. 'My dear chap, who knows how many murderous impulses have withered in the shadow of the gallows?'

'Our noble policemen would endorse that sentiment,' acknowledged Stanmore drily; and Hampstead rounded on him.

'Good heavens! I hope you don't set too much store by them! Vested interests, to say the least.'

'Tell us, George,' Lord Eaglesfield demanded, 'How'd you like to don the black cap? Sleep easy, would you, havin sent some chap off for stretchin?'

Stanmore eyed him indulgently. 'I don't make the law, William, I only sit in judgement. I've put men down for thirty years; sometimes the hangman might seem more humane.'

'Why, George,' exclaimed the minister, 'I do believe you're with the angels.'

'I didn't say so.'

47

'You're very quiet, old man,' remarked Jarvis, thrusting Nigel into the limelight. 'Not boring you, are we?'

Nigel smiled and spread his hands. 'Gentlemen, forgive me. It's not the time or place for private practice.' The sally earned a ripple of appreciative laughter.

'A pretty evasion,' Marsden allowed, 'but rather typical, I fear, of the whole issue. A man kills, stands proven in guilt. Society, we agree, must be protected. Very well, lock him up, feed and clothe him, heal him when he's sick. Let him watch television, study at the Open University, have his wife in. Society will pay. A pretty evasion, as I said, but costly.'

'Society, in this case, meaning voters, we assume,' said Jarvis, and Lord Eaglesfield chortled.

'Touché, Reggie. He's got your number!'

The minister smiled, but his eyes were cold. Not a good loser, Nigel decided.

Hampstead began. 'Society has a responsibility . . .' And Marsden cut straight across him.

'To whom, the normal or the aberrant?'

'To all its members, as your party conveniently forgets!'

'Gentlemen, gentlemen,' interjected Stanmore smoothly, 'let us not sour the wine.'

Lord Eaglesfield, peevish and not quite sober, asked, 'So it's no decision, is it? You really reservin judgement, George, or just creasin the old derrière?'

'Creasing *what*, William?'

'Squattin on the fence.'

Stanmore sighed elaborately.

'Dear oh lord. I expected you chaps to resolve this your-selves. Perhaps we've wined and dined too well.' A nicely weighted pause, and they all murmured dutifully. 'There *is* an argument, you see, and it's incontestable. It needs no great rhetoric; I'm sure Mr Buxton can enlighten us without compromising his ethics.' Nigel glanced up sharply. Stanmore regarded him expectantly.

Nigel felt a pang of resentment. Surely this could not have been contrived to test him? Dismissing the thought, he never-theless longed to say something outrageous. So much hot air demanded a cooling blast. Nothing to be gained, he realised reluctantly; and besides, it would be rank bad form. In the manner of a deferential junior, he murmured, 'I assume milud refers to the matter of Timothy Evans.'

Stanmore beamed, the benevolent don on a favoured pupil. 'Just so. Christie kills and Timothy Evans walks to the scaffold. It's really that simple, gentlemen. It's not a question of civilisation or morality or social responsibility. It's straightforward and pragmatic. As long as we are fallible, as long as an innocent might hang, the death penalty must remain in suspense. And that, Reggie,' he deferred to the minister, 'despite a restive electorate and a Boadicean leader, is why Britain will not reintroduce capital punishment. Now, I suspect the ladies, too, are restive, and I would rather provoke the electorate than them.'

Very adroit, Nigel conceded. He'd led them on, saved his best for last, left them laughing; and allowed no time for closer inspection. An enviable command of expertise, both legal and social. Yet, as he strolled towards Theresa's welcoming and somewhat relieved smile, he reflected that the outcome had been by no means as conclusive as Stanmore implied.

Not for the first time recently, Evans was nursing a hangover, and the hunt and peck of Beddoes's typewriter did nothing for his concentration. The stuffy room made him lethargic, the greyness outside oppressed him. The phone jangled, touching raw nerves like a dental drill. Beddoes grabbed it, grunted, and began scribbling on a pad. Evans passed a hand over his eyes and struggled vainly for coherence in his own report. Beddoes set the phone down.

'You fit?' he enquired cautiously.

'Not specially. Why?'

'That was Wharf End nick. Someone snatched a bird earlier on. She's there now, shaken but chatty. Fancy a trip?'

'Aye. You drive, mind.'

Beddoes picked his way through congested streets. There was a lowering overcast and a biting wind. The mass of humanity heading workward looked hurried and cowed.

'They picked up Smythe's bulletin on the Yardley girl,' Beddoes explained. 'Putative sexual assault, right area.

49

Actually said that, putative, would you believe? Nice to see some efficiency, though. Makes a change.'

Evans grunted.

'False alarm, like as not. But still. Watch the lorry!' Beddoes opened the window, spoke harsh words and received a derisive V-sign for his pains. Icy air swept some of the fog from Evans's brain.

'Cheeky sod,' Beddoes muttered, 'good mind to take 'is number.'

'Fabian of the Yard,' Evans said, and Beddoes grinned.

'Back among the livin, are yer?'

Wharf End police station had seen better days. Bleak and ugly, straddling the corner of two mean streets, it smelled faintly of Dettol and cabbage. The desk sergeant ushered them in. Lean, sharp-featured and grizzled, he addressed Evans alone, clearly considering Beddoes beneath his dignity. His prominent Adam's apple bobbed like a cork in a whirlpool.

'On 'er way to work, she was, bit of a state. Bin mucked about, like. Gave her char and she perked up. Doesn't want to press charges. Old man'll belt her, she says. Your Super's message caught me eye, like, stuck in me mind. Got a teenager meself. Thought I'd give you a buzz.'

'You did well. Thanks.'

'In the rest room, sir, with a WPC. You're welcome.'

They followed him down a gloomy passage, their heels clacking. The rest room was dark and bare.

'Inspector Evans,' announced the desk sergeant, and the WPC stood up. She was young and brunette. Beddoes gazed openly at her tight tunic.

'OK, Palmer,' said the desk sergeant, 'you can go.'

Evans glanced at the victim. White tearstained face, rumpled clothing, ridiculously short skirt, torn stockings.

'If it's all the same, sarge,' he said, 'I'd like her to stay.'

The desk sergeant shrugged. 'No problem, sir.'

In the hiatus as he left, Evans muttered to Beddoes, 'Usual form, you first.'

Beddoes winked, tossed his coat over a chair and told the WPC, 'You're 'ere to see fair play. Sit tight and say nothing.'

The brunette nodded, colouring at his tone.

'Now then, sweetheart,' Beddoes began, 'What's this about your Dad beltin yer? What you bin up to?' The girl clutched an imitation leather jacket round thin shoulders and absurdly prominent breasts. Her green-tinged hair hung spiky, her eyes were wide and feverish. She looked frail and fearful and sulky.

'Don't want nuffin in the papers. I'm OK, honest. Missin work, ent I.'

'Name?' snapped Beddoes.

'Dorofy Wallis. My friends call me Dot.'

'Age?'

'Seventeen.'

'Address?'

She gave it, shivering, and watched while Beddoes wrote.

''Ere, yer won't tell, will yer?'

'We'll see. So what 'appened? Come on, we haven't got all day.'

Halting and disconnected, her story emerged. She worked in a factory, early shift. The bus stop was dark and cold, so she'd walked a bit for warmth. Passing a derelict building, she'd got edgy and started to trot. Evans pictured the thin legs flashing and the breasts bouncing, and leaned forward, listening intently. Beddoes stood over her, prompting and hectoring.

''E come outa nowhere. 'It me an' grabbed me an' pawed me about.' She fingered a darkening bruise on her right cheekbone.

'Come from behind you, did he?' demanded Beddoes.

She hesitated ducking her head. 'Musta done. Never seen 'im. Dragged me along, 'e did. I wuz ollerin an' kickin but 'e wouldn't leave orf.'

'Dragged you how? Your hands, your hair?' She hunched into herself, head down.

'Me jumper,' she mumbled. 'Barstid ripped it. Me Mum'll kill me.'

Beddoes's hand snaked out and flipped the jacket open. A yellow sweater, the wool rent and ragged, a pink bra, heavily reinforced and very grubby. She struck at his arm, hissing like a cat, wrenching the jacket together.

''Ad a good look, fuzz?'

51

'Just checking,' said Beddoes with a sly leer. 'Be a big girl when you grow up.'

She showed him her teeth, sharp and feral. 'Pig!'

Beddoes wagged a finger in her face and she flinched. 'Watch yer lip, sweetheart. Keep talking, but civil, right?'

Smouldering, her eyes resentful, she snarled, 'I'm tellin yer, if yer'll give me a chance. I think 'e 'ad a car.'

'You see it?'

She shrugged, keeping her arms linked. 'Seemed to know where 'e was goin. Down the alley, like.'

'Big, was he? Strong?'

'Yeah. Nah. I dunno.'

'But you got away?'

She was growing more defiant by the moment. 'Course I did, else I wouldn't be 'ere, would I?' The WPC smiled and Beddoes shot her a vicious glare.

'How d'you do it, then, Kung Fu?'

'Kicked 'im.' She met Beddoes's eye for the first time, knowing and triumphant. 'In the goolies. 'E flopped about an' I 'oofed it.'

Beddoes straightened, strolled a pace or two and whirled on her, chin out-thrust in accusation.

'You were 'avin a snog! Some little berk 'oo fancied you. Passion in the bus shelter, excitin! Lost your nerve, tried to cool 'im and 'e planted you, right? *That's* why yer Dad'll 'ammer you.' She gaped up at him, momentarily speechless.

Quietly Evans said, 'OK, Sergeant, I'll take over.'

Beddoes stamped off, plunked himself in a corner and glowered. The brunette stared as though he'd just oozed out of a sewer.

'Now, Dot.' Evans gentled her. 'We want the truth, everything you can remember. No stories, mind, it's important.'

She watched him warily, confused by the sudden shift.

'Look at me,' she whispered. ''Look at me face an' my tights. Don't think I'd 'oller fuzz if me feller got shirty, do yer?'

'Course not,' he soothed. 'You had a rough do. Take your time and get it right.' He walked her through again, slow and easy. She'd been in a dark patch midway between streetlights.

Pressed, she recalled hurrying footsteps, a sudden blow, painful hands at her breasts.

'I'm sore,' she whispered. In the struggle, she'd raked at his fingers. She paused, looked surprised. 'Gloves, 'e 'ad, woolly ones.' Evans bent to her; one nail was torn, but there was no trace of wool.

'Careful now,' he advised her. 'How big was he?'

She swallowed, made small fists in her lap. 'Little bloke, I reckon. I mean, 'e caught me a fourpenny, 'ad me down an' I got away. Wiry, though.' Her eyes widened in revelation. ''E smelt nice! One o' them aftershaves, spicy!'

'Good girl. Go on.'

''E wuz awful quick.'

'Aye, he would be. See him at all, did you?'

A frown of concentration. 'Not reely. Just a glimpse, like, when 'e wuz lyin, moanin. I didn't 'ang about, know what I mean?' She lowered her eyes, fiddled with her skirt. 'Didn't get 'im like I said. More a knee in the guts, I reckon. Lucky, reely.'

'His face,' Evans prompted, patiently.

'Thin. Pointy. Like a bleedin weasel.' She hesitated again, said softly, ''E wuz wearin a suit. Greyish. Little stripe, like a toff, you know?'

'You said it was dark,' snapped Beddoes.

'I seen it,' she retorted. 'Greyish with a thin stripe.'

'Know him again, would you?' Evans asked. She shook her head doubtfully.

'I dunno, honest.'

'One more thing, Dot. I want you to show us where it happened. Do that for me, will you?' Her eyes darted around the room, flicking quickly over Beddoes, resting on the WPC, finally returning to Evans himself. She sighed, bit her lip and nodded.

'Orlright. Can I go then?'

'Probably.'

They dropped her at a terraced house in dockland. She wouldn't let them in, no one would be there. By the time her Mum and Dad came home, she'd be 'sorted out'. She'd make up for the lost shift on Saturday. Piteously, she implored them, 'You won't tell no one, will yer? I gave yer everythin, honest.'

'Garn with yer,' Beddoes said; when she smiled, she was quite pretty. In the car, Beddoes warned, 'Walk soft. Could be a pack o' lies.'

'No chance, boyo. She was telling the truth, as she saw it.'

'Pinstripes an' pouf mixture up 'ere? Do me a favour.'

'Look, if there's any connection, it's a nutter we're after. They come from both sides of the tracks, mind.'

'Don't push it, sir. Likely some brickie havin a quick grope.' Beddoes very rarely gave him the courtesy of rank. Evans studied the sharp profile curiously.

'Something on your mind?'

'She's right, y'know. Old man'd knock seven bells out of 'er if 'e knew. Wouldn't fancy the competition.'

Evans grimaced.

'Darro, bach, you've a nasty tongue.'

'Homeground,' Beddoes grunted. ''Appens more'n you'd think.'

They pulled in opposite the place she'd shown them, one more cramped and dingy street. Halfway along, two houses had crumbled, gaps in a row of rotten teeth. They climbed out and prowled the pavement silently, hunched against the cold. Evans wove between tumbled masonry and stopped, the wind whipping his coat around his legs. The air smelt of soot and decay.

'Aftershave,' Beddoes growled, in vast contempt.

'He was here,' Evans said slowly, 'I can feel him.'

'Cheese on toast,' Beddoes retorted.

'Huh?'

'Welsh rarebit for supper. Gives you bad dreams.'

'Remember the map. River's only half a mile away.'

''Appy 'untin ground, you reckon?'

'It might be, boyo. It just might be.'

Chapter Six

Evans, restored, embarked on a paperchase. Armed with the necessary docket, he took himself to the computer section in headquarters.

'Missing persons,' he told the girl. 'Females of light build between the ages of twelve and twenty who've gone adrift in the last eighteen months. Home addresses within a three mile radius of the docks.'

'Anything else? How about the winner of next year's Derby?'

She was a bored, synthetic blonde in a white coat and her early thirties. She didn't interrupt her self-administered manicure.

'What's that supposed to mean?'

She jerked a freshly tinted thumbnail at a row of consoles behind her. 'His name's Dirk, not Merlin.'

'Dirk?'

'Data Intensive Retrieval and Checking. D I R C. Get it?'

'Very clever, I'm sure. On strike, is he? Paid-up union man?'

'You'll have to break it down.' She drew in another careful purple line.

'Listen,' Evans said reasonably, 'I apologise for imposing on your valuable time. Only a working copper, me. Evans, by the way, Inspector Evans. Suppose you put the warpaint away and run up a few answers.'

'My, aren't you the big cheese.'

'Just busy. Course, I could always tell the Super you're busy, too. Doing your nails.'

Very deliberately she replaced the brush, screwed down the

cap and set the varnish aside. Fluttering her left hand limply, she adopted a drawling monotone.

'Dirk stores a wide range of information. Personnel data, electoral rolls, traffic control systems, accident statistics, court proceedings, pending files, criminal records and case archives. Which d'you want?'

Evans shrugged.

'Suit yourself.'

He was halfway to the door when she called, 'Hold on! No need to be stroppy. Look,' she said huffily, 'Dirk can't work miracles. You have to feed him small portions.'

'Seems to me that's *your* job.'

'Tell me again, slowly.'

He came back to the desk.

'Manage the buttons, can you? Hate to spoil the artwork.'

'You made your point. Ask your questions.'

It took the best part of two hours. Once she stirred herself, the girl seemed deft and competent. They whittled away the search area and finally she produced a teletyped list of twenty missing person files.

'There,' she said still petulant, 'now you can pull rank at the registry.'

'Aye, thanks. And you can get on with your perm.'

The registry clerk, in complete contrast, located files cheerfully and rapidly.

'Here you are then, sir. You can't take them out, naturally. Have a seat. Fancy a cuppa?'

'Lovely,' said Evans, sitting down gratefully. Opening a file at random, he glanced at the top folio. He read more carefully, his anger mounting. Leaving things as they were, moving briskly, he strode back to the computer room. The blonde looked up from a woman's magazine.

'That was quick.'

'I've seen one file,' he snapped. 'Janet Towns, 43 Dockside Terrace, aged sixteen. Went missing 23 February, came home 26 February. Been for a weekend with her Gran and forgot to tell Mum.'

'So?'

'Dear God! I said missing persons!'

She nodded.

'Which is what you got. Exactly.'

Furiously he said, 'I'm after a nutter, a rapist and murderer!'

'Then,' she replied sweetly, 'you should've asked for those *still* missing, or dead, shouldn't you. Dirk's not a mind reader, you know.'

'Run them through again, fast!'

This time there were only four indices. Back at registry, the clerk checked smartly and the pile melted away. When she'd gone, he spread the four folders out. Caroline Yardley's was among them. Sipping tea, he steadied himself and went to work.

The other three girls came from relatively poor homes and seedy areas. Two of them, like Caroline, had simply disappeared, at night, in bad weather. The third had been found, dead. If it wasn't for the rain, the body would've vanished under the foundations of a new supermarket going up only a few hundred yards from Ernie Potts's barbel swim. A downpour had flooded a trench; the remains had given a navvy recurring nightmares. The forensic evidence was sparse and unhelpful. The child had been raped and strangled. Methodically, he noted days and dates. April, February, July, September, and every one a Sunday. Now, mid-October and Dot Wallis. It didn't fit. Shove it on a back-burner, let the subconscious have a crack.

That evening, alone in a flat grown masculine and quirky with bachelordom, he sipped whisky and worried his findings. The punk music from upstairs didn't help; the infants of Eirwen's time were teenagers now. After a while, he blanked them off; and perceived the beginnings of order. Next morning, he tried it for size on Beddoes.

'OK, Sherlock, what d'you think?'

Watching him carefully, Beddoes said, 'I know what *you* think; far too much. Buildin sandcastles, mate, fittin facts to a theory.'

'Oh aye? Which theory?'

'One, it's down to the same guy. Two, 'e's a taste for little uns and 'is own bit of territory. Three 'e 'as a standard MO. And four, the time lag's gettin shorter.'

57

'There you are then. Classic nutter's pattern, bach.'

'Cobblers. You forced it. Fool yourself if you like, you don't fool me. *Course*, they're all little and living in dockland. That's what you asked Humphrey.'

'Dirk.'

'Whoever. If the Wallis bird hadn't escaped, you'd've had to draw them bigger. Leave 'er off the list and your pattern's blown. Anyhow, she was done this Tuesday. How does that jell?'

'Shorter time lag, remember? He's out of control, not planning any more, see, grabbing where he can. A psycho, mind.'

'Assumption. Not a scrap of evidence. Prob'ly three other blokes.'

'So it won't wash?'

Beddoes paused thoughtfully.

'Aint sayin that. But it's all on Wallis, innit. You reckon 'e's stuck to small game, never missed before. If you're wrong, you're back to square one, just unconnected hits. You gotta tidy it.'

'Proceed, thou cockney guru.'

'Over to Richard, mate.'

'Dirk.'

'All right, Dirk. This time you ask for *attempts*, right, unsuccessful ones. After, maybe, you can talk about timing.'

'Aye. Off you go, then.'

'Me? Ah, I getcher. No way I'll 'ave you for forcin, eh?'

'Sort of,' said Evans, and grinned.

Beddoes returned at four, perished but reflective.

'Dirk's on your side. So far so bad.'

'How come?'

'No sexual assaults, hit or miss. None on the files and unsolved, not in dockland, anyhow.'

'None?'

'You've 'ad a sheltered life, mate. In dockland, rape'll pass for slap'n'tickle.'

'Aye, well you should know.'

58

''Ark 'oos bleedin talkin! Whatcha do to Dirk's playmate? Gettin on famous we were, till your name dropped. Benidorm to Siberia in no time flat.'

'Interrupted her manicure,' said Evans, grinning again.

'Funny you should say that. Doin 'er toes, she was, when I looked in. Glimpse of the promised land. She's not a natural blonde, y'know.'

'You'd do better keeping your mind on the job.'

'Exactly where it was, mate, I tell you. You want to go steady yourself. *She* 'as 'er way, ole Dirk'll log you public enemy number one.'

'Speaking of which ...'

'Yeah. Like I said, so far so bad. Theory's 'oldin up.'

'Pity Dirk can't do the next bit, mind.'

'Which bit's that?'

'Ought to suit you lovely, boyo. Legwork.'

'I'm a tit man, meself.'

Sporting fur-lined gloves and carrying a hipflask, Evans went public and nocturnal. And froze anyway. Each day, he pored over maps; every evening, he embussed for dockland. From seven to midnight he walked, skirting the fringe of the derelict port. He was accosted by several women and one man; and once, a persistent and officious beat bobby. Mostly, he avoided bright lights and spoke to no one, stopping for a pie and a pint at some mouldering tavern. It was desolate and bone-chilling work, but a sense of urgency drove him. Theory had become fact. Somewhere in the night a second shadow prowled; a shadow cloaked in menace.

He visited the market where Caroline made her last purchase. He surveyed the building site where the first victim had surfaced. Late one evening, he paced the mildewed wharf and watched the eddy revolve. He was trying to invade a warped mind; warped but by no means feeble. In his head, he re-drew the map, plotting the dark and lonely places, the hides from which a man might pounce and strike. They were surprisingly few. Even in this weather, people of the night went abroad; most of them, he saw, were watchful.

It took him a fortnight. On the fifteenth morning, he slept

late, primed his wits in a session with Beddoes, and went to beard the Super.

Smythe's office was the highest, biggest and best appointed in the building. On a clear day you could see across town to the bend in the river. Today, a cutting wind pushed sleet against the picture window; you couldn't even see across the street. Nevertheless, Smythe faced outward, hands in pockets, as though contemplating the most sylvan of views. He didn't turn, but his voice and his scepticism carried clearly.

'Correct me when I err, Inspector. A psychopath, you say, slight and wiry. He therefore selects undersize victims. And underage, of course. Operating in dockland, he has raped and murdered at least four times. His appetite is becoming less controlled and more frequent. He accosts teenagers at night, performs his rituals, and covers his tracks efficiently; bodies have been discovered by sheer accident. Thus far it's circumstantial and largely unconfirmed, but just credible, I suppose. Enter the Wallis female. She's bigger and older than the others, was attacked at dawn by a man wearing aftershave and a suit; and she survived. Hardly consistent, is it?'

Evans nodded at the motionless silhouette.

'That's the point, see, sir. A break in the pattern. I'd say he was heading for work. She caught his eye and the urge took him. *Because* she was stronger, because he wasn't hyped, he missed. He went over the top, sir.'

'Hm. What's this about Sundays and bad weather?'

'Just precautions. See the two things for their effect. Less people about.'

'Ingenious. I'm expected to divert men from regular duty and set up a scenario straight out of *Kojak*, I gather. Where's the sense, man? He's over the edge, you say, running wild.'

'Was, sir. Had a fright, see, steadied him down. He's bent but not stupid. He'll go back to the places he knows and the methods he trusts.'

'And give up aftershave?'

'Couldn't say, sir.'

'Oh? You seem pretty damn certain of everything else.'

'Not certain, sir. No.'

'Very well. Let's concede the principle, shaky though it

60

may be, and consider practicalities. Patrol the area, you say. Leave one or two key spots clear and march some poor WPC in mufti up and down in dockland. Here I am, take me. Christ, she's supposed to be a school kid, not a whore!' He pronounced it 'hoor', with deep distaste. Very righteous man, Smythe.

'Nothing so crude, sir. Only three nights, see, Friday, Saturday, Sunday. You put the girl in at dusk and she makes a single pass. It's a fair old walk, mind, takes a few hours. Shift the patrols around, leave a different opening every time.'

'And you, presumably, cover likely ambushes?'

'Me 'n' Beddoes, sir.'

'Of course, you know them all.'

'Aye.'

'Just "aye"?'

'Bit of research, sir. My own time, naturally.' Smythe shifted slightly but still didn't turn. Somewhere nearby, a telephone rang unheeded.

'All these uniforms wouldn't scare him off, would they?'

'Might do, sir. For a while.'

'Ah, I see. A lengthy campaign.'

'Give it a month, I reckon. He'll be nicely wound up by then.'

'A month, yes, why not? Handle it ourselves, d'you suppose, or should I call in the military?'

Doggedly, immune to sarcasm, Evans proposed, 'Ten men and a new girl each night, sir. Four weekends. Beat bobbies'll do nicely. Just shuffle them a bit.'

'You seem to have found all the answers.'

'I've tried, sir.'

At last, Smythe swung round and stalked to his desk. Still standing, leaning forward, he asked, 'How do you make a skinny teenager from a husky policewoman?'

'We must have a few under the cruiserweight limit. Ankle socks, a blazer, tam-o-shanter and pigtails. It's only an impression in the dark we're after, to draw him, like.'

Smythe settled in his chair, toyed with a paperweight; butterflies in perspex, an incongruous touch. Reflectively, watching the gaudy insects, he said, 'We have just two bodies.

61

The others could still be alive.'

'It's possible.'

'If it's one man, he could be six foot and fourteen stone.'

'Beddoes said the same. Three other blokes.'

'Hmm. Smart lad, Beddoes. Talented, wouldn't you say?'

'Oh indeed, sir, very.' For some moments, Smythe seemed wholly engrossed by this assessment. He set the paperweight down, just so, and folded his hands.

'I'm glad you appreciate the uncertainties, Inspector. And the difficulties.'

Evans grasped the opportunity.

'I'll take responsibility, sir. You can have an official request, written, mind.'

Smythe studied him, his expression unreadable. Finally he said, 'You're functioning again. Good. What size is your collar?'

'Pardon, sir?'

'You heard me.'

'Ah, seventeen, sir.'

'Mm. From here, your neck looks longer and thinner.'

Evans allowed himself a tight smile. 'Aye. Thank you, sir. Friday then.'

November. With traditional English perfidy, the weather relented. The wind died, the clouds lifted, the bleakness of the city eased. A bad omen.

'Cheer up, mate,' Beddoes advised. 'Be pissin down by Friday. Guy Fawkes.'

'Dear God,' breathed Evans, 'I forgot.'

'Yeah, well we all 'ave our moments.' Smythe offered no such charity.

'Ah, Inspector. Where's the wet-night monster now, sunbathing?'

'It's only a hypothesis, sir.'

'Changed your tune, haven't you? Last I heard it was a fundamental law of nature.'

'Aye. See, I was selling the idea, wasn't I?'

Smythe gave him a frosty smile. 'Just remember, salesmen are expendable. You propose to continue the charade?'

'Won't do any harm, sir. Rehearsal, sort of.'

'Hmm. Make sure it comes right on the night.'

Beddoes lost, Smythe won and Friday the fifth proved a write-off. A mild, almost muggy evening, the streets packed with kids of every age. Rockets and starbursts, pinwheels and jumping jacks, the smell of woodsmoke and gunpowder. Fire engines clattered through dockland, claxons blaring, blue lights ablaze. Movement, noise and confusion. Like the bloody Arms Park on international day. Keeping tabs on the bait was a nightmare; one large schoolgirl among countless minor editions.

Finally, the WPC forgot herself, giving comfort and first aid to a badly burned ten-year-old. As the ambulance pulled away, Evans sidled up to her. 'Might as well go home, luv. Your cover's blown.'

'I couldn't leave the child, sir. He'll be lucky not to lose some fingers.'

About to deliver a rebuke, Evans noted her tautness and the blood on her skirt.

'Aye. Demands of duty. Off you go, then.'

Beddoes, watching sardonically, enquired, 'Beddy-byes?'

'Too risky. Kids'll be out till midnight. Chummy could get lucky in the small hours.'

'Course 'e could. Question is, where?'

'Any bloody where. Super'd have my guts.'

''E'd like that. Look, page the beatmen, make it blanket coverage, no loopholes. Match postponed till tomorrow. If Chummy's got any sense 'e'll stay outa this lot.'

'Any sense? He's a nutter, man!' But it figured; the best of a bad job.

Saturday was calmer, a more reasonable traffic. The air remained unseasonably warm, the city went about its pleasure. By ten, the WPC had become a forlorn and solitary figure. They stuck to the script, walked her past the danger spots and collected her at eleven, footsore and dispirited. Not a hint of trouble. By Sunday they had it pat. Another pseudo victim made the long hike unhindered and apparently unremarked. Beddoes was stoical. On Monday morning, Smythe's silence was eloquent.

During the next week, Evans found himself irresistibly drawn to the docks at twilight. A refinement occurred to him, and he put it to Smythe.

'Blenheim Terrace, sir. They've demolished one side. Proper little concrete jungle. Now, if you could fix a blackout Sunday,' he shrugged, 'well, it might encourage him, see.'

Smythe shook his head in wonder.

'I'll say this for you, Evans, no half-measures.'

'Nothing to lose, sir.'

'Except my reputation. Oh very well!'

Beddoes, as always, had a pert comment.

'If Chummy's black, let's 'ope 'e's got big eyes and a smile.'

Friday and Saturday nights were clear but much colder; and uneventful. On Sunday, they trailed the girl awhile then cut ahead to the darkened terrace.

'Jesus,' whispered Beddoes. 'Must make you 'omesick. Like a bleedin coalmine.'

Evans had miscalculated badly. Accustomed to glaring streetlights, they were as blind as moles. For two breathless, heartstopping minutes, crouched beside crumbling masonry, they charted the target's progress by her footfalls. When she reached them unscathed, Evans's sigh of relief might have flattened the undamaged row.

'Nasty that,' he muttered.

'White scarf and gloves,' suggested Beddoes, 'would make 'er a bit more conspicuous.'

'Aye. Hindsight's a marvellous gift.'

'I'd've settled for any kind o' sight just then.' It hit them both simultaneously.

'Darro, boyo, she's not home yet!' But she made it, and another weekend was lost.

The intervening days dragged, time seemed suspended. At night, sleepless, Evans balanced probabilities, counting the ways he might be wrong. Sometimes he thought of Grace Yardley; her image lent him strength.

Friday's girl was petite, willowy and Irish. Kitted out, she passed for a mature fourth former. As she exchanged banter with Beddoes, Evans caught the underlying tension and asked, 'You all right, luv?'

'Ah, now sorr, 'tis a mite nervous I am. 'Twill pass, for I'm a divil with the Tae Kwon Du.'

'And flied lice,' grinned Beddoes, and she went for him, prettily indignant.

''Tis a martial art, me boy, so mind your manners.'

'Take you on any day, two falls or a submission.'

'Is that so? And who'd be helping the Inspector during the convalescence?'

Tonight, Blenheim Terrace was lit, and Evans went there alone. They'd decided to split, a variation to save walking.

'Time and motion,' Beddoes had groused. 'Too much of one, not enough of the other.'

The derelict side lay shrouded in shadow, and Evans entered cautiously. The wind, a nor'easter, gathered weight and ferocity by the minute. He hunched in the lee of a ragged wall and waited, conscious of a million stealthy rustles and a stench of drains. Strain and fatigue had weakened him; he felt exhausted. His mind wandered ahead to Sunday's blackout and the need for faster visual accommodation. Change the route, he thought, get her here earlier while we're alert. Despite cold and discomfort, he dozed. Only a flicker of white, far off, revived him.

If she was still edgy, she hid it well, approaching boldly but not too fast. He had to face the wind directly, and light blurred as the tears trickled. She came on, her shadow lengthening ahead and retreating behind as she moved from one pool of light to the next. She passed almost close enough to touch and he relaxed. In fifty yards she'd be clear.

The speed of it appalled him, a moment of paralysing disbelief. A bigger darker figure overwhelmed her, the sound of a blow, a cry, and she was down and struggling. As a surge of adrenalin thrust him forward, he registered another error; his steel-tipped heels crashed on the flagstones like gunshot. The scrimmage heaved and separated, the girl prostrate but moving, her assailant breaking clear. Too fast, too many options. In fury, he sensed initiative slipping away.

'You OK?' he shouted, running, and she cried, ''Tis just a bump.'

He shoved the walkie-talkie into her hands and left her,

bellowing over his shoulder, 'Get Beddoes here quick!'

An impression of angry eyes and a worm of dark blood on a pale cheek.

'Catch the divil, sorr! Don't let him away!'

He pounded on, conscious of the widened gap and the network of alleys all around. Chummy had panicked; had he taken to the shadows he'd be long gone.

A prop forward in his youth, Evans had trained for strength and stamina, not speed. He cursed the restraining overcoat, the clinging trousers and the pain in his chest. At full stretch, he was making no impression. The dark flying figure swung abruptly left and disappeared, soundless. Evans skittered round the junction, flailing for balance, veering on to the road. He was alone now, Beddoes could only guess at his whereabouts. The thought gave him a yard of pace. He was holding on, perhaps gaining a little. The map flashed into mind; Chummy was making for the river.

Evans drove onward, drawing on a last reserve. His quarry doubled left again and he sprinted for the corner. The signboard caught his eye, Waterloo Close, a cul-de-sac blocked by a fifteen-foot wall to the railway cutting. He steadied himself, gasping, preparing for the end-game. A single streetlamp cast dim light along the alley. Chummy's outline stood clear against whitewashed brick; spreadeagled, reaching upward, feet scrabbling for purchase. Beside him, a tarred slogan, *City rules, OK?* Evans side-stepped a dustbin and moved forward, catching his breath.

''Ard lines, boyo,' he called. 'Nice try. No way out, though. Let's be sensible, shall we?'

Chummy whirled, hands spread, knees flexed, back to the wall. A black tracksuit over a slim frame, black gloves and jogging shoes. Nightgear. His face seemed short and shadowed; a beard! So Wallis *was* a one-off, after all. Evans edged nearer, primed. Dark eyes watched him, close-set and strangely vacant. Using the wall for leverage, Chummy exploded right, checked and accelerated. Evans, off balance, lunged wildly, cursing aloud. An instant of frantic, febrile resistance, a rending sound, and Chummy was past, a shred of black trailing from one shoulder. On his knees, spent, Evans watched dull and unbelieving as two figures merged under the lamp. A despairing swerve, a flailing tackle, the distinctive whoomph of a winded man. Then he was there, dropping his knees into the narrow back, forcing limp arms into a vicious full nelson. A moment of pure, insensate rage. Dimly, he heard his own laboured breath and the thin, pig-like squeal. Beddoes touched his elbow.

'Easy, sir. 'Ere, slip the cuffs on.' Cold metal in his hands and a voice of reason; a double click, the squeal fading to a whimper. Beddoes stood wringing his wrist and grinning like a dervish.

'Bit o' luck,' he confessed. 'Ole biddy saw you go in. Window-watcher. Din't believe it, to be honest, but I 'ung around anyhow.'

'Hurt, are you?'

'Scraped me 'and a bit. Daft game, bloody rugby.'

'Pity. England hath need of you.'

'Count me out, mate.'

None too gently, Beddoes prodded the supine figure with his boot.

'Up you come, Chummy. Let's 'ave a look at you.'

He faced them, mouth twisted with pain, chest heaving, bare shoulder grazed and oozing. Beddoes leaned closer, made a quick grab. A gasp, a soft tearing noise, and hair dangled like a scalp from a naked and receding chin.

'Santa Claus, I presume,' murmured Beddoes.

'Name?' demanded Evans. No answer. He turned to Beddoes. 'Chatty, isn't he? Got your radio?'

'Sure. 'Ad a bit of a clatterin, though.' He drew out the aerial and pressed a button. A roar of static startled them both; even Chummy blinked.

'Stone me, good as new! Clever people, these Nips.'

'No wonder the Common Market's crumbling. Colleen all right, is she?' Beddoes smiled.

'She'll 'ave a lovely shiner in the morning. She'll get over it, when she sees 'is nibs 'ere.' He gave terse directions into the battered equipment.

The car arrived in short order. They bundled Chummy into the back, one each side. He still hadn't spoken. Evans leaned back, more thankful than triumphant. The long shot had come home, but only just, mind. He closed his eyes, welcoming the gentle sway of the car and the warmth back to his bones. Then, incredulous, he sniffed. Faint but definite, beneath the tang of fear and exertion, a distinctive spicy odour. Beddoes caught it too.

'Bleedin Brut,' he crowed. 'Our 'Enery'll 'ave a seizure!'

Back at the station the medical officer, summoned from hearth and TV, gave brusque treatment to minor injuries. O'Brien and Beddoes, comrades in small pain, traded insults somewhat giddily. The desk sergeant, a calm and avuncular character known to all as Jack Warner, kept a stern eye on proceedings. Evans lolled in a corner, his attention focused on Chummy, who submitted dully to the doctor's ministrations, his eyes blank. The black clothing emphasised his facial pallor and physical slightness. There was a bovine passivity about him which, coupled with his lack of stature, made him a curiously innocuous figure. He looked a most unlikely murderer.

The doctor left and Beddoes escorted the WPC across the room.

'She's a bit shaky,' Beddoes said defensively, 'I'll see 'er 'ome, OK?'

'Bless you my children,' Evans murmured, and they went out sniggering.

'Warner' caught Evans's eye.

'Charge room, sir?' Evans shook his head.

'Here'll do fine.' He turned to the suspect and intoned the caution.

'You're under arrest. You'll be charged with felonious assault pending further enquiries. You're not obliged to say anything, but if you do it may be taken down and used in evidence. You're allowed one phone-call.'

Briefly, the dark gaze flickered, whether in fear or relief Evans couldn't tell and didn't care. Sensing a clash of wills, he had neither the inclination nor the resources to provoke it now.

'Search him. Take him to the cells. He can have tea if he likes. Keep an eye, mind.'

At home, he downed a mammoth Scotch in milk and waited for sleep to come. His legs ached, his brain felt dislocated, but he couldn't rest. Had he, after all, trapped a casual prowler? There had been no real resistance, no denials, no reaction of any kind. Indeed, Chummy's stubborn, eerie silence had been the most impressive thing about him. They still didn't know his name.

I hope you catch him, Grace Yardley had written. Well, he'd done that. Hadn't he?

Chapter Seven

Evans awoke feeling his age; slow-witted, stiff-legged and unrefreshed. He'd been bloody lucky, no doubting it. The trapping of Chummy owed as much to a nosey crone, a blank wall and an unlikely tackle as to any thoughtful planning. Funny how things turn out.

Grey light filtered through the curtains. Somewhere close a stranded dog mourned the cold. As he lay there, half awake and cosy, a thought of Caroline crossed his mind. She would have been up by now, combing her hair and packing her satchel. Anger kindled, and with it, renewed resolve. Today, Chummy will talk. Creakily, he clambered out of bed ...

Apart from a bandaged hand, Beddoes looked improbably bright, and Evans sighed inwardly for lost youth.

'Tough little bird, the O'Brien,' announced Beddoes.

'Oh aye? Gave her the injection, did you?'

'You got a dirty mind, mate. Steady Catholic, waitin for Mr Right.'

'She'll be waiting still, then.'

Beddoes shrugged, moved a downturned palm this way and that. 'Lose some, win some.' His expression tightened. ''Ow do we 'andle Chummy? Usual style?'

Evans shook his head.

'I don't know. Tread carefully, play it by ear. Make it up as we go along.'

Chummy sat in the charge room, his tracksuit crumpled and unrepaired. His fingers, bitten about the quick, picked ceaselessly at the handcuffs and a facial tick fluttered below his left eye. Evans, reading the signs and, knowing what a night in the cells could do, moved very slowly indeed. He seated the stenographer precisely, enquiring after her comfort and the quality of the light. Acting up nicely, Beddoes slouched against the wall and eyed the prisoner fixedly. At snail's pace, Evans removed his jacket, rolled up his sleeves, laid out his notebook and pencil; and, with a vast sigh, sat down. Chummy, chewing at his lower lip, followed the performance apprehensively.

Finally Evans asked, 'Understood the caution last night, did you?'

Chummy nodded, an eager dip of the head.

'Want to call a lawyer?'

'What's the point? You caught me. There's nothing to be said.' The words tumbled out, running together. A high-pitched and not unpleasant voice, a classless Home Counties accent. Evans, secretly very pleased, recalled the dictum of a former mentor; once they start talking, you're halfway home.

'Aha,' he said comfortably, allowing the Valleys into his own speech, 'You're wrong there, see. I like a nice chat, me.'

'Been inside before?' asked Beddoes casually, and Chummy stiffened, clearly mistrusting the question.

'No, never.'

'Thought not,' said Beddoes, with a wolfish grin. ''Omely, innit?'

'I don't follow. And I'm dirty.'

'Relax, boyo,' Evans told him. 'Just gettin to know each other. Preservin the social amenities, like. Not goin anywhere, are you?' Chummy made a quick nervy gesture. The hand-cuffs clinked and caught the light.

'Look, this isn't necessary. I know what I've done and – well, I'll talk about it.'

'No hurry. Let's start at the beginning, shall we, and work through. Name?'

Evans bit off the last word and Chummy blinked.

'Morris, Edward Charles.' The stenographer went to work.

He was an accounts clerk who lived with his mother in the suburbs and commuted. He gave his age as twenty-nine, height five six, weight a hundred and thirty-two pounds.

'Like to call your Ma?' enquired Beddoes. 'Spect she'll be wonderin by now.'

71

'Not to worry,' said Morris quickly. 'I've been out nights before. I'd like a wash though.'

'Ah,' breathed Evans, and wrote laboriously. Without raising his head, he murmured, 'Pop out and check the address, will you, Sergeant?' Taking his time, Beddoes obeyed.

'Um – he's not going there, is he?'

'No, no. Only to the desk, see. All sorts of records we keep here, you'd be surprised.' He sat, motionless and sphinx-like until Beddoes returned. A good five minutes, by which time Morris could hardly keep still.

'Mrs Thelma Morris, widow,' Beddoes declared. 'She your Ma?'

'Yes.'

'Good,' said Evans warmly. 'Nice to get the facts straight. Now, tell us about the girls.'

Morris licked his lips, darted a glance at Beddoes.

'One was early in the morning a few weeks back. And the policewoman last night.' He hesitated, and added, 'I don't know what came over me. I just – needed it. I'm not very good with girls.' He lowered his head.

Evans studied the stenographer's pen. When it stopped, he told her regretfully, 'Sorry, luv, I've wasted your time.' And to Beddoes, 'Come on, Sergeant, we've better things to do.'

'Right you are, sir.'

'Wait! Where are you going?'

Evans rose and stretched. Standing over Morris, he said, 'Look, boyo, we got you cold on assault. Give us credit. If that was all, you'd be in front of the beak, not sitting here comfy. It's the others we're wanting.'

Morris's lips thinned.

'I don't know what you mean.'

'Aye. Pity, mind. Well, you toddle off downstairs and we'll get back to the salt mines. Further enquiries, like I said.'

'Could take a fair bit o' time, sir,' mused Beddoes.

'Aye. A month, maybe six weeks. Mills of God, see.'

'You can't keep me here six weeks!' Morris cried. Evans eyed him, suddenly cold.

'Can't I? Tell him, Sergeant,' he ordered, and walked out.

72

Ten minutes later, Beddoes, very chuffed, relayed the conversation.

'You read 'im lovely, mate. Bustin to talk. 'Ates bein cooped up, he says, it's why 'e prowls at night an' falls into temptation.'

'Oh sure.'

'Anyhow I fed him the medicine. 'F'd 'ad the caution and declined a mouthpiece. 'S'all here, I told 'im, in black 'n'white. Talk or rot.'

Evans was flicking through the file, refreshing his memory.

'Sir?'

'Mmm?'

'What about the car?'

Evans grinned. 'Clever boy. A commuter.'

'Yeah, well. Stands to reason, don't it. Gotta be a motor around somewhere, 'ed've used it last night. I'll page the uniforms, shall I, get 'em to keep an eye?'

'Think about it, bach. Where there's a car there's a key.'

Beddoes snapped his fingers. 'Warner!' Together they headed for the desk.

'Warner' was off-duty, but he'd left an envelope for the inspector. In it, a ring of keys and a note: 'Found these in his hip pocket. Thought you'd come looking, sooner or later.'

'Cheeky old berk,' said Beddoes indignantly.

'Honour thine elders, boyo. He's a good copper.'

'Geriatrics united. All right, let's get to it. Datsun, it says here. I'll 'ave a session on the blower, check out the dealers an' try for the registration.'

Evans sighed. 'Walk, don't run.'

'Huh?'

'I'm for the easy life, me. Look, we know what it is and we know, more or less, where it is. So we send a uniform up there with the key. Not too many cars about at this time. Working hours, see.' And within the hour, the lab boys were taking a blue Datsun apart.

Back in the office, Beddoes, somewhat subdued, asked, 'What's the next step?'

'The turning of the screw.'

''Ow d'you mean?' Evans told him and Beddoes whistled respectfully.

'Bit dodgy, innit? S'pose 'e blabs?' Evans had a fallback for that, too.

Shortly after lunch, they were called to the cells.

Morris, very agitated, cried, 'I'm making a complaint. Someone in there's been beaten up.' He pointed, shaking.

'That's a serious charge, boyo.' Evans turned to Beddoes. 'Check it. Find out who's next door,' and Beddoes left without a word.

'By the way,' Evans said conversationally, 'we've found your car.'

'But I didn't tell you ...'

'Not very clever, really. You know what they say – it's better by bus. It's the blanket, see. Boffins are working on it right now. Wonder what they'll come up with? Why d'you say someone was beaten? Not our style, is it?'

Morris hesitated, not knowing which thread to pick up; and settled for the safer.

'I heard noises. Blows, something metal, groans and screams.'

'It's the quiet, you know, and the loneliness. The mind wanders, doesn't it? I expect it was a daydream.'

'It was real, I tell you!'

Beddoes entered, looking, to Evans's experienced eye, a good deal too innocent.

'Cell's unoccupied, sir. 'As been for a week.'

Morris's voice rose, shrill and girlish. 'You're lying! You're covering up!'

'Take it easy,' Beddoes advised him. 'Cleaners, I reckon. Mops and pails and 'eavy feet. They sing sometimes. They're *awful* singers. What time'd it 'appen?'

Morris eyed him narrowly, his suspicions almost tangible. 'Around midday.'

'Ah, well, there you are. Cleaners. Gotta be. Oh, I forgot, yer Ma phoned.'

'What?' Morris looked stunned.

'She was worried, she said. Oh, she's used to you bein out

74

nights, you told us, but not the 'ole day after. Usually gets a call, she said. Considerate, aren't yer.'

'What did you tell her? What did you say?'

Beddoes shrugged. 'Tricky, innit. Well, what could I do? I mean it's limbo, you not talkin. Told 'er I'd let 'er know soon as we 'ad somethin definite. OK?'

Morris was standing rigid, arms dangling, eyes everywhere. He looked ashen. Evans, gauging the moment and mindful of the risk, murmured, 'Sally Brooks, Edna Clark, Doreen Childs, Caroline Yardley. Wonder what they'll find on that blanket.'

The cell was suddenly still and quiet. Morris went slack, the apathy of the previous night reborn. Presently, he said sulkily, 'You know. You've known all the time.'

'Come on, boyo,' Evans coaxed. 'Get it off your chest. It's what you *want* to talk about.' Morris nodded like a clockwork toy.

'Yes. Yes, I do.'

In the charge room the atmosphere was altogether more businesslike. The stenographer waited, poised. Beddoes hunched forward expectantly. Evans himself played it absolutely straight, repeating the caution and putting the words 'voluntary statement' into Morris's mouth. Jerkily at first, but with gathering fluency, the prisoner spoke.

Evans had witnessed confessions before; the evasions and histrionics, the despairing pleas for vindication and understanding. An untidy slurry of emotions from which facts had to be sifted like gemstones, and then scrutinised for truth. Morris merely talked, a thickening catalogue of horror delivered in the detached, almost languid, tones of a stock-market report.

He liked them young and clean, he said. He avoided tarts and the willing ones, he had a mortal dread of disease. Sunday evenings were best, especially when it was wet or cold or both.

'The buses aren't so regular, you see. They get impatient and start walking. Youngsters can't keep still for long, I find.'

He would draw alongside and offer lifts. If they refused, he

75

smiled and drove on. Those who sat watchful and alert on the edge of the seat, he dropped as promised. He insisted on the front seat, naturally. Only when they grew relaxed and chatty, distracted, could he detour. In some ill-lit street, he would feign worry about a puncture. He'd get out, stroll round to the passenger side and open the door.

'There's a torch in the glove compartment, my dear. Could you pass it please?'

He would lean in, wait for the forward movement, the exposed neck. A quick judo chop and away to his special place.

In the same awful monotone, he told of the blanket and a pyjama cord and the problems of undressing an unconscious girl. And more; the pleasures of passivity and sweet young flesh. The stenographer looked bloodless and sick. Beddoes sat like a man in a waking nightmare.

The worst part came later, Morris assured them; driving to a suitable place of disposal. That was the word he used – disposal. Once he'd been lucky with construction work, once he'd used the river. The other four, he said smugly, would never be found. Here Beddoes stirred. 'Four?' – and Evans shot him a fierce warning stare. The Wallis girl, Morris continued, had been an aberration, a spur of the moment urge.

'She looked nicer than the rest,' he confided wistfully. 'Rounder. I wouldn't be here if I hadn't been so stupid.'

Nevertheless, he looked contented, a man reminiscing over a few drinks.

'Funny, really. I only knew the name of one, Yardley. Before they were printed in the paper, I mean.'

Evans paused, mostly to control his voice. 'Very interesting. She must've been different in lots of ways, mind.'

Morris smiled, looking suddenly very young and pure. 'Oh, you know about that, too.'

He'd been on his way to dockland and had seen the pair of them, hand in hand, walking in the rain. He'd never had two at once. He'd read of it in the magazines he hid from his mother and the idea excited him. Racking his brains for a plausible approach, he trailed them to the market and parked. He watched while the slim, dark one bought a gee-gaw, close enough to read the embroidered name tag on her white socks.

He was disappointed when the chubby one trotted off; he'd have to make do with what was left.

At the fringe of the crowd, he'd asked if her name was Caroline, Mrs Yardley's daughter. Told her there'd been a slight accident, her mother was safe but in hospital. Could he drive her there? She'd been frightened and eager, so easy really. He'd thrown the china away – some blue and white thing, he said.

Standing under the strictest control, his fists bunching at his sides, Evans took the signature. Then, to Beddoes, he said, 'Book him.'

Outside, fittingly, was fog and dreariness. From his habitual listening post, Smythe could have seen only his own reflection. Even so, he stood like a sentinel and spoke, as usual, without turning.

'You were wrong on a number of counts. Four more, you say. They'll play havoc with your pattern.'

'Details, sir. The *principle* held, didn't it?'

'Of course. Don't mistake me, an admirable piece of work. Not your normal handwriting though, that's what bothers me. You used to be a belt and braces man, Evans. Not going fey and Celtic, I hope?'

'A bit harsh, sir.'

'I mistrust hunches, Inspector. I don't hold with stake-outs and elaborate traps and Hollywood street chases. Obsessions leave me cold, too. You over yours?'

It was an awkward question, cutting the ground from under Evans's feet, and he fumbled haltingly.

'Ah, as a matter of fact, sir, I was wondering ...'

'Speak out, man!'

'Miss Yardley's in Eastbourne, sir. Convalescing, you could say. See, the papers'll have a field day with Morris. The whole truth and nothing but the truth, no matter how ugly.'

'You're not asking for censorship, surely?'

'Course not. They'd dig it out anyway, and hammer us for withholding news.' He spat the last word away like phlegm.

'I'm glad you see that.'

77

'It's just I'd like to break it myself, sir, so she gets it straight. From someone she – well – trusts, see.'

Smythe paced to his desk.

'I've already given you too much rope.'

'I didn't hang myself, sir.'

'Not yet. It's no part of your duty.'

'No. Call it a favour then.'

The Superintendent settled heavily and stroked the paper-weight absently.

'She must have impressed you a great deal.'

'It's in the file, sir. No husband, no one close. Often, it's the strong ones who break.'

'Couldn't help the daughter so you'll try to save the mother, eh?'

'If you like.'

'I don't. Still, I suppose you've earned it. One thing, though. Draw a line, Evans. Love her, leave her, but get yourself sorted out. An end to obsession, do I make myself clear?'

'Aye, sir. Thanks.'

It was a foul drive. Visibility on the motorway down to fifty yards and the fast-lane cowboys raising spray in buckets. He stopped for a greasy and exorbitant snack, and the prices at the self-service pumps made his eyes water. More than once he thought of turning back, the news he carried didn't hold much joy. Later on, he toyed with buying flowers, and dismissed the idea as wishful thinking. The assurance he brought to professional issues deserted him. This was a personal mine-field and he'd lost the map. Soldier on, boyo, what else is there?

He found the place easily enough, a superior type of boarding house at the up-market end of the promenade. As he reversed to the kerb, the weather was lifting. Tide's turned, he thought, recalling a piece of Aberystwyth folklore. He asked for Miss Yardley and was ushered into 'the conservat-war', an over-furnished room containing two geriatrics, some blighted palms and a meagre coalfire. He felt lumpish and conspicuous, wholly out of his element.

The clack of high heels alerted him; he had just a moment to observe her before she saw him. There was a touch of colour to her cheeks and a freedom in her movements he'd not noticed before. He knew at once he'd been wrong to come, bringing his recipe for relapse; but someone had to tell her.

She came towards him, a smile of real warmth lighting her eyes. The trip was worth it for this alone.

'Inspector, what a pleasant surprise.'

Not for long, he thought.

'Ma'am. It's mutual, mind.' An awkward, rather uncomfortable pause; they'd never had much small talk. He asked inanely after her health; then, 'There's something I have to tell you. Not here, though.'

Her face fell.

'I see. I'll get my coat.' She turned away, purposeful and poised. He couldn't keep his eyes off her.

Outside it was brighter but cooling. There'd be a frost inland, and ice on the roads; it wouldn't be wise to drive back. Briefly, he allowed himself a fantasy; a mid-week break, his woman at his side. And shrugged it off angrily. Don't be bloody daft, man. Keep your feet on the ground. He glanced down, saw her struggling and slowed abruptly.

'Sorry. Copper's pace.'

'It's good for me.' The breeze had ruffled her hair. She looked very young and quite lovely. They picked their way along a front dotted with wheelchairs; piles of blankets with sad eyes.

'It's nice here,' she said, guessing his thoughts, 'but a bit depressing.'

He crossed the road, steering her to the railings. They were alone now and he sensed an all too familiar tension. Gripping the rails, gazing out over the leaden sea and pitching his voice above the tow of wave on shingle, he said, 'You asked me to do something. In your letter. Well, it's done.'

'You caught someone?'

'Aye.'

She closed her eyes and he had to bend to hear her. 'Tell me about him.'

So it began again, the careful phrasing, the euphemisms, the attempt to clothe naked evil in some guise of decency; the kind of account in which silence is more eloquent than sounds. She listened, taut and still, her face austere.

'So you see, she didn't suffer, not as you might have imagined.'

Salt air and seaweed and the squabbles of gulls. Beside him, she seemed absurdly fragile; at any moment, the wind might rise and whisk her away. He sensed the inner struggle as she, in turn, hunted the words she needed. At last she lifted her eyes to him, and he was stunned at their serenity.

'I think I knew I'd lost her, even before you arrived that night. It wasn't something I could ever admit. Do you understand?'

He felt the full power of her appeal and nodded, his voice thick.

'I think so. Aye.'

'She can't be hurt any more, Inspector, and neither can I. The worst is past.'

She fumbled in her handbag, showed him the picture. 'You were right. This *is* Caroline, as she was and always will be. Nothing else matters.'

'Well – if you're sure, mind ...' he muttered, and won another smile.

'I'm sure.'

It was a wholly unexpected reprieve, and from it he drew fluency. Walking back, she spoke of local shopping difficulties and made an occasional deft comment on her fellow-boarders. For the first time, there was ease between them, the closeness of survivors.

Off-handedly, she asked, 'What will happen to him?'

'Hard to say. He's not normal, see – well, that's obvious – so he may not go down.'

'Go down?'

'Sorry. Prison.' Glimpsing her expression, he added, 'Don't worry. He'll be out of circulation a good long while.'

'Perhaps I should pity him. I don't, though, not a bit.'

'There's very few'd blame you for that.'

Already it was much colder. The day, and certain other things, neared an end. Draw a line, Smythe had told him, and he was ready. Ready as he ever would be.

At the front door, she turned sharply, struck by a wayward thought.

'You're sure you have the right man? I mean, absolutely sure?'

'Yes.'

'You say he's - abnormal. I believe, sometimes, people confess to things they haven't done. Is that true?'

'It happens.'

'Surely you understand? How can you be certain?'

Casually, his mind elsewhere, he said, 'It was the vase, see. No one else knew about it.'

In the blankness of her expression he saw the ruin of the afternoon. *No one else knew.* Not even Grace Yardley. She'd been wrong, she could and would be hurt again; and again he must be the instrument. For now he must remind her that a gift for her had cost her daughter's life; and like the child, the gift had been despoiled and broken.

Chapter Eight

From her fifth-floor window, Grace Yardley overlooked the sea. She had come to know its every mood, to revel in the storm and grieve in the calm. Tonight the water scarcely rippled, lying beneath a quarter moon like beaten silver. Briefly, her mind returned to other beaches; buckets and spades, candy-floss and donkey rides. Evans had done this, she thought, with his clumsy, well-meaning concern. She had stored these images away in rooms of memory too empty to enter; he'd forced a door which she had tried to close.

Somewhere below, water-pipes thrummed and gurgled; the colonel in his evening bath. Solitary nights had taught her the heartbeat of the building. Presently, Mrs Ponsonby-Walker would yodel for her cats, then chain and bar the door. And woe betide the latecomers.

Soon she would leave, she realised, the interlude was over. She must pick up the remnants of her life; however threadbare they may seem. She had no place among the wealthy who waited so listlessly for death. Evans had prompted this resolve, too. A visitor from the real world, a walking symbol of things now past and those which might yet lie ahead. Someone, perhaps the only one, who cared.

She need only crook a finger and he would come running. In a vague, unfocused way, she'd sensed this from the start; only recently had she analysed and accepted it. Under the pretext of duty, he'd trailed her steadily, offering comfort and support where neither were possible. An unstated, perhaps unacknowledged promise of companionship on any terms she cared to dictate. She sighed. A good man, solid, dependable and constant. There was a resilience to him, a refusal to yield before loss and tragedy, a bedrock of common

82

sense and dignity which would always endure. Idly, she wondered what hidden sorrow had forged him. A broken home, a failed marriage, a stillborn ambition? He would never tell, and she would never ask. She remembered what he'd said; and what he hadn't. There *were* consolations. Caroline had met death with a daughter's concern in her heart and a present in her hands; and hadn't suffered. Poor, dear Caroline.

The thought brought her up short, shocked at her own resignation. Grief, she suddenly knew, is finite, can only be sustained so long. Then it becomes mourning, an altogether gentler and more lasting condition. In quiet moments, she would mourn Caroline for the rest of her days. But grief was no more.

A cloud covered the moon. Somewhere above, a radio blared pop music. In the abrupt blackness, a new conception touched her; the man who killed Caroline. For the first time, he existed in her mind. Not a beast, not a freak, but someone who lived with his mother and used a calculating machine and drove himself to work each day. A man who, for nothing other than his own gratification, could issue cruel lies, subject a little girl to mental and physical torture; and casually destroy her final gift. She fell to the most futile of wishes. If only Caroline had been ill, if only it hadn't been raining, if only the market had been closed ...

The moon blew clear again, the radio ceased in mid-wail. Grace Yardley stirred and dried her eyes. Moving briskly, she crossed the silvered carpet into the bathroom and pressed the switch. Squinting in the sudden brightness, she took a plastic pill-box from the medicine chest and emptied its contents into the lavatory. Distantly but clearly, she had glimpsed a purpose which might fill the void in her life; and had no further use for Valium.

'Go on, taste it.'

Nigel Buxton peered at the morsel on his fork, then up into Theresa's eyes. No prisoner at the bar had awaited judgement more anxiously. In vain had he pleaded indifference to curry. Goan cuisine, she'd stated blithely, like Goan blood, sprang from a marriage of Europe and Asia, the best of both worlds.

Gingerly, he bit into the skewered prawn – and nodded in surprise and relief.

'Delicious,' he said, meaning it, warmed by the pleasure in her face.

'There, you see. Think what you've been missing all these years.' The meal progressed, small portions delicately spiced and cunningly blended, proving her point beyond dispute.

Theresa had moved in two weeks ago. 'Bag and baggage,' she'd said with a knowing smile. He wasn't quite sure how it had happened, he couldn't remember making a decision. She simply took over, with a practical touch which belied her exotic looks. Already she'd established a routine. His personal life had seldom been so organised.

And yet ... Sprawled in a favourite chair, he felt a curious unease. Order bred sameness, a subtle lack of uncertainty and variety. Very agreeable, but a rut nonetheless. Just as he savoured the cut and thrust of courtroom battle and the modest fame it brought him, so he needed the stimulus of sexual challenge with its promise of less public rewards. St Paul's words came to mind: *O Lord, grant me chastity; but not yet.* There was something rather *too* comfortable about his present circumstances; Chopin on the stereo and the sounds of washing up. He imagined the awful Dame Stanmore: 'So nice to see young Mr Buxton settling down. It'll be the making of him.' Perhaps, thought Nigel, but he still had doubts of domesticity.

Theresa's arms slid round his neck and a musky perfume stirred him. She had somehow found time to shower and squeeze into something frivolous.

'Tired?' she murmured throatily.

'I was,' he admitted, reaching for her. 'Men of my age need plenty of rest.'

'Then you'd better come and lie down. In that order.'

He followed her into the bedroom, marvelling anew at the texture of her skin and the tautness of her hips. As the négligé floated free and her heat enveloped him, he believed he might, after all, tolerate this particular rut a little longer.

*   *   *

84

The interrogation of Morris foundered on bland and unbending obstinacy. It was as though, having confessed, he had forsaken all claims. He spoke only to complain; of stale clothing, of dirty furniture, of dull food. Despite verbal traps, psychological pressure and increasing hostility, he refused to reveal anything new. He wouldn't identify those still missing, he'd 'forgotten' how, when and where he'd 'disposed' of them, they might never have existed. Forensic studies drew a blank, and the river, in spite of comprehensive dredging, preserved its mysteries.

'I told you you'd never find them,' Morris said. Evans was hard put to keep hands off; even Beddoes was getting physical. The charge room became a prison for them both. At this point, the lawyer, a public appointee, made his appearance. Coming late to the feast, he denied them even crumbs. His client had already said far too much; henceforth he would say nothing at all. And he needed toilet requisites. Morris simply sat there, a blank wall against which their questions echoed hollow.

After two days, Smythe called them off. Seated, for once, at his desk and looking uncharacteristically benign, he told Evans, 'I've been dickering with the law men, it's over bar the shouting. The Yardley case is unshakeable, Morris will plead guilty. Diminished responsibility. The tame shrink's got him bang to rights. Classic syndrome, it seems, Krafft-Ebing in spades. Perversions in pig Latin, precedents galore. Defence counsel's biddable, doesn't care for grime on his hands. We'll trot it through on the double, clear the slate by Christmas. Amazing what they can do when they try, usually takes months. Prosecutor's booked a skiing holiday, apparently.'

'Nice for some,' Evans grunted. 'Goodwill to all men, is it?'

Smythe cocked his head, testing the nuance; the heater bubbled fitfully.

'I'm sorry you don't approve, Inspector. Desolated, in fact.'

'Diminished responsibility,' mused Evans, undeterred. 'Manslaughter, mind, not murder.'

'I'm aware, actually.'

'He's irrational then, poor dab.'

'You said it yourself, man. A nutter!'

85

'Read the confession, have you?'

'Just skimmed through, in an idle moment. Of course I have!' The intercom buzzed and Smythe ignored it. From the corridor, marching feet approached, passed and faded.

Reflectively, Evans said, 'It's the Wallis affair I'm thinking about. He's pottering along in the Datsun ready for the office. Pinstripes and pouf mixture, according to Beddoes. Very fussy, Mr Morris, see. Tidy. Along comes our Dot, bouncing lovely. He hits the anchors and jumps all over her, right there in the road. I mean, *anyone* could've seen him. I think that's irrational, me.'

'Brilliant. Excellent. I'm glad we agree.'

'Ah. But he missed, didn't he. A few bruises, a bit of a shaking, she'd do worse at the Palais Saturday night.'

'Make your point, d'you mind? I've one or two other things to do.'

'Aggravated assault at the worst. Six months, suspended if he's lucky. First offender, see. Hardly manslaughter, then.'

Smythe raised his eyebrows and waited.

'Take Caroline Yardley, now. Something else again. It's Sunday night, he's spent all day getting ready. Checked the oil, filled the radiator, blanket and strangling rope in the back. Time's right, weather's right, he's *planned* it, see. He trails her to the market, reads the name on her socks. Standing there, he thinks up the one story which'll really get her worried, bring her to the car itching to go. He's still got the torch and puncture trick up his sleeve. Don't know about you, sir; in my book that's murder. Premeditated.'

'What is this, Evans, the male menopause?'

'Not just yet, thanks. Thing is, it's not logical. We're doing him for a miss and turning a blind eye to the big one.'

'Good God, man, you know the score! Even you concede he's psycho. The hell difference does it make, murder or manslaughter, so long as he's off the streets and out of harm's way? He pleads. It's easier, cheaper and quicker for everyone.'

'Specially the St Moritz set.'

'I'll pretend I didn't hear that, Evans.'

'Oh sure. Look, sir, he won't even get a proper sentence. The nuthouse till he's better. Better than what? Better says

86

who? In five years he could be cured, pronounced normal, whatever that is. Off he goes, free as air, an older and wiser man. Then one day he spots a well-turned gymslip and he's away to the Home Stores for the tracksuit and pyjamas. It's happened before, mind; don't tell me it hasn't.'

Smythe got up and strode to the window. There was nothing to see but weather. He stood, hands in pockets, shoulders hunched, rocking gently on his heels. Evans thought he was considering; when he turned, the illusion vanished. His eyes were icy and there were dull red patches on his cheeks.

'I don't care for lawyers, Evans, the barrack-room type least of all. You're not a psychiatrist, you're not a solicitor, you're not even a superintendent. You're no kind of expert, and you'll keep your place! Hold your tongue, man! I don't need any more legal advice from you. Since your education is so sadly lacking, I'll remind you of the copper's code. *We* catch 'em, *they* cook 'em, right? We're enforcers, you and I, nothing more. Now, I just whiled away an hour driving a bargain. It wasn't easy and I didn't enjoy it; my salary only runs to Margate. But it's a good bargain, the very best I could get. Morris will plead, the judge will decide, *and you will forget the whole damn issue!* Now go and do something useful. Bloody woman's turned your head!'

Not so much turned his head as opened his eyes, Evans thought later, lying low in the office. You spend a lifetime chasing villains, you grow calluses. Had to, really, or you'd end up making baskets and staring at the wall. Trouble is, it hardens you to victims, too. After a while, the robbed and the bereaved become mere names in a file, figures in a table. You develop the face and the manner; outward sympathy, inner indifference.

It had started that way with Caroline Yardley, just another runaway on a wet weekend, just one more deceived mother. Then Grace Yardley turned it inside out. Through her, he'd experienced the worry and the agony, become something of a victim himself. Because of her, he'd gone beyond the limits, made the hunt for Morris a crusade, taken the role of judge and jury on as well. It wasn't sensible, mind, he didn't need Smythe to tell him. He'd been arguing from the gut, not the head, and none the worse for that, either. As a copper, he'd go along with Smythe; but as a man, he didn't have to like it.

He ought to call her, really, no expectations, just to see how she was managing. Somehow, he couldn't quite find the nerve. He'd hardly be a welcome voice – the man whose every intrusion in her life had aggravated the tragedy. So it was with considerable surprise and no small pleasure that he lifted the phone and heard her speak.

'Inspector Evans? Grace Yardley.'

'How are you, ma'am?'

'Back home and in work. As well as can be expected, I suppose. Improving.'

'Glad to hear it. Can I help?'

'It's something I'd rather not mention over the telephone. Could you possibly come here? Would it be an imposition? At your convenience, naturally.'

'I'm not overburdened at the moment,' he confessed, smiling grimly at himself. 'Tonight suit you?'

A short, rather sticky pause.

'Well – I'm sorry. I have something on ... An important meeting.'

'No problem. Tomorrow, then?'

'Yes, fine. And thank you.'

He took extra care over his appearance, once more rejecting the idea of some small gift. He hadn't the right, not yet. She looked a little strained, he thought, despite the usual grooming. Composed, of course, more vital than before, and something else. Purposeful? Different, anyway.

Off-duty, he felt able to accept a drink.

'Sherry?' she offered, and, seeing the distaste he couldn't quite conceal; 'Or would you prefer Scotch?'

'Now you're talking,' he said, and basked in her smile.

He watched as she busied herself at the cocktail cabinet. Perhaps he was imagining, but he fancied there was more freedom in her, a little more sway in her walk. The drink came in a cut-glass tumbler, a generous tot. She seated herself, sipped her sherry and said, 'I believe the trial is due soon.'

'Next week.'

'I want to go.' Her directness hadn't changed, anyway. He nursed the glass, chunky in his fingers.

'It's your right, ma'am, a public occasion. No one can stop you.' She was watching him closely, her grey eyes sombre.

'You don't sound very encouraging.'

'Look, it's just a formality, see. He's confessed, there's nothing to prove.'

'I've never been in court.'

'You haven't missed much. It's mostly dry stuff. Boring.'

'I hardly expect to be bored, Inspector.' The light stress reproached him and he cast about for amends.

'Sorry. Bad choice of words. What I meant was *cold*, really. Very factual, very clinical. Nasty.'

She'd gone paler, but there was a determined set to her mouth.

'It's a question of truth, you see. I don't want the edited version.'

He cropped at the whisky, weighing his words.

'He's pleading guilty. No defence, see. Even so, the prosecution has to spell it out. Chapter and verse, mind. No holds barred. There'll be medical evidence, post mortem reports. He'll be in the dock, of course. You'd have to see him, listen to him. Might last a couple of days.' He paused, asked quietly, 'Up to it, are you?'

She'd finished her drink and rose to get another. At the cabinet, she whirled, her hand coming to her mouth, her eyes wide in distress.

'Oh, forgive me, my manners! Would you like some more?'

He held up his glass. 'Still going, thanks.'

She settled again, crossing her legs. As she bent, breast and flank thrust briefly against her suit and he caught his breath, mortified at himself.

'This isn't a whim, Inspector. I've thought about it very deeply.' She placed her glass on the table and leaned forward, suddenly alight with fervour. The sheer impact almost over-whelmed him. 'There has to be an end, you see. I don't want to read about it. I don't want to look at photographs. I have to watch and listen and reach a personal judgement. It's not a question of whether I can; I must. I owe it to Caroline – and to myself.' She held his gaze a moment longer, then sighed and bowed her head. An errant strand of hair touched her face and she brushed it away, the most feminine of gestures.

He'd seen it, then; a fleeting glimpse of the passion beneath the calm and beautiful mask. He found it disturbing and compelling, felt himself falling inexorably under her spell. He shrugged, helpless and disarmed.

'Well, if you feel that way … no one can stop you, like I said.'

'I'm sorry,' she murmured, 'I have no right to harangue you, of all people.' Hesitation, an intake of breath. 'Will you be there?'

'Me?'

'I thought – well, I assumed you'd be a witness.'

'Oh aye, certainly. I'll give evidence and push off, that's the form. No need to hang about, see. The court gives us a buzz when we're wanted. Don't call us, we'll call you.'

'Oh.' His attempted humour fell quite flat. She sounded very downcast.

'Ma'am?'

'Oh for goodness sake, I'm not a maiden aunt! The name is Grace!'

The outburst rocked him, left him speechless. Hurriedly, she added, 'I'm sorry, I'm not used to drink, I shouldn't've …' She broke off and her expression shifted like quicksilver. Suddenly, she looked no older or less mischievous than her daughter. 'No, I'm not sorry. I should have said that *months* ago. I'm not a piece of Dresden, I'm a perfectly normal woman!'

Breakthrough, he could scarcely credit it. Cautiously, conscious of the gleam in his own eye, he said, 'We're trained to notice things like that.' A gentle blush climbed her cheeks, and she gave him a quick, long-lashed sideways glance.

'I sincerely hope so!' A moment of suspense, dare he push his luck?

As though reading the thought, she pleaded, 'I'd like you to be there. With me. I make brave speeches, but I don't know if I can take it alone.'

90

Enslaved, he spoke without the smallest pause for thought. 'I'm sure it can be arranged. Grace.'

He'd driven halfway home before the implications hit him, bringing him to earth. He'd need Smythe's consent – an unlikely favour in the light of their last encounter. To hell, he thought, I'll go on my knees if I have to. Instead, he made his approach on carefully professional grounds.

'Funny things happen in court, sir,' he began the following morning. 'Prisoners get overawed, or boastful, or just plain careless. Morris is a nutter, unpredictable. You never know what might slip out.'

Whatever his faults, Smythe was not a vindictive man. He listened neutrally, his rage of yesterday forgotten.

'What are you suggesting, Inspector?'

'Someone should be there, sir. Keeping an eye.'

'The records are kept punctiliously, as you well know.'

'Ah, records. They'll give the facts all right, but you don't get the tone, see, the inflection. Could be just a hint, mind. Easily missed in the records, hints.'

'Voluntary service, Inspector? Usually takes wild horses to drag you into court.'

'Just a thought, sir. Not important, really. Only seeing as I'm a witness anyway ...'

'It'll take several days, man, even the expurgated version!'

'Aye, time-consuming, no doubt. But then, I'd have to hang around, wouldn't I, waiting for the call.'

'I don't see why. I'd expect you to be on early. No cross-examination, remember?'

Evans waited, staring out of the window where a fitful sun pierced the clouds.

'This Morris character's really got to you, hasn't he?'

Evans, sensing sympathy, played up for all he was worth. 'Unfinished business, sir. It upsets me, like.'

'Keen to be in at the kill, eh? See him go down?'

'Not that so much, sir. It's the girls we never found. I'd like to *know*, see.' In this he was wholly sincere and Smythe relaxed perceptibly.

'Understandable, I suppose.' Then, elaborately casual, he asked, 'Not still goose-chasing, I hope? How's the obsession?'

It was a shrewd sally, and Evans had difficulty meeting his eye.

'All done, sir. History.'

'It'd better be. At my age and rank, Evans, I'd hate to be conned.'

'Have to be up early for that, sir.'

'It's happened. Not for a very long time, though.'

Chapter Nine

Evans loitered in the grey and windswept street. He wasn't alone. Presently, a blue van inched through and the noise started; an ominous, high-pitched mutter. Morris was hustled past, shielded by heavies and hooded in a blanket. The crowd, mostly women, became hysterical. The voices were harsh, the language unbelievable. Evans glanced at the chapped, hate-filled faces and shivered, not from cold. You could swop Morris for any of these, he thought, and hardly know the difference. Nutters.

He followed, at a discreet distance, into the building. Imposing enough from outside, he reckoned, but a swine to heat. Huge lofty rooms, a draughty maze of corridors, one radiator every half mile; or so it seemed. A gaggle of reporters overtook him, and several spoke his name. He kept within earshot, his mind on the doctor's campaign for anonymity. So far, it seemed to be working; Grace Yardley wasn't mentioned. Just as well, he thought. Even she'd be easy meat for these vultures.

She sat in the public gallery, solitary, and, to him at least, very conspicuous. He glanced around warily. No one else paid her the slightest attention. Much relieved, he sidled towards her.

A powder blue suit today, setting off her hair and bringing subtle highlights to her eyes. Very becoming. A tense but welcoming smile, an appraising glance.

'I've never seen you in uniform before. Most impressive.'

'Only for court, mind. Smell the mothballs?' She frowned slightly, not disposed to humour.

'Doesn't it defeat the object?'

'How do you mean?'

93

'I assume you wear plain clothes to avoid being taken for a policeman.'

'By the time they get here, it's too late to matter.' She gave him a doubtful look and he hurried on. 'I'll be called early, the Super says, first or second. Not allowed in till after my evidence, see. Manage for a bit, will you?'

'Of course.'

He wasn't long on the stand. He gave details of the arrest and the confession, flat and factual, suitably deferential, mindful of her presence. Routine stuff, your friendly prosecutor, a piece of cake. He was much too old a dog to be put off by wigs and pomp, but he did wonder how she was taking it.

He needn't have worried, she wasn't in the least overawed. When he reached her side, she was staring intently at the slight figure in the dock. Morris sat easy but absent, ignoring the proceedings. He might have been on a park bench.

Wonderingly, she murmured, 'He is so utterly insignificant. It's hard to believe he could be – responsible.'

'He's not. That's the point.'

She made a small gesture of impatience. 'You know quite well what I mean. But if what you say is true, why the charade?'

She was whispering, but forcefully, and one or two heads had turned her way.

Setting aside his own reservations, toeing the line, he replied, 'Don't worry, he'll be put away, it's only a question of where. First, justice must be seen to be done.'

'Oh.' She sounded distant and sceptical. The magic in her sitting room seemed years away.

The ritual unfolded, the archaic modes of speech, the urbane tones, the unhurried pace. Every time a witness entered, a chilly draught pierced the courtroom; Evans's feet were numb. Grace Yardley didn't notice. Having dismissed Morris, she reserved her attention for the witnesses, each of whom she watched with fierce concentration. Evans felt like an intruder at some private ceremony.

Mrs Morris was called towards midday, a plump, distraught-looking woman in tweeds and rhinestone spectacles.

94

'Mrs Morris,' began the prosecutor briskly. 'Was Edward a normal child?'

She began to recount an idyllic boyhood. Light flickered from her restless, bejewelled hands. She seemed in the grip of a kind of shocked bewilderment. The prosecutor cut her short.

'He was never in serious trouble?'

She became indignant, her spectacles glinting as she emphasised her points.

'But he did often stay out at night?'

'He's a grown man. I try not to burden him.'

'Did he talk of girlfriends?'

'No.'

'Did he ever bring a girl home?'

'No.' She hesitated, started on a qualification. The prosecutor, a tall, deceptively languid man, pressed her relentlessly.

'He is how old, please?'

She broke off, sullen. Evans counted three gold-capped teeth in her partly open mouth.

'He'll be thirty in March.'

'And you don't find it surprising, this indifference to the opposite sex?'

'I told you, it's his own affair.'

'Mrs Morris, you are a widow, you have time on your hands. Can we assume you read newspapers, watch television, keep yourself in touch with events?'

She misread his tone, took it as a compliment.

'Well actually I like to be well informed. I read very widely really, only the quality ...'

'Indeed. You could hardly fail to be aware of the publicity given to the missing girls. Could you?'

'I *do* seem to recall ...'

'Quite. Did it occur to you that Edward's absences coincided with the attacks?'

'Never!' The answer came fast and forceful, in sharp contrast to her earlier ramblings.

The prosecutor glanced meaningfully at the judge. Grace Yardley muttered, 'She knew.'

'Wondered, maybe,' said Evans cautiously. The prosecutor

strolled a pace or two, peering at his notes. He turned sharply and spoke accusingly.

'Mrs Morris, did you at any time suspect Edward of these murders?'

'Of course not.' She spread her hands, leaning forward in abject appeal, 'He's my son!'

Evans was conscious of movement at his side: Grace Yardley trembling, dabbing at her eyes. From then on she sat like a statue, lost in a world he couldn't presume to enter. After the adjournment, she left without a word; he wondered if she'd return.

He should have known better. She met him at two, shamefaced and full of apologies. He guessed she'd had a bad couple of hours and had prepared her speech.

'You were right, I shouldn't have come. But I can't back out now. Don't take any notice of me. Just – stay – please.' Not much he could say, really.

So, for a further day and a half, he remained a witness; to her iron, inflexible will. She sat as if tranced while the forensic expert told of semen and pubic hair from the blanket; while two psychiatrists spoke of dark moods and ungovernable impulses; and while the prosecutor laid it squarely at Morris's door. Only when Morris himself took the stand did she wake, a quick, involuntary recoil, an expression of deep disgust. Evans touched her arm. 'Steady, girl.'

She bit her lip and nodded.

'All right. I'll be all right.'

Morris stood upright and impassive, his hands resting lightly on the rail, his eyes vacant. In eerie, monotonous tones, he detailed Caroline's last hour. During a casual, off-hand exchange with the prosecutor, he first admitted and then confirmed his guilt, sounding completely unconcerned. Through this, with an effort Evans could only guess at, Grace Yardley held her head up and kept her eyes dry. She even managed an appearance of interest in the final defence submission.

'There,' said Evans, in no small relief, as the judge swept out and the prisoner's escort formed, 'all finished.' And once again underestimated her.

96

'Not yet,' she said tiredly. 'When will they pass sentence?'
He opened his mouth to protest and she waved him to silence.

'Please, no arguments. Surely you don't expect me to miss it?' Unwilling, he went in search of an answer; and received a wan smile for his pains.

'Next Tuesday, then. I'll see you here.' She hesitated, indecisive for the first time. 'I'm afraid I'll be – rather busy – until then.'

'Better for you really,' he said comfortably. 'Being occupied, I mean.'

'Oh yes. And thank you.'

It rained on Tuesday, a chill and icy drizzle which kept the crowd down. Even so, Evans had to pick his way over electrical cables that snaked everywhere, and between media men bawling instructions and calling each other darling. He was skiving. Only an hour, mind, Smythe wouldn't know. He couldn't desert her now.

Grace Yardley wore a sleeveless light grey dress; curious choice, he thought fleetingly, on such a vile December afternoon. Still, it revealed what he had always suspected – a superb figure. Her arms were smooth and slender, the handbag seemed out of scale, too cumbersome for her. There was a tautness about her, a feverishness in the eyes which permitted no social pleasantries. Edgy, then, and who could blame her?

Punctual to the minute, the judge took his place. The usher called, the whispers stilled. Milud produced a pair of half-moon spectacles, polished them vigorously, adjusted his robes; and began to read. As the pages turned and the dry, pleasant voice continued, Grace Yardley shifted and whispered, 'Does it always take so long?' Evans saw the gooseflesh on her arms, the lines of rigid discipline at her mouth. He nodded and raised a finger to his lips. Someone at the front coughed, on and on, each sound echoing in the hush like punctuation. The judge raised his head and waited, expressionless, for silence. Satisfied at last, he returned to his notes. Grace Yardley's slim fingers bunched and twisted in her lap.

Quite suddenly the tone changed. An actor's pause, a clearing of the throat, and a steady gaze for the accused. The atmosphere was heavy with tension.

'Edward Charles Morris, you plead guilty to the murder of Caroline Yardley. In the judgement of this court, however, you are found not responsible for your actions. You are therefore guilty of manslaughter, but unfit for preventative custody.' Another pause. Grace Yardley craned forward, her face ashen. 'I hereby order you committed to a suitable institution pending further psychiatric reports.'

Bedlam. A scrimmage of reporters headed for the door, a gavel pounded furiously but ineffectually, an usher's plaintive demand. Grace Yardley slumped motionless, her arms cradling the handbag, while the gallery chattered like magpies. As Evans reached out a hand, she roused herself, hauling herself back to reality.

'Well,' she said dully, 'now we know.'

'It's what we expected mind,' he told her gently. 'No surprises.'

'Yes. An end to uncertainty.' She sat, remote and listless, while order was slowly restored. Presently, escorted by a phalanx of uniforms, Morris began his retreat from society.

'Where are they taking him?' she demanded.

'Out the back. Trying to dodge the press, see, and the crowds. It's hopeless. They'll be there.'

'I want to go. I want to see.'

'Look, it's cold, you're not dressed for it. It could be rough, too. Let it go. Enough's enough.'

She gave him a strange look, half sympathy, half challenge.

'Yes. You've been very patient. I'll go by myself.'

He sighed. What the hell, he'd humoured her this far; might as well see it through.

He guided her through the building, receiving nods and salutes. She walked beside him, silent and determined, the bag bumping against her legs. Outside, the harridans had gathered. For all he knew, they could be the same ones. Bare-armed in the wind, Grace shivered uncontrollably.

98

Finally, a door opened, and Morris came out, heavily shrouded. Flash bulbs flared, camera booms swung and steadied, the crowd grumbled ominously. Grace Yardley drifted forward like a moth to candlelight. She wants to be sure, he thought, wants to see him safely out of her life. The van inched up, blue light throwing angry eyes and baying mouths into garish relief.

As Morris drew level, she turned, peering over Evans shoulder.

'Someone's looking for you, Inspector.' He pivoted, scanning the confusion behind; so he didn't see it happen. He heard the shots, a single scream, and a man's voice cursing softly and fluently. Sick with horror and realisation, he saw her held and elbowed to her side.

''Ands off, boyo,' he warned a white-faced constable. 'You're hurting her, see.'

She looked up at him, her eyes luminous. 'Now it really is over.' Then, with a quite terrible urgency, 'He *is* dead, isn't he?'

Evans glanced down. A St John's man knelt beside the body, his busy hands slick and red. He caught Evans's eye and shook his head.

'Yes,' said Evans heavily, 'he's dead.' He took her arm and led her away. She was smiling.

Later, on the six o'clock news, he watched, in slow motion, as she opened the bag, drew out a heavy pistol, moved closer and shot Morris twice. He saw the body crumple and sprawl, saw her calmly reverse the pistol and pass it to the nearest uniform, then take a delicate, fastidious pace away from the widening pool of blood. BBC colour was very true.

Evans reached the office ten minutes late after a bumper-to-bumper crawl through the early fog. He slung his coat over his chair and went straight upstairs. Better to volunteer than wait for the summons. Smythe looked rumpled and unshaven and coldly furious.

'Ah, Inspector Evans, the man of the moment. Nice of you to drop in. Slept well, I trust, in the pink and so on?'

Evans knew enough to keep quiet. Showing admirable control, Smythe began almost sorrowfully.

'I warned you more than once, didn't I? Beware of involvement, forget the obsession, don't try to con me. But you knew better. You'd touched the hem, hadn't you, learned how to feel again. So I switch on the six o'clock news and what do I see? A man gunned down in cold blood while a full-dress inspector stands a yard away and gawps like a moron. One of *my* inspectors. Then he takes the heroine by the arm and strolls into the sunset in full view of forty million viewers. Are you sleeping with that woman?'

'No, sir!'

'Well, the time you've spent, you bloody well should be!'

Evans had stood by her as long as he could, holding off the media and his own outraged colleagues. She seemed completely removed, existing somewhere far beyond the chaos she'd created; silent, slack, yet strangely peaceful. Over and over he instructed her.

'Tell them nothing. You're not guilty, you want a lawyer. Got it?'

For some time, she ignored even him, and he grew quietly heated; until at last she sighed and repeated tonelessly, 'Not guilty.'

He'd shouldered through the mob outside, gone straight home and taken the phone off the hook. Over a massive whisky, he'd tried to make some sense.

As shock and numbness faded, neat spirit on an empty stomach fuelled a bitter anger. She did you lovely, boyo, the sweetest sucker punch in history. You read the signs and looked the other way; literally. The sleeveless dress for ease of movement, the outsize handbag, the refined come-on over sherry in her lounge. She *needed* you, see. She could go where she pleased and do as she liked. With a uniform at her side, who'd suspect her? Clever, fair play, classic sleight of hand. While everyone watched Morris, Grace Yardley turned the trick. She'd planned it to the last detail, tame cop and all. Jesi Mawr.

He couldn't sustain the emotion, couldn't allow himself to

100

believe it. When had it started, then? When had she ceased to grieve and turned her acute mind to revenge? *Not* from the start; her need had once been genuine, he'd swear it on a stack of Bibles. She *had* deceived, but only partially and recently. He would tell Smythe none of this, he'd rather be damned for a conspirator than a dupe. He held his peace and took his hiding as the Superintendent tallied the charges.

'You fell for her, Evans, you didn't care who knew it. You went along every step of the way, publicly. When the storm broke, you went to ground, incommunicado for all of twelve hours. What were you doing, covering her tracks? Don't answer that! I'd rather face the Commissioner in ignorance. He wants a full-scale enquiry, Evans, Special Branch breaking plates in *my* china shop. You should be cashiered, he says, done as an accessory.'

'Aye,' said Evans. 'Nasty for you, no doubt. Resign, then, shall I?'

'You'll hold your water! I'm not finished yet, not by a long chalk.' Smythe stood up and marched to the window. Number of times he's done that, thought Evans, light-headed, there ought to be a track in the carpet. Wonder if he turns it weekly like a mattress? Smythe spat words in short acid bursts.

'I rated you, Inspector. Sharp, dedicated, reliable, grade A promotion material. I'm on record with that, would you believe? My neck's on the block as well, d'you see; God help you if it wasn't.' He paused, took a grip on himself, spoke more reasonably.

'Had a hard night, thinking. You should try it sometime. Had words with the Commissioner, an up-and-downer. Bought time. I'm getting to be quite a negotiator. A last hope, then, and a faint one. Something which might possibly redeem us both. Not,' he added with some asperity, 'that I consider myself particularly culpable. However.'

'My responsibility, sir. We agreed, mind.'

'I'm tempted, believe me, but it won't wash.'

'I'm obliged.'

'You don't know the price yet. She's made a statement. The gun was her father's, a war souvenir, been kicking round the house for years. You believe that?'

'Belief's a bit tricky just now.'

'Pity you didn't think so before. In my view, it stinks. What would they want with a shooter, a respectable housewife and teenage daughter? She's lying. She's capable of it, wouldn't you say?'

'No question.'

'Still comes hard, doesn't it, still carrying the torch. Too bad. Because that's your assignment, d'you see. Find out where and how she got the gun.'

Evans, his mind reeling, mumbled, 'A tall order, sir. Have to give it some thought.'

'You do your thinking here and now, man! There's only one way to show you aren't the gormless moon-struck oaf you appeared to be. You stand up in court and *prove* her a liar! Is that perfectly clear?'

'Haven't much choice, have I?'

'Choice? My God you've got a bloody nerve! You ride roughshod over every convention for the sake of a fair lady and end up raising her sleeve while she kills. Live, on television!'

A long silence. Smythe's posture altered subtly. He wheeled slowly, made his way to the desk and slumped behind it. In the fluorescent light, he looked washed out and rather sad.

'No copper can be that stupid, Inspector. My story, and I'm sticking to it. The Commissioner's been told you were a victim, you're eager to earn a reprieve. He might even believe it. Anyway, there's your choice, take it or leave it.'

Briefly and dizzily, Evans considered the grand gesture. If they already accepted his complicity, why not act it out? Take the rap for her, cook up a story, it was me what put her up to it, sir. It's the strain, see, the disillusion, too many Chummies sprung by the law men. Serve the time, then whisk her back to the Valleys, raising kids and chickens. Drivel, he realised, pure Arthurian fantasy. If he baulked now, Smythe would throw the book. Rightly so, mind. The Super'd been very decent really. Covering his own back, no doubt; but still. Anyhow, where did a discredited middle-aged ex-copper go for the mortgage? No takers, boyo. You're snookered. Wearily, he asked, 'When do I start?'

'You just did. And Evans, a caution. I expect results. No stalling, no backsliding. I'll be watching you every minute. I won't be conned again, ever.'

Chapter Ten

Nigel Buxton had watched the 'newscast of the decade' with growing absorption. It held the promise of a major legal event, a case of epic proportions. A wronged woman, an appearance of police collusion, and the debate on crime and punishment in full swing. The trial and everyone involved in it would make world headlines. And, as Theresa rather tersely observed, 'She's beautiful, too.'

Back in the studio, a 'legal advisor' enlightened the masses. Nigel knew him slightly, a sleek, over-indulgent man given to velvet jackets and polka-dot bow ties. He was wearing both for the occasion.

'Dandified charlatan,' Nigel growled, and Theresa made cat noises.

'Miss Yardley will doubtless elicit the sympathy of millions,' intoned the advisor, gazing earnestly into the camera. 'She has suffered appalling loss and endured weeks of strain. Few, on the other hand, will mourn the passing of a convicted child-killer. Nevertheless, on this point the law is implacable.'

'He is rather pompous,' observed Theresa. 'Occupational disease?' Nigel shushed her impatiently. The camera panned in, filling the screen with large and improbably regular teeth.

'Homicide,' the advisor continued, 'becomes justifiable only when defending life, kin or territory against immediate threat. *Crime passionnel*, while not formally defined in English law, could be invoked in defence of an impulsive, spur of the moment act. All indications suggest that Miss Yardley planned her revenge carefully and in advance. I would therefore expect her to be charged with premeditated murder.'

'Has he got it right, Nigel?' Theresa asked, her face alive in reflected colours.

'More or less.'

The advisor took a sip of water, a smooth, practised gesture. 'After a recent and rather similar incident in Belgium, the perpetrator was found guilty and given a severe but suspended sentence.' The picture faded to the newscaster, who got as far as 'Meanwhile, in the Middle East ...' before Nigel switched him off. Theresa stretched and yawned voluptuously.

'How exciting. I'm ready for bed.'

'Clarence Darrow ...' murmured Nigel, ignoring the hint.

'Pardon?'

'A very famous American defence counsel.'

'Never heard of him.'

'In the twenties, I believe. He saved two college boys from the electric chair.'

'I don't see the connection.'

'They kidnapped and murdered a teenager, claimed they'd got the idea from Nietzschean philosophy. Brutal and motiveless, you see. At the time, their actions were considered indefensible. There is a parallel, and it made his name.'

'Delusions of grandeur, Nigel?'

He had the grace to smile. 'No more than usual. But it wants thinking about.'

'If you're going to lecture, I need a drink.'

Nigel went to the bar and opened a bottle. 'Our mutual friend in the dicky-bow just put paid to *sub judice*. The BBC, in their infinite wisdom, actually showed her pulling the trigger. The prosecution case requires virtually no burden of proof. It's a unique situation, unprecedented.'

'Vodka and lime, please, and lots of ice.'

He glanced at the glass in his hand. 'Oh yes. Sorry.' He mixed the drink and poured himself a generous brandy. Theresa had kicked off her shoes and spread herself along the sofa; a favourite pose. She sipped delicately, her eyes warm and inviting.

'Will the CJ hear it?' she asked casually. 'Good old Courthouse Interruptus?'

She was being openly provocative, the actress in her well to the fore.

105

'Probably,' he said, deliberately aloof, 'public pressure will demand it. A first-class prosecutor too, no doubt. Which means, in the interests of balance, a defence counsel of outstanding ability.'

'You're fishing, Nigel, and I'm tired.'

'In which case, old thing, I suggest you pop off to bed. I'm busy.' Her expression changed. She finished her drink at a swallow and strode, wordless, out of the room.

For his own benefit, he shrugged and grimaced in comic resignation. He hadn't really meant to be abrupt; a clash of moods, no more. He gave himself a refill, swirling the liquid and watching the play of light. There *were* times when company, especially company as determinedly female as Theresa's, could be irksome. He put something soothing on the stereo and re-entered his train of thought.

Stanmore, in a social context, had made his views on capital punishment clear; and, in effect, Grace Yardley had acted as executioner. The Chief Justice, in Nigel's opinion, was very conscious of both position and His Master's Voice. Not biddable, of course, that would be unthinkable; but definitely conscious, which brought him to a crucial question. If Miss Yardley chose not to plead but to face a jury, could any credible and acceptable defence be assembled? He sipped brandy, enjoying it's mellow burn. He was moving now into unknown regions. Did she *want* a defence? There had been an air of finality about her: I've done it and I don't care what happens to me. Why was she *Miss* Yardley? Where and who was Caroline's father? What of the policeman who seemed so protective? Was that how she got the gun?

The house was very quiet. Theresa might well be waiting for him; they seldom left differences unresolved. Probably, he would be shamed into amends – but not just yet. He turned the tape over and stood thoughtfully beside the machine, frowning in concentration.

On the face of it, a trial like this could do him little damage. Everyone, Stanmore included, would confidently expect a conviction. A gallant stand and an honourable defeat. Suppose, just suppose, against all the odds and in defiance of the Establishment, he could win. What of his long-term hopes?

106

He'd never courted favour with Stanmore, but he'd be a fool to jeopardise it. In the background, Clayderman vamped 'Climb Every Mountain', and Nigel smiled at the irony.

He finished the brandy, suddenly very tired. Give it a rest, he advised himself. Nobody's asked you yet.

The extent of Evans's fall was soon upon him. The shooting had happened on City Central turf. Pursuing Smythe's strategy, he went there, cap in hand. Headquarters was a bright and modern building, its personnel considered themselves elite. They put him over the obstacle course.

The divisional superintendent, a craggy, raw-boned Scot named McKay, was known for his terseness and nationalistic fervour. He and Smythe had been at odds for years; Smythe referred to him as the Pillock of the Glen. He kept Evans waiting for half an hour, then addressed him with rasping disdain.

'I'll no pretend tae like ut, Jummy. You're here on the Commissioner's say-so and no blessing from me. Be about your business and take yersel off. I've no use for boobies on my patch.' Thus welcomed, Evans kept his head down; but drew attention anyway. Everyone had seen the broadcast, no one wanted to know him. Denied McKay's 'blessing', he encountered all the delays of petty bureaucracy.

Eventually, on a hard chair in an outer waiting room, he laid hands on the transcripts and knuckled down. Grace Yardley, he discovered, had wasted very few words.

'He raped and murdered Caroline,' she'd said, 'so I killed him.' And declined to elaborate. An old hand at interrogation, Evans pictured the scene. Tight, watchful faces, bright lights and tobacco smoke, hard questions coming from every side. Of the gun, she'd said, 'My father was an officer during the war. I found it among his papers sometime after he died.' The tempo increased. Why had she kept it? A felony, didn't she know? You're a criminal, Miss Yardley, why not come clean? Where had she got ammunition, when had she learned to shoot? Her replies were sparse and unconvincing. The bullets had been with the gun, she'd forgotten she had them until after Caroline's death. Then, with an irony which transcended the written word, 'I didn't need to learn. I had no intention of missing.'

The inquisitors had hammered on. Was there any more ammunition; had she cleaned it, how did she know how to load, how to work the safety?

'I deal with computers every day. The pistol is a very simple tool, comparatively.'

They'd been to her house, looking, and had found nothing. Ripped the place apart, Evans thought grimly; vandals.

Towards the end of what must have been a frustrating session, someone had mentioned Evans himself.

'Tell us about the boyfriend.'

'I've no idea who you mean.'

'Come on, Grace, luv! Your fancy man, Inspector Evans. Don't tell us it was all your own work, a respectable lady like you!' For the first and only time, she'd displayed emotion.

'What utter nonsense! The Inspector investigated my daughter's disappearance. He was at least civilised! He was needed in court as a witness and I begged him to stay. He knew nothing whatsoever of my plans.' And, despite further grilling and much snide innuendo, she'd held to this truth. Tougher than she looked, fair play; but he knew that already.

As he trudged the centrally heated corridors, a police-woman, tall and plain, detained him.

'You're Inspector Evans, aren't you?'

'Aye,' he admitted warily.

She lowered her voice. 'I thought you were great. Poor Miss Yardley, I do hope she gets off. For two pins I'd've shot him myself!'

It bucked him, no question. Even for the wrong reason, he could do with a lift. Because he was on his way back to McKay.

'Still here? What is ut now?'

'With your permission, sir, I'd like to interview the prisoner.'

'Oh aye? Fancy yersel smarter than my lads, do ye? Or mebbe you've some *special* talent denied us lesser mortals.'

He leered suggestively. Evans didn't hold with baiting senior officers. Futile, really; spiting your face. Only, he'd had enough.

108

'The Commissioner gave me the job, see. Tell him I can't do it, will you; or shall I?'

'Och, it's a hard wee mon y'are with the brass at your back.'

'Aye, sir. You'll pass the word, then?'

'I dinna have the choice. You'll not go there alone, though. I'll bide no trysting in my lock-up.' He grinned, mocking. 'Enjoy yersel, Jummy. An' don't come back!'

Pity, really, Evans thought. Could've done with a private word. Like, when had she gone off the rails, why had she chosen *him* as the straight man? Simple things, how are you, do they treat you well, and don't let the questions get you down. No chance; not with the stolid, grim-faced sergeant listening in.

Her appearance shocked him. Not unkempt, exactly, but for her, definitely neglected. Her skin was tightly drawn, almost translucent over the bones. The prison weeds swamped her. She looked small and lifeless. Her eyes flickered briefly as he entered, but by the time his chaperones had settled, the moment had passed. Even so, she made the effort.

'Inspector Evans. I'm sorry you were dragged into this. I've told them already.'

'Sure. Thanks.' He hesitated, not much caring for what he had to say.

'This is a formal visit, Miss Yardley. On the record, mind.'

She nodded wearily. 'I understand. I'll try to help; the least I can do.' Listless and apathetic, going through the motions. He had to jolt her, chivvy her out of it.

'Tell me about the gun,' he suggested, wasting no time.

'There's nothing to tell.'

'Look, nobody believes you, you're not making sense. Darro, girl, you're up for murder, not possession!'

Dully, repeating a lesson, she mumbled, 'It was my father's.'

He tried another angle.

'You'll be needing a lawyer. He'll have to know everything, to give you a chance, see.'

She smiled, a grey shadow of the expression which once had warmed him.

'A chance, Inspector? A chance for what?'

On his own, he might have persisted, but the stenographer

sat poised; in another moment, he knew, Grace Yardley would say something to put her fate beyond doubt. Quickly he said, 'Think about it. The truth won't hurt, you can't be worse off. I'll check it out, see, everything you've told them. Duty, mind, nothing less. Be sensible, girl, it's your only hope.' He wanted to add a bit of humanity; mind how you go. Her awful blankness frightened him.

Outside, the sergeant lingered.

'Word in your ear, sir.'

'What is it?' Evans grunted, still on edge.

'She's lying. The pistol's a '53 model, didn't make 'em in the war.'

'Who says so?'

The sergeant winked. 'Big ears, sir. Heard the Laird chatting up a boffin.'

The Laird, Evans thought, Smythe'll love that. He drew closer, welcoming this unexpected ally.

'Have you thought, Sergeant, maybe her old man was the liar?'

The sergeant gave him a respectful glance.

'Benefit of the doubt, eh? Between you and me, sir, I'm sorry for her. Bad bugger, Morris.'

'Keep it dark, boyo. A bit sensitive, your Super.'

'Ole Hamish? A right bastard, I don't mind telling you. Bloody Jocks.'

Cashing in on flagrant disloyalty, never mind the cause, Evans let the sergeant draw the file and noted the vital points. The gun was indeed 1953 vintage, by which time Captain Yardley had long since donned his civvies. McKay had been holding out; in a statement dated yesterday, Grace Yardley had shifted her ground.

'When I found the gun, I assumed it was from the war.' Have to do better than that, girl, he thought, they'll crucify you in court.

Which led his mind in a new direction. He consulted the file. She hadn't named a lawyer. 'Anyone will do. It makes no difference.'

But in Evans's book, she needed and deserved the best. A name teased at his memory, a new QC with a reputation for retrieving lost feminine causes. Burton? Something to check on, anyway, something positive. Not an entirely wasted trip, then, despite the Laird.

'Tell me something, Nigel,' Theresa murmured contentedly, 'I gather you're serious about defending this Yardley woman.'

He hadn't woken her last night, and breakfast had been a decidedly off-hand meal. This evening, however, the spat apparently forgotten, she'd provided a fine dinner and a bout of athletic lovemaking. Now, sprawled in her usual graceful abandon, she eyed him quizzically.

'It's crossed my mind,' he admitted equably, 'as you may have noticed.'

'Who me? Listen, won't it cause you some mental gymnastics?'

'Child's play after what you just put me through.'

'Didn't hear you complaining. Let's take it a step at a time. She's guilty, no one can doubt it, half the population saw her do it.'

'Live, in glorious six-two-five colour.'

'Exactly. So how can any responsible barrister offer to defend?'

'*No* barrister may *offer*, old thing.'

'You know what I mean. Don't hedge.'

'Look, if you're going to grill me, I need a drink. And it's your turn.'

She grinned impishly.

'Touché.'

Naked, she crossed the room, and he watched happily. He heard her clinking at the bar, aware of the rather foolish grin on her face. If you must have a woman around, it's nice to be on good terms. She came back carrying the glasses, poised and very beautiful.

'There. Are you sitting comfortably? Then I'll begin.' She sat cross-legged on the carpet, unselfconscious as ever. 'I've always thought,' she said slowly, 'that you couldn't take a case believing the client to be guilty.'

'Aha. Confessions of a Perry Mason addict.'

'My darkest secret. You're merely a substitute figure.'

111

'Nonsense. The man's paralysed from the waist down.'

'That's Ironside.'

'My, such knowledge!'

'You're wriggling, Nigel.'

Nigel sighed and heaved himself into a sitting position, propped against the quilted headboard. Subdued light made a poem of her body; he felt mellow and expansive.

'Very well. Buxton's Jurisprudence, introductory chapter.'

'Oh, how thrilling.'

'You insisted, remember? Buxton's Law states: for every fundamental tenet, there exists one which is equally valid and wholly contradictory. Cheers.'

She toasted him sardonically, and murmured, 'Frightfully confusing for you.'

'Not so. You have only to resolve the paradox. Take the example you've quoted; the barrister must believe in his client's innocence. Contrariwise, the accused has a right to a competent defence. In Miss Yardley's case, as you say, the first prerequisite may be impossible to meet. In which instance, the second is automatically forfeited. Hardly fair to Miss Yardley.'

'Well, when you put it that way...' She had rolled on to her stomach and was picking at a thread in the pile.

'Oh I do. Inverting the argument, if *every* barrister accepts her guilt, it doesn't matter who defends her. Except, of course, it does. Like anyone else, she's entitled to the best. Ergo, me. If you carry on like that I'll buy lino.'

She stuck her tongue out, an absurdly childish and appealing sight.

'And so modest with it. See, I've stopped. No hands.'

Her smile faded, and she looked genuinely puzzled.

'Don't dazzle me with rhetoric, Nigel, there's a real problem here. I mean, if *you're* not convinced, how do you sway a jury?'

Nigel nodded approval.

'Enviable instincts, Theresa. Albeit unwittingly, you've struck the nail on the head. Hole in one. Bull's-eye.'

'Thanks a million.'

'Don't pout, pet, no condescension implied. You see, in purely legal terms, she cannot be defended. Only her sentence remains to be decided. If, however, she refuses to plead, the issue becomes *entirely* moral; if you like, a matter of swaying the jury. And as we well know, juries can be thoroughly insensitive to judicial imperatives.'

'Very cogent, Nigel,' she made a wry face. 'There, you've got me using the jargon now. I'm not convinced, though. How do you salve *your* conscience? Can *you* afford to ignore judicial imperatives?' He sipped his drink, impressed. More to her than met the eye, which was plenty. She looked almost pagan; smooth, dark skin against the creamy rug.

Distracted, he mumbled, 'The first duty, old thing, is to the client.'

'Brilliant, Nigel, Stanmore would be proud of you. A marvellously pompous evasion.'

Irritated, he demanded, 'What more do you want?'

'A straight answer to a simple question, just between you and me. How do you get her off? And if you succeed, haven't you abandoned all your principles?'

She had risen on one elbow and was leaning towards him. Perfume wafted over him and her breasts invited his touch; but her eyes were cool and intent. Clearly, the answer mattered very much.

'That's two questions.'

'Nigel!'

'Very well. I demonstrate that if they convict, the jury will condemn her to retribution beyond their power to temper; and that her action does not warrant their condemnation.'

Theresa sat up slowly, looking stunned. Thinking it through, she murmured, 'You leave them only one alternative. On moral grounds, you said. How very devious. Tell me, do you believe it?'

'What?'

'That her action is morally justifiable.'

'Theresa, we're talking about winning or losing.'

'Do you?'

'I will if I have to defend her.'

She shook her head, incredulous and miserable.

'Orwell called it doublethink.'

'Orwell wrote fiction. We're discussing reality.'

113

She sat, head bowed, long hair flowing like black silk over her shoulders. He got up and went to her, trailing his fingers lightly down her thigh. For a moment she watched his hand, her expression curiously bereaved.

'You've exhausted me, Nigel.'

'Well, it makes a change.' But she wouldn't even smile. Poor Theresa, he thought, lying beside her in the darkness, another illusion betrayed. She'd kissed the prince and he'd turned into a frog.

Chapter Eleven

A man's chambers, Nigel believed, ought to reflect his tastes. It had taken some time to achieve, but these days he could survey his surroundings with satisfaction. A second home, almost. A thick-pile fitted carpet in dark tan, a walnut desk of impressive bulk and antiquity, a glass-fronted and well-filled bookcase of like vintage. The books looked used; tools, not ornaments. Velvet curtains of old gold, an unobtrusive pastel tint to the paintwork, and a single Blue Period Picasso print. Functional aspects kept to a minimum, two easy chairs for visitors, and a small bar for those overcome by whatever he might have to tell them. Normally, he enjoyed working here; today, he was hearing a sad and all-too-familiar tale.

Mrs Goldstein was middle-aged, clearly well off, nicely preserved and not unattractive in a severe and county way. Twining a handkerchief through her fingers, she sounded thoroughly upset.

'She's a bitch, Mr Buxton. I'm sorry, there's no other word. She married Clive for the money – *our* money – and she's led him a merry dance ever since.'

Clive was the younger brother, an expert in financial disaster.

'Clive was the baby, you see, and I suppose we all spoiled him. He's not *bad*, really, just weak. Oh dear.' She blew her nose delicately.

'Mother's will was perfectly fair until *she* went to the hospital. Mother was near the end, in constant pain and wandering. *She* didn't care. "Clive's in a fix, Mrs Goldstein, the others don't need the money." She won, of course, she always does. The properties to Clive and loose assets divided between Geoffrey and me. A pittance, Mr Buxton.' She sniffed, touched her eyes, collected herself and continued more calmly, 'She's right in a way. One can always use more, the hounds are so expensive these days, but we're not exactly destitute.' She fingered a Gucci handbag as if to emphasise the point. Nigel knew what to expect.

'Geoffrey's livid. A matter of principle, he says, we're obliged to contest. The solicitor claims we can win on mental grounds.'

Nigel tapped a document on his desk. 'Geoffrey's man has done a competent job. One can't make promises, but I'm confident of a judgement on this.'

An unhappy but decisive shake of head. 'Not me, Mr Buxton. Mother's dead, Geoffrey says, she's beyond hurt. But *I* won't stand in court and call her crazy. Is there no other way?'

Nigel offered a sympathetic sigh. 'I'm afraid not. Once you concede she was of sound mind, your mother's will has to be respected. It's not really a legal issue at all, just something for you and your brothers to decide.'

'If only it was! Left to ourselves, I'm sure we could agree, but *she'd* never stand for it and Geoffrey's wife can be wilful, too. Whatever happens, the family's doomed. It would have broken poor Mother's heart.'

He made soothing noises, knowing the matter was already settled. Clive's 'bitch' would prevail and the enmity would outlive them all. He ushered her out, a minor casualty of petty greed, smelling of lavender. Typical of the business he'd handled lately: mundane, non-volatile, lucrative – and dull.

He moved into the bay window, which overlooked the street. Another beastly day, bleak and claustrophobic. The passers-by looked perished, even the traffic seemed muted. The scene depressed him, he was conscious of a vague, general dissatisfaction. A plateau in his life; the absence of challenge.

A buzzer sounded discreetly and he moved to the desk. 'Yes Joyce?' The speaker hummed and his secretary said, 'A Mr Evans to see you. A criminal matter, he says. He doesn't have an appointment.'

'Send him to Fortesque.'

'I've – suggested – that, Mr Buxton.'

116

Nigel's eyebrows lifted. Joyce's 'suggestions' tended to emerge as orders, daunting all but the most persistent. She sounded miffed.

'He won't listen. Says it's a barrister he wants.'

'How's my schedule?'

'You're free until lunch.'

'Oh, all right. Show him in.'

A square, blocky man, taller than he seemed. Thin sandy hair and freckles, pale blue eyes, a slow assessing gaze. A quite forbidding physical presence, at odds with the comfort of the room. He looked ill at ease; and strangely familiar.

'Please sit down, Mr Evans. What can I do for you?'

'A delicate business, sir.'

The habitual courtesy gave him away; a public servant. Nigel smiled easily.

'You'd be surprised how many people say that.'

'Aye. A murder trial, then. Someone needing the best advice. A Miss Yardley.'

The penny dropped.

'Ah, of course. Inspector Evans. Isn't this somewhat irregular?'

The faintest of rueful grins.

'More than you know, sir. Witness for the prosecution, me.'

'A prosecution witness acting for the defendant? How do you reconcile that, Inspector?'

The grin widened, inviting complicity.

'With difficulty, sir.'

Very drily, Nigel said, 'I hardly think your superiors would find it amusing.'

'I'm here as a private citizen. Free country, mind. Or so they say.'

'You have the right to consult a solicitor on behalf of a friend, yes.' As Nigel intended, Evans caught the inflexions and his face tightened.

'Miss Yardley's in need, see. I'm looking out for her, nothing more.' Phrased as an excuse, it rang like a warning. With a quiet force of his own, Nigel said, 'We're playing hide-and-seek with professional ethics – yours and mine. I told you, see a solicitor.'

117

Evans shifted in the chair, settling, not rising. He had planted his feet broadly, uncomfortable but fixed. Already, he seemed less awed by the luxury.

'Not sensible, really, is it?' he asked rhetorically. 'I mean, it's murder we're talking about, not breach of promise.'

'Nevertheless, convention must be observed. We're not permitted to tout for trade.'

'Very proper, I'm sure, sir. Thing is, I'm ready to pay. Call it a consultation, shall we?'

Neat, Nigel conceded inwardly, and just about acceptable; but he didn't care for the tone. As though sensing this, Evans leaned forward, his big hands lifting in appeal.

'Hear me out, sir. No harm, is there?'

'I don't come cheap, Inspector.'

Evans cast a knowing, almost impertinent glance around the room.

'I can see that. Nice place.'

'I'm delighted you approve'

Evans's eyes gleamed sardonically.

'Getting them off pays better than catching them, sir. Make a round of the cat-houses, I will, ask for a bit on the slate. We're both honourable men, see.'

'Your money's as good as the next man's?'

'Or woman's. Better than some you've dealt with, I'd say.'

'Very well, Inspector, we'll call it a draw. Tell me about Miss Yardley.'

Evans collected himself. For some reason, his gaze fell on the Picasso and rested there.

'She's tough, sir. Not hard, mind, no. She bends to the wind; like a withy.'

'A what?'

'Sorry, local term. You'd say willow, I expect.'

'Very poetic, Inspector.'

Evans coloured quaintly.

'Not intended, sir.' He took a breath and tried again. 'She's gone to ground, see, drawn herself in. She'd never thought beyond her one moment in the court. Obsessed, I'd say; know a bit about that myself.'

118

He didn't elaborate, and Nigel waited.

'I'm only a copper, not telling you your job, mind. I reckon she must stand a chance, given a jury and a good mouthpiece.' He paused, discomforted. 'Sorry again. A manner of speaking. No offence.'

'Console yourself, Inspector. It's an accurate idiom and I've been called worse.'

'Me too,' breathed Evans feelingly, and Nigel pounced.

'I can imagine. She made you a public fool, undermined your career. Even here, you are compromised, to say the least. Very well, why are you doing it? You must be something of a withy yourself.'

Again the ghostly grin.

'More like oak, me. Thick all through, skin and head. It's hard to explain. How much have you heard?'

'I've read the papers.'

'Good for you. No, fair play, strip off the scandal and they've got it about right.' He paused, frowning, hunting the words. 'Look, maybe she's done wrong, but I know what she went through. Duw, she had every cause! There's something about her, see; something worth saving.'

Nigel knew a momentary insight; a Welsh deacon in his tabernacle of slate. Quietly he asked, 'It's no more personal than that?'

A flicker of anger in the pale eyes, quickly suppressed.

'I know what they're saying. Chance'd be a fine thing, believe me. It's crazy talk, mun. A cat can look at a king, and I did. My hat's off to her, I *admire* her, see. No more to be said.'

Nigel considered. With Theresa last night, he'd been teasing it, doing some legal press-ups, a purely abstract exercise. And furthering her education, of course. The *idea* intrigued him; he hadn't envisaged the reality. Suddenly it was upon him, in this gracious room with this infatuated policeman. I should back out now, Nigel thought, there's every justification. A clandestine, almost improper approach from a man who couldn't see the issues, let alone the defendant, in any perspective. Evans sat awkward and glum and anxious as an expectant father.

And yet there was drama afoot, he could sense it in his

bones. The audience buzzed, the stage was set, most of the principal roles were already cast. Only hero and villain remained unknown; would remain so, he realised wryly, until the final curtain. The Inspector's question echoed in his mind – *No harm, is there?* Not here and not now, at least.

A squall of rain struck the window, startling them both.

'December!' muttered Evans, in comic disgust.

'Season of goodwill,' agreed Nigel; then, 'On that basis, and as a private citizen, give me the evidence so far.'

Evans sat straighter, filling the chair. As he gathered fluency, the Welsh became more pronounced. He did it well, observant, perceptive, and concise.

'So there we are,' he concluded. 'She hasn't been quite straight, even with me. I'm doubting her about the gun, see; more to it than she's saying. I'll find out, mind, make her a liar in court. No option, really. It's why she needs the best, the reason I came. She won't ask, though. She can be bloody stubborn.' He gave the phrase a curious wistful pride; not exactly an objective witness. More than ever wary, Nigel took refuge in convention.

'Not good enough, Inspector. We're already close to the wind; let's not go overboard on unethical conduct. The approach must be correct. I'd try Fortesque, of Fortesque and Blakemoor. A sound man.'

Evans rose abruptly and prowled across the room. For a big man, he moved very lightly. The picture absorbed him. He examined it closely, reading the name.

'Never knew he did people,' he confessed. 'I've only seen the poached egg and tadpole stuff. Quite good, isn't he?' And, turning into Nigel's ironic smile, added, 'See what you mean. He'd have to be, wouldn't he.' Then, quite diffidently, as though asking the time, 'Take it on, would you, if she went by the book?'

'I can't say, at this point.'

The window had misted over, the room had darkened and closed. Evans stood wide-legged, weight slightly forward, arms linked behind him. His figure seemed to draw in the light as he rocked gently on his heels. The classic British copper, large, comfortable and just a little threatening. He nodded

120

slowy, confirming a suspicion. 'Don't blame you, really. Open and shut, isn't it?'

This is how he works, Nigel realised suddenly, when he wants something badly; he's shown me his technique. The slow build-up, deferent, polite, flattering. A bit of cajolery, a glimpse of hardness, then the facts laid out. A distraction, and the vital question tossed in casually. And finally, the needle, a hint of intimidation, and the gauntlet thrown down. Whatever he's done, he's still very good. Aloud, he said reasonably, 'Inspector, anyone who defends Miss Yardley could be inviting trouble. There's a lot at stake here.' Evans gave him an old-fashioned look.

'Ah, come on, sir. Only a game to you blokes. Slanging each other one minute, off to the boozer the next.'

'Inspector, that's heresy. Lawyers don't *booze*.'

'Oh sure.'

'Seriously, you are mistaken. Even where I live, this will cause passions to rise. It might be better to plead guilty and invoke the mercy of the court.'

'Better? Better for who?'

In spite of himself, Nigel chuckled.

'Whom. But I take the point.'

Evans had drifted to the window and cleared a small patch with his sleeve. It was still raining.

'She's been in a few days, sir. That'd be the line, if you'll pardon me saying. There's still a world outside, see.'

'I think I can manage, thank you. If I decide to.'

'Right up your alley, sir.'

'Don't press, Inspector. You could be on the opposing bench.'

'Suits me lovely, sir.'

His tone gave Nigel pause.

'I hope you're not suggesting ...'

Evans, silhouetted against the window, waved a placating hand.

'Relax, sir. Honourable men, remember?'

'Not entirely. If you *do* find out about the gun, I'll want to know. First.'

Evans stiffened, whistling softly.

121

'Now who's cutting corners?'

'I like a few aces up my sleeve, Inspector. If and when I play, I play to win.'

'I can't promise, mind.'

'Nor I, yet.'

Two days later, Fortesque phoned.

'Hello, young Buxton. Well, I trust?'

Unthinking, Nigel murmured assent.

'Ah, the blessings of rude good health. As for myself, alas, at this time of year ...' And he was off. Elderly, pallid, stooped and emaciated, Fortesque was also a hypochondriac. Nigel had a sharp mental picture of him hunched over the receiver in his poky, overheated office, clutching an inhaler and reeking of menthol. His dry reedy voice droned on, detailing symptoms real and imaginary. In truth he was as strong as a horse.

'Prospective client for you, m'boy,' he said at last, the list of ailments temporarily exhausted. 'Name of Yardley. Ring any bells?' Fortesque had tutored Nigel at law school, and always addressed him as a pupil. His lectures had been notorious for pedantry and tedium. Entering practice in middle age, he'd astonished everyone by doing very nicely, thank you. Relieved of the necessity for personal involvement, he'd revealed a sound if abstract understanding of the criminal mind, a shrewd financial touch, and an unexpected worldliness. In spite of everything, Nigel liked and respected him. Patiently, he said, 'I saw the action replay.'

'You and half the world. Trial by television. Couldn't have happened in my day, thank God.' He paused, and the wheeze in his chest carried clearly. 'Curious business. A man called on her behalf. Welsh, a Morgan or a Thomas or whatever.'

'Evans,' corrected Nigel.

'That's what I mean. How do *you* know? Curious. When I arrived she acted surprised. Wasn't interested. What's going on, m'boy? I'm too old for mysteries.'

Nigel had long since learned to ignore difficult questions.

'What did she say, Fortesque? How did she behave?'

'She said nothing. Thin, fragile, withdrawn. Feeling martyred and misunderstood and not too partial to lawyers.

122

Solicitors, anyway. Pretty, I suppose, if you like them pale and interesting.' He coughed, hard and throaty, and railed the weather. Nigel doodled on his blotter, waiting.

'I think you'd better see for yourself,' Fortesque advised, back on track. 'If you're feeling inclined, that is. Personally, I'd pass.' He coughed again, more affectation than infection, Nigel thought.

'Incidentally, m'boy, how's our beloved leader? I'm told you two are *very* close these days.' A typical Fortesque sally, the most delicate of hints, delivered in the guise of a social enquiry.

'Don't believe everything you hear. Look, you're not very forthcoming.'

'Neither was she. I'd advise you to keep out; of course, should you decide otherwise, I'll be at your disposal.' He sniffed disdainfully. 'Though not at hers, I suspect.'

'What d'you mean?'

'Go and see her. You'll find out.' A pause, a rather horrid rasping chuckle. 'Prefers younger men, I dare say.'

Sleet tapped at the windows, driven by a fitful wind. Periodically, the antique radiator shuddered and dripped, making a single muggy corner in the frigid room. Evans glared at it morosely.

Beddoes, picking at his typewriter, stopped and looked up. 'Cheer up, mate. Christmas is comin.'

'Christmas!' echoed Evans, in massive contempt. 'The annual orgy. They'll all be at it, shelling out for mountains of trash. Tinsel, fancy lights, robins in the snow. Turkey and plum duff, and cold cuts on the motorway. Don't talk to me about Christmas.'

'Bah humbug,' murmured Beddoes. Evans affected amazement.

'Duw, don't tell me you've read a book!'

'Nar. Saw the movie, didn't I. Lionel Bart.'

'Dear God, that was *Oliver*, you moron.'

''S all the same to me, Shakespeare. 'Ere, 'ows 'e going to get in then?'

'Who?'

123

'Santa. I mean, there's no chimneys any more, right? So what does 'e do? Trickle up the pipes, ooze down the elements, plop on to the 'earthrug and bobsyeruncle. North Sea Gas, ho ho ho.'

'Aye, go on, laugh. A *Christian* celebration, mind, and what do you get? *Straw Dogs* on the box, punch-ups at the boozer, vomit in the gutter. Lovely.'

Beddoes eyed him appraisingly.

'Eno's, mate. Just the ticket when you're feelin liverish. Me, I'm off shoppin. Lookin for stockin fillers.'

'Oh aye. Blonde, cup size 36C, no doubt.'

'That'd do nicely,' said Beddoes, leering. 'Listen, if it gets too bad, don't fight it. Shoot yourself.'

It *would* get very bad, he knew. Since Eirwen left, Christmas had become the low point of his year. Early on, he'd volunteered for duty rather than sit home alone. The gesture had passed into ritual, taken for granted by everyone. Nobody bothered to ask; his name appeared automatically on the night roster, 25 and 26 December.

He'd laid it on a bit for Beddoes, but not too much. The festive season was a copper's nightmare, he'd lived a few himself. Santa Claus in the charge room, nicked for feeling little girls' bottoms and cursing like a navvy; a vanful of skinheads, intercepted on a Paki-hunt: 'Teachin 'em a lesson, we wuz. They ent like us, are they, soddin heathens'; broken glass glinting under frosty lamplight, a small twisted form in black blood, a driver babbling and reeking of booze; and later, the whey-faced, dry-eyed mother saying over and over, 'We bought him a bike for Christmas, what are we going to do?'

Give over, bach, if you don't like it you shouldn't've joined; there'll be plenty worse off. Grace Yardley, for one. Not too much cheer where she is, either.

He'd've liked to visit her, really, pass the time, take her something a bit special. Flowers, chocolates, a magazine. It wasn't on, of course. Smythe had been as good as his word: watching every minute. In a way, Evans was still looking out for her, bearing in mind what the lawyer had asked. He would help her best by keeping his nose clean, being free to pass on whatever he learned.

124

So he'd stay away and do his stint while the flotsam of the city revelled in the Christmas spirit. They would come out of the woodwork in droves, thugs and conmen, shoplifters and whores. Meanwhile, he'd sit at the nick and enter them all, the singers and complainers, the humble and the haughty. And bless them every one. Oh sure.

Chapter Twelve

From outside, Nigel reflected, Her Majesty's Prisons probably look much as they did a century ago. It was only inside you saw the differences. Though hopefully just as secure, the bolts and bars were a good deal less obtrusive. There was light now, and air, and even a kind of comfort. An institution, certainly; but it could have been a hospital or an old folks' home. The same quiet, the same lack of urgency, a forgotten backwater calm. But hardly durance vile. A phrase from Stanmore's celebrity party came back – *Seems to me we should concern ourselves with victims, not psychopaths.* It was not an argument he cared to examine. His failures came here, and no man likes to dwell on failure.

He had been before, of course, and never felt at ease. Despite Radio One and ping-pong and the new pastel shades, it remained confinement. Nothing could ever wholly disguise the fact, and rightly so, he supposed; otherwise, why bother? On his way to Grace Yardley's quarters, he pushed these thoughts aside. A time for decision, not speculation.

She sat forlorn in a narrow, spotless room. The single high window let in cold, brief, watery sunshine. Against it, she looked small and frail and utterly ordinary. Somehow, listening to Evans, he'd imagined a bolder creature, capable of passionate emotion and violent action. He hesitated, feeling cheated, almost betrayed.

She took his hand, a cool, impersonal touch, a glance of studied indifference.

'You shouldn't have come, Mr Buxton. You're wasting your time.' A clear, educated voice, classless and dismissive.

'If I thought so I wouldn't be here.'

'I didn't ask for you, or for Mr Fortesque. I'm perfectly capable of saying what must be said myself.'

'Your friend disagrees.'

'My friend?'

'Inspector Evans.'

She sighed, and her grey eyes watched him disdainfully.

'Mr Buxton, I have covered that ground very thoroughly and much more directly.'

'I didn't mean to imply ...'

She cut him off without rudeness or aggression, simply talked through him.

'Inspector Evans is scarcely a friend, merely a decent man who tried to help.'

She shifted, crossed her legs; admirable legs. 'Besides, I've brought him enough trouble already.' The sun disappeared abruptly, and her face took proportion; good bones.

'Miss Yardley, may I ask what, precisely, you think must be said?'

The faintest of shrugs, the same lack of inflexion. 'I killed a man, I'm in their hands.'

'Taking the consequences of your actions?'

'Exactly.'

'Hmm,' he murmured sceptically. 'I wonder if you are.' A standard gambit, which she completely ignored. Pressing the point, he added, 'Law and order is much in the public eye at present. I know judges who'd be very severe.'

'It's not important.' The implication scarcely touched her. She looked and sounded utterly apathetic.

Briskly, he demanded, 'How old are you, Miss Yardley?'

She blinked, surprised. 'Thirty-six.'

'Do you realise you could spend the next fifteen years in a place like this?'

She met his stare steadily.

'Yes.'

'It's longer than you think. Do you consider that just?'

'I broke the law.'

'Indeed you did. Tell me, how did you feel when you shot Morris?'

A swift, suspicious glance.

127

'Completely myself, physically and mentally. Fully aware of what I was doing. What I *did*.'

He waved an impatient hand.

'Taken as read. I'm not trying to trap you.' Outside a door slammed and someone passed, whistling; a popular carol. She listened, head cocked, eyes moist and distant. The sound faded and she stirred, coming back.

'Peaceful,' she said. 'I felt peaceful.'

'Not guilty? Not remorseful?'

'No.'

'Why not?'

She shook her head listlessly.

'Do you really have to ask? He was walking away, Mr Buxton, untouched and unconcerned. *He* felt nothing; why shouldn't I?'

Nigel sat straighter, making a start.

'Very well, you *don't* feel guilty. In fact you propose to enter a courtroom, take an oath; and perjure yourself.'

Her eyes widened, her hand came slowly to her face; and with it, mobility and colour. She *was*, he suddenly saw, a very attractive woman.

'I – hadn't thought of it that way.'

'Then you should.' He collected himself, speaking weightily. 'I don't normally offer gratuitous advice, Miss Yardley, but I'll say this: only fools or saints represent themselves in court. Frankly, I don't think you qualify as either. It is your privilege, of course, to submit, take the easy option; but a defence *is* possible, should you choose to present it. It might even succeed.' And, recognising a fitting exit line, he left her.

Twenty-four hours ought to be enough, he reasoned, and he was right. This morning she looked animated, even eager. Without preamble, she began.

'I've been thinking about what you said, the easy option. I'm afraid I don't understand.'

Nigel settled himself, conscious of a smell no amount of window-dressing could ever disguise; wax polish and carbolic.

128

'Inspector Evans gave you a glowing reference. Your courage impressed him. So far, I haven't seen it.'

'You're very direct, Mr Buxton.'

'As you said, I haven't time to waste.' For a moment he thought he'd lost her. Her face closed, she seemed about to drift away again. Quickly, he added, 'Whatever your state of mind, the physical part wasn't too difficult, was it? You were anonymous, shielded by a senior police officer; taking advantage of someone who'd been kind.'

'You have no right! I didn't – it simply never occurred to me! You must believe me!' She leaned forward, a pose of passionate appeal. Suddenly, she was alive, and the transformation dazzled him.

Softly, he suggested, 'Wilful blindness?'

She nodded gratefully.

'Yes. Yes, that's what it was. I had only one thing on my mind, you see. No thoughts beyond what I might have to do.'

'Might?'

'It depended on the sentence.'

'You'll have to explain.'

She stood and tried to pace, hands clasped, head bowed in concentration. Even in this minute space, she moved with a curious sensual freedom.

'How could he do it?' she cried. 'The judge, I mean. He sat like a Buddha and heard it, the whole vicious obscenity. And what did he say? Not murder, not even a proper sentence. Just – you weren't responsible. Responsible to whom?' She was standing straight, her arms flung wide, her face twisted in anguish.

She had echoed Evans almost verbatim, and Nigel wondered. Had there been something between them? Better not to know. Either way, it would sound impressive in court. Evenly, he said, 'You were under considerable strain, Miss Yardley. Anyone can understand.'

Her eyes darkened and narrowed; gunmetal.

'I tell you I was completely rational!'

'Though obsessed. Come, you just admitted as much.'

'No! Single-minded, if you like; not obsessed, not abnormal.'

He watched her, expressionless, and she relaxed.

129

'A test, Mr Buxton? A taste of what I might expect in court?'

He allowed himself a slight smile.

'*If* you so decide, things will be much tougher. The easy option, remember?'

She inclined her head and sat down, composed and intent.

'I want you to understand this clearly, Miss Yardley. The safest course of action is to plead guilty with mitigating circumstances. There are plenty of precedents, and though you clearly broke the law, your actions were understandable, maybe forgivable. I would expect a suspended sentence. You would, however, become a convicted criminal.'

She made a small sound, very expressive. Colour infused her cheeks; even prison drab became her. Softly she said, 'The library here is very good. I've been reading law. It passes the time, you see. Apparently, had I been able to kill – that creature – while he was molesting my daughter, the law would absolve me. Instead, I shot a man already found guilty of murder. A premeditated act for which I must be punished. Correct me if I'm wrong.'

'He wasn't convicted of murder. You are wrong.'

'Then so is the law! Tell me, please, how I may plead not guilty.' She faced him steadily, chin high, a hint of challenge in every line of her body.

'We've covered this ground, Miss Yardley; you don't *feel* guilty. Look, if courtroom practice depended only on law-books, barristers would be superfluous. The jury is the great strength of the system; it concerns itself with living justice, not words on paper. In the end, the jury will decide your guilt or innocence. As *people*, not lawyers.'

The tension eased, leaving her drawn and pale in the fitful daylight.

'What are you offering, Mr Buxton?'

A bell rang stridently and he started.

'Visiting time,' she explained. 'It always makes me jump.'

There was a brief, tenuous warmth of shared emotion between them and it gave him unexpected satisfaction. He held nothing back.

'I'm offering an ordeal, Miss Yardley, I can't pretend

otherwise. A rehash of everything that's happened. A protracted trial in the full glare of international publicity and a prosecution hellbent on conviction. You'll be spared no pain. It's not an inviting prospect, but I honestly believe you have a chance to go free.'

A long, not uncomfortable silence. Nearby, a key rattled and someone shouted an excited greeting. She seemed to retreat into herself, as if assessing her own reserves. Presently, she stirred.

'A question for *you*, Mr Buxton. I gave you no encouragement, you came here uninvited. Why?'

Again, the echo of his confrontation with Evans. Motives. He shrugged, carefully casual.

'Call it professional curiosity. It's an – unusual – situation.'

'Don't patronise me, please. You've been honest up to now; the contrast is very obvious. Shall I be crude? It's the modern way, isn't it. What's in it for you?'

'My dear lady ...'

'Let me guess. Whatever happens, you can't lose. A gallant failure will be applauded, success would send you into orbit. Don't look so shocked; I haven't been in here *that* long. It's quite all right, Mr Buxton. Self-interest is something I'm beginning to know about.'

Taken aback and off-balance, he retorted, 'My services are costly, Miss Yardley. However, since we're talking practicalities, I'd point out that money has very limited value in gaol.' He regretted it at once, a rare and mortifying lapse. To his astonishment, she smiled; wan and without much humour, but a smile none the less.

'Thank you for calling, Mr Buxton. You'll hear from me soon, one way or the other.' Picking his way through the fog-bound city, Nigel began to comprehend what might have happened to Evans.

That evening, Theresa, attentive and conciliatory, coaxed the details out of him.

'I think you might be missing something, Nigel,' she warned, sitting more sternly than usual.

'Oh? And what might that be?'

131

She paused, worrying the nub of the sofa, gathering lint and thoughts.

'She's a solitary, not by choice, perhaps; but still. She brought the child up – alone. She sat out all the agony and uncertainty – alone. She made her plans, went to court and shot Morris. Alone. Perhaps she wants to see it through the same way.'

He nodded equably. 'You may be right. But look where it's landed her.'

'Has it occurred to you that she might want to be there?'

'What is this, amateur psychology? Back to the womb?'

'Not exactly amateur. It was part of my degree.'

'My, hidden depths!'

Her lips tightened. Wordlessly, she got up and went to the kitchen. He heard the rattle of crockery. Presently she came back, carrying coffee. Still mute, she set a cup beside him and returned to her chair. She sipped, eyeing him over the rim.

'You don't have to be snide, Nigel. It's not a competition.'

He grinned, shamefaced.

'Good coffee. Sorry, old thing, I'm a bit stretched at the moment. Pray continue.'

She studied him for sarcasm. Finding none, she said, 'She's been under tremendous strain. This insistence on normality seems suspect.'

'Methinks thou dost protest too much?'

'Well, don't *you* think so?'

'Perhaps. What's your point?'

Theresa leaned forward, her eyes warm with persuasion. The pose reminded him of Grace Yardley; and invited comparisons. Theresa's dark beauty and voluptuousness seemed suddenly obvious and overblown.

'Suppose you drag her into court against her instincts. More limelight, more questions, more trauma. She might just fall apart.'

'Perry Mason rears his toupeed head. Dramatic collapse in the final reel, the babbling maniac condemned out of her own mouth. Come *on*, Theresa!'

'Go ahead, sneer. You'd never live it down.' Her concern, he realised belatedly, was for him. Gently, he explained.

132

'You haven't met her. Evans was right, amazing resilience. She simply won't let it happen.'

Theresa sniffed. 'And of course, she *is* pretty.'

'Yes. I hardly noticed, at first.'

Theresa drank cold coffee and grimaced. 'She's worth the risk, then.'

Testily he snapped, 'Don't be absurd! The risk would be no less if she looked like Quasimodo?'

'Really?'

'Yes really! Look, old thing, you know I'm not one for gossip with the boys. Even so, I keep in touch. No one's frightfully keen on Miss Yardley. This is *England*, you see. You don't just shoot a man down, even a rapist and a murderer. Awfully bad form. No one's likely to volunteer – they're all shuffling backwards at a rate of knots.'

She toyed with her spoon, turning it this way and that to catch the light.

'You're joking! The great English public adore an underdog. Or should I say bitch.'

'Dear me, language! Unfortunately, the great English public can't influence judicial appointments. To a barrister, common acclaim is about as welcome as gonorrhoea.'

'Poor old Nigel. Even if you win, you lose.' Abruptly, she dropped the teasing tone and asked in deadly earnest, 'So why *you*? Heaven knows, you don't need the money!'

He shook his head in exasperation; he'd heard the question too often.

'Reasons! Suppose I said – a sense of justice. You wouldn't believe me, would you? Why are you living with a middle-aged rake?'

Her eyes narrowed.

'Oh, so it *is* that sort of commitment.'

'For God's sake, Theresa, don't use Freudian claptrap to justify hormonal pique!'

She set the empty cup aside and stood up, taut with anger. From the doorway, she delivered the last word.

'You're a lavatory snooper, Nigel, as well as a rake. Why indeed!'

Next morning they went their separate ways like strangers.

Nigel pottered around his chambers, dictated a couple of letters and read a solicitor's brief. A messy divorce, petty and sordid. He gave thanks that he and Theresa hadn't reached *that* stage. He buzzed his secretary.

'Joyce, send Brown versus Brown back to old Fortesque. Elaborate regrets and I'm much too busy.'

'Right you are, Mr Buxton. Oh, the prison called. A Miss Yardley would like to see you at 2.30. You have a prior appointment – Mr Wigmore.'

Nigel hesitated. The Wigmore case was complex and months away from court readiness. Grace Yardley was here and now. Even so, it wouldn't do to appear eager – if she'd decided so early, she was probably pleading anyway. Let her stew for a while. Astonished, he heard himself say, 'Put Wigmore off. Tell him something urgent cropped up. I'll go to the prison.'

'Very good.'

He sat for a while gazing at the Picasso and thinking of willows. It was worrying when you didn't understand your own impulses.

Grace Yardley was waiting, calm and expressionless. Under the bland light, she looked drained and waxen. A sleepless night, he guessed. She came straight to the point.

'When will the case be heard?'

'Depends on your decision. If you plead guilty, it could be quite soon.'

'How soon?'

'Say, two months.'

'And if I don't?'

'Then we have a lot of research to do.'

'It will take longer?'

'Certainly. March at the earliest.'

She bowed her head briefly, a study in dismay. There were dark half moons beneath her eyes and her cheekbones thrust against the flesh.

'What do you mean, research?'

He leaned back, counting on his fingers.

'I have to look for precedents. A brief must be prepared.

134

Prosecution statements must be studied, witnesses must be interviewed.' Gently, he added, 'I know very little about you, Miss Yardley.'

She made a limp, tired gesture and he caught a whiff of perfume. Something light and subtle, and in this setting, wholly incongruous.

'Why should my private life be important, Mr Buxton?'

Nigel sighed. Sometimes she behaved like a clever child; wilfully obtuse.

'You'll be put in the dock. Be assured, the prosecution will mobilise every possible weapon. There's an old courtroom maxim; never ask a question if you don't already know the answer.'

Unexpectedly, she smiled, faint and ironic.

'How dull. You spoke of a brief.'

'Prepared by Mr Fortesque. We barristers are only actors; the solicitors write the script.'

Suddenly she awoke and took command, another of her improbable rallies.

'I have no intention of baring my soul to *two* confessors.'

'Miss Yardley, it's a question of time. I do have other clients, you know.'

She was up and moving again, lithe and nervous; feline. He could feel her resentment of confinement.

'I told you I've been reading. There *are* no precedents, Mr Buxton, my position is unique. As you pointed out, I'm employing you. Very well, I'll state my terms.'

'Now just a moment ...'

'Please let me finish.' Still pacing, vibrant and certain, she said, 'Let the prosecution do their worst. I will not make an emotional exhibition of myself. I will not be party to legal tricks, I will not be coached or rehearsed. *You* made me understand this, Mr Buxton. I have done nothing, not one single thing of which I am ashamed or which I would not willingly do again. Let them judge me on those terms.'

He shook his head, incredulous.

'Forgive me, Miss Yardley, but you are frighteningly naive. Reading a few books in no way qualifies you to override counsel's advice. You are making quite impossible demands.'

135

She swung to face him, alight with fervour, her body taut and strangely provocative. The sudden beauty appalled him.

'You set me on this road,' she accused. 'You defined the issue – people, not law. All right then. I can live with myself if I must, my conscience is clear. I'd rather spend the rest of my life in this contemptible place than trade on the pity of twelve honest men!'

Now is the time, he thought. All you have to do is get up, apologise and walk away. She stood erect and imperious, a fierce proud spirit trapped and fretting under harsh prison light. Evans's sing-song spoke in his mind. *Something worth saving.* Doggedly, he clung to pragmatism.

'Mr Fortesque will prepare the brief. He will assist me in court and out, as always.'

She made a brief, dismissive movement.

'As you wish. But I will speak only to you. If you agree, I will plead not guilty, place myself in your hands, and accept the outcome, whatever it may be.'

He was, he knew, contemplating supreme folly, the unnecessary censure of his peers in a cause almost certainly lost. But a part of him recognised the challenge, the ultimate test of professional skill; and more, an element he was not yet prepared to acknowledge even to his innermost self.

She slid back into the upright chair, a neat, quintessentially female wriggle.

Meticulously, he declared his own position.

'Miss Yardley, you would deny me three-quarters of my usual armoury. The prosecution, you may be sure, will suffer no such handicap. In return, I demand two guarantees: you will answer *all* my questions, no matter how personal or irrelevant they may seem; and you will allow me to determine what you are pleased to call the "emotional content" of the final plea.'

Her eyes flashed and he felt the profound force of her will.

'I have no desire to appear a distraught woman driven to madness!'

He smiled wearily.

'Even if I were shallow enough to attempt it, they would glance at you and dismiss the idea.'

She inclined her head, and an errant strand of hair shaded her face.

'Forgive me. I am being presumptuous.' And that, he thought, might well qualify as the understatement of the year.

She lifted a fine hand and pushed the hair back. The movement thrust her breasts against the drab material. She was, he realised, one of those women who, in seeking to conceal her feminity, actually drew attention to it. One more trap to be avoided in court. She glanced at him under long lashes.

'Have we reached a compromise?'

He swallowed, nodded, and muttered gracelessly, 'I suppose so. However, it is customary to refer to yourself as my client, rather than my employer.' From the corridor came the measured tread of heavy boots. The room seemed suddenly cramped and mean; he felt loutish and somewhat ridiculous. Not a muscle in her face had moved, yet he sensed her contained amusement. She let him rise, cross the room and approach the door.

'Mr Buxton? We'll be seeing a lot of each other. Please call me Grace.'

Though her voice was tentative, her eyes warmed him like a spring sun. On his way out, he visited the warden and made a request – on behalf of his client.

Chapter Thirteen

Grace Yardley rose to greet him, transformed. A sleeveless black dress outlined her figure, her hair looked soft and lustrous.

'Mr Buxton, how can I thank you? It's so nice to wear something of my own.'

'You had only to ask.'

'But I didn't know that.' She smiled. 'Another thing. Since you arrived, I've been left alone. No more questions, no more insinuations. Did you arrange that, too?' Her warmth embarrassed him.

'Coincidence, I expect.'

'Anyway, I'm grateful. I've suddenly realised how much I want to get out.'

She sat down, ankles crossed, hands in her lap; dependent. The meanness of the room was irrelevant, a mere back-cloth for her. This is how Evans must have seen her, he thought, bereaved and vulnerable, a living challenge to protective male instincts. How she'd escaped them so long was something Nigel meant to discover.

'You mustn't count on it,' he warned her. 'We will need your full co-operation; and some help from the gods.'

'What do you want to know?'

He began the litany – and immediately met an unforeseen obstacle; her compulsive sense of privacy. Despite her best intentions, answers came slowly and reluctantly. It was like drawing teeth. He trod very lightly as he approached the first important area of ignorance.

'Forgive me, but I find it strange that you are so completely alone.'

'I am used to it.'

138

'Perhaps. But wouldn't you have expected some support from Caroline's father? He must be aware of what's happened, surely?'

'No.' She made it flat and final, covering both questions.

'How can that be?'

'He never even knew I was pregnant.'

So that was it.

Her head came up, the familiar defiant tilt. 'I wouldn't have wanted him near her, ever. He was charming, amoral and ... irresponsible.' The word caused her obvious pain; no wonder she detested Morris so.

'You're absolutely certain, are you? Remember what I said about surprises.'

'I've never named him and I never will.'

He was beginning to sense her motives, to test the force of her emotions. Her courage might prove a useful weapon; her habitual reserve would have to be overcome. The genteel interrogation stumbled forward to the next hurdle.

'Now, Grace,' he savoured the word, 'tell me about the gun.'

She avoided his eye.

'It was my father's.'

'Look,' he said. 'Concealment can be excused in certain circumstances, deceit never. Candidly, I don't believe you. More important, and more damaging, neither will anyone else.'

Still staring at her hands she mumbled, 'I can't help that.' The same irritating and childish stubborness.

He let the silence lengthen; then, 'Inspector Evans has a special assignment. The history of your pistol. You mustn't underestimate him. He's a formidable policeman, and he has every reason to succeed.'

'Why is it his business?'

Concisely, he told her. She seemed to shrink; hugging herself miserably.

'I suppose I did use him. It wasn't calculated or malicious, I never meant him any harm.' Her whole attitude invited reassurance and he couldn't withhold it.

'You're very lucky. He seems to understand. I'm sure he

wouldn't want to condemn you, but he hasn't much choice.'

She faced him at last, composed and unyielding. 'There is nothing for him to find.'

She had been badgered on this before, he guessed, and had buried her secrets somewhere deep inside. It had been a hard session, he'd gone as far as he could.

'Very well,' he told her. 'Let's leave it for the moment. I won't be seeing you for a while, so you have time to reconsider.'

She stared at him, unable to hide surprise and disappointment. Even now he hadn't appreciated the full extent of her alienation. Very gently, he told her.

'It's the holiday. Christmas, you know.'

Her confusion was painful to behold.

'Please forgive me, this place makes one – selfish. I'd never even considered your personal life.' She made the effort, reaching for brightness. 'Of course you must think of your family.'

'I'm not married, Grace. But I do have certain commitments.'

'I see.'

Something in her tone arrested him, and he glanced at her quickly. She sat severely, troubled but innocent.

Impulsively he asked, 'Would you like me to visit? Socially, I mean.' Briefly, gratitude and hope touched her eyes, but she shook her head.

'Not here, please. I would be – very poor company.' He felt relieved, and just a little rejected.

Back at chambers, still preoccupied, he answered the phone to Stanmore.

'Compliments of the season, m'boy, and to the delightful Miss Da Silva. I see you're making headlines again.' The slightest hint of disapproval beneath the hearty words.

'I hadn't seen the papers, sir. They don't waste time, do they.'

'Indeed not. Still, the case is news, no denying it. Interesting, what?'

'I must confess I'm intrigued.'

140

'Hmm, Good-looking woman.'

'I didn't mean . . .'

Stanmore laughed, and Nigel, wincing, held the receiver away. 'Of course not, m'boy. You meant the legal implications, I'm sure.'

A pause, a change of tone.

'Not contemplating anything *rash*, are you? No American dramas?' Stanmore held the American judiciary in great contempt. Having made his point, he hurried on. 'Don't answer that. I'll be sitting, d'you see. Can't avoid it.'

'I'm delighted, sir,' said Nigel, dutifully but not untruthfully. 'It will be a privilege.'

Stanmore grunted, mistrustful of flattery as ever. 'Don't be too sure. Thing is, m'boy, it puts us in a personal dilemma. Not a matter of choice, do you see, but social contacts are taboo. At least until it's over.'

'Understood, Sir George.' The title still gave Stanmore satisfaction – Nigel could hear it in the silence.

The exchange faltered and dwindled to a close. Nigel replaced the phone, very thoughtful. Cunning old bugger! The faintest stress on 'at least', the most subtle of warnings. And a Merry Christmas to you too.

Grace's intransigence and the CJ's message sent him home in less than festive mood. All he wanted was a stiff drink and an uncluttered evening. Theresa, bright-eyed and very fetching with achievement, led him into a flat festooned with Christmas decoration. He ooed and aahed half-heartedly, feeling middle-aged and stodgy, shamed by her girlish enthusiasm. Amazing creatures, women, he thought, she still hasn't acknowledged the inevitable. The female of the species is not more deadly – merely more tenacious. Wilful blindness; and he pictured Grace alone in her cheerless cubicle.

Fortesque had sent transcripts of the Morris trial. After supper, declining Theresa's offers of coffee, brandy and other services, he set himself to read. It was stark fare, clinical but graphic, and Evans once more spoke in his memory – *God knows, she had every excuse*! Pity about Evans; he'd've made a useful witness for the defence.

'You've taken the plunge, then,' Theresa interrupted his

absorption. She was sitting quiet but expectant, her posture a claim to attention.

'No, she has.' Marriage would be like this, he thought; partnership in disharmony.

'You didn't give her a push?'

'Well, maybe a gentle nudge.' He moved the file aside, permitting the discussion. It never hurt to think aloud, to test the echoes; and Theresa was a good audience. When he finished, leaving out the last part, she made a doubtful face.

'She sounds very demanding – paranoiac, almost.'

'Don't let's start again. From now on, she's the client, for better or worse.'

'Interesting phrase, Nigel. Her wish is your command?'

'If you have something to contribute, Theresa, I'll be grateful; if you're going to snipe, I'd be better off alone.'

She raised her eyebrows, cool and enquiring. 'Take up thy bed and walk?'

'I didn't say that.'

There was hurt in her eyes now, and a trace of sadness.

'What's happening, Nigel? I thought we were doing rather well.'

He shrugged, keeping it casual. 'First things first, old thing. It is my daily bread, after all. I can do without domestic complications for the next few months.'

'Is that what I am, a domestic complication?'

His attention wandered to the file. 'You haven't been, up to now.'

'I see. Wanted, a handmaiden and bedmate, temporary only.'

'As I recall, Theresa, you volunteered.'

'Oh yes! In the face of fearsome resistance!'

Pointedly he opened the file. 'I see very little merit in prolonging this discussion.'

She came and stood over him, hands on hips, eyes ablaze. 'Know something, Nigel? You can be unbearably pompous.'

He leaned back and looked up calmly. 'I am a dirty old man, a middle-aged rake, and pompous with it. There, we can agree for a change. I'm also an allegedly distinguished barrister prepping a critical case. It's Christmas Eve, old thing, go and

142

hang up your stocking. You'll feel better in the morning.' He actually felt the wind of her furious movement; the door crashed like artillery. Soon it will end, he thought, with insults and recriminations; Brown versus Brown. I wonder how Grace is feeling.

Somehow, Smythe had acquired a complete duplicate of McKay's investigation, two inches thick and growing. Evans knew much of it by heart. Central squad had given Grace Yardley the works. Their mounting frustration screamed between the lines, as did her regal calm. If she'd been a feller, he mused, they'd surely've laid hands on her. Denied this resort, they'd ravaged her psyche and raided her subconscious; to no effect. Inches of paper notwithstanding, her story held. She'd obtained the gun by inheritance, kept it by default. And a plague on all your houses. Good for you, girl.

But not for Evans. Smythe, edgy and watchful, needled him unmercifully.

'How's the courtroom conjuror? Found a rabbit for your hat?'

'I'm trying, sir.'

'Very.'

Even Beddoes observed a distance, laid off the smart talk and called him sir. It was like having some contagious disease.

He received one guarded phone call.

'Inspector. Recognise the voice?' He didn't.

'It's coming from the mouthpiece.'

'Aye, it would. With you, sir.'

'Our mutual friend is adamant, the source of supply remains obscure. Do you follow?'

'Aye, sir, I know.'

'I don't believe her.'

'Makes two of us.'

'You know the rules of the game? Relevant details are open to both defenders and strikers?'

'Sure.'

'I need time, d'you see. It's entirely in your hands, investigation and communication. Just a hint would do.'

'I'm snookered myself, sir, up to now. If I get a break ...'

'I'd appreciate it.'

Lawyers, double talk. Jesi Mawr.

He spent time with a ballistics man in a dingy, acrid-smelling laboratory, hearing of lands and grooves, twists and grains, momentum and muzzle velocities. Very entertaining, mind. The Yardley gun was army issue, part of a 1956 consignment. It had vanished from an armoury four years later along with five others. Dirk and his sulky handler completed the tale. The NCO responsible, cashiered, had proceeded to drink himself to death.

Thus informed, Smythe bestrode a favourite hobby-horse.

'Ah. This would be our bog-trotting, spud-stuffing cousins from the Isle of Poteen. Vicious, demented scum. Be nice to follow this one home.'

'Not a hope, sir. The trail's cold.'

'It always is, with those lads. Still, it knocks your Calamity Jane's story on the head, doesn't it?'

'Sorry, sir.'

'D'you mean, sorry?'

'The serials were filed down. The gunpowder boffin used acid. Even then, the numbers weren't perfect. An educated guess, see. Defence'd drive a bus through it.'

Smythe's small face tightened.

'Straws in the wind, eh. You no forrader?'

'No, sir.'

'Then don't waste my time, man!'

And so to a 3D Christmas; depression, duty and drunks.

It was the bells that woke her, the bells and the stillness. She came slowly from a dreamless sleep, lost and disoriented, her mind shrinking from some unknown ordeal she knew she must face. The wild pealing stopped, echoed and faded. For a moment, there was utter stillness and silence. She lay wide-eyed in the dark, warm and uneasy, waiting. Something was coming, something familiar but unwanted, something she had tried so hard to keep away. Memory. Nothing stirred, not a car, not a dog, not a human voice.

Then, faintly, from an early radio down the corridor, a tune, 'Away in a Manger'. The voices rose, sweet and high and

144

childish, every word clear. In a little while, it would be upon her, the small joyful tornado, bouncing on her bed and babbling of Sindy and the doll's house and a new dress. Oh Mummy, Mummy I love you, Happy Christmas. Then downstairs to a room rich with spice and cooking, the tree and the parcels, the excitement and the pleasure. The floodgates were open now, the images took her, one after another: a toddler in Bambi pyjamas, cuddling the new teddy bear but frightened of his growl; at six, wobbling across the lawn on the gleaming two-wheeler – Look, Mummy, it's snowing! And the twelve-year-old at her first midnight mass, face pure and lovely, mouth open in song, eyes solemn with the wonder and mystery of it all. Just for now, it was all right to lie here and smile; and remember.

Gradually, stealthily, the world intruded. Water sluiced in the pipes, keys jangled, boots stamped. The carols faded, drowned by the sounds of awakening. But most of all, it was the smell, an essence she would never, ever forget. It seeped from the floors and the walls, it pervaded the furniture, it rested in the blankets like an unwanted pet. Not offensive, not obtrusive, but always there, cold and antiseptic. The smell of prison.

She closed her eyes and called back the images, but they had gone, banished by the first taint of reality. She clutched at the blankets, fighting; she had sworn it wouldn't happen, steeled herself against it – and failed. All right, she told herself, just this one last time it's all right. And, as the bells rang out once more, she surrendered and wept for Christmas and her loss.

Chapter Fourteen

Inspired by company, Theresa made New Year's Eve her own; gracious, intelligent and easy on the eye. As host, all Nigel had to do was pour drinks and accept compliments. Fortesque, leaving frisky, unsteady and last, spoke for everyone.

'Well done, young Buxton,' he whispered much too loudly. 'Found a goddess at last. Hang on to her, m'boy. I envy you.'

They cleared the debris, silly with fatigue and drink and shared triumph. Afterwards, they made languid love and she fell asleep on his shoulder. Strange, he thought while her breathing tickled his ear, how the holiday had fashioned the truce. Temporarily free of Grace Yardley's burdens and buoyed in the social swim, they'd recaptured something of their former closeness. Yet, even in this intimacy, he sensed an Indian summer. Stanmore, not Fortesque, had seen the truth -- *not counted among your long term plans.* Soon, he would see Grace again.

He returned one brutal January evening to a flat bare of decoration. Theresa was unusually subdued at supper; later she made her announcement.

'I've been auditioning, Nigel. I've got a part.'

He looked up from his case notes enquiringly.

'Nothing earthshaking, but a start, at least.' If she was overjoyed, she hid it well.

'Thing is, it will keep me occupied.'

'I'll be tied up myself.'

'I've noticed. I'd like to know her secret.'

'Me too. Don't be childish, Theresa. She's a client, nothing more.'

'Really?'

'Yes, really.' It sounded much too definite, even to him. 'The show opens next month, they're hoping for a good run. It means day rehearsals and performances at night.'

'I see.'

'Do you? Then why make me say it?' She was willing him to argue, her eyes soft with hope and sadness. Ask me to stay, Nigel. It would be so easy to let things drift, to remain together but distant. He knew a moment of real regret; then grasped the nettle.

'The trial starts on 1 March, St David's Day. Evans will be pleased. Until then, old thing, this place won't be much more than a dormitory for either of us. But you're welcome to stay, of course.'

'My, how could I refuse an offer like that!'

'Well, it's better than throwing plates about. Perhaps, afterwards, we could try again.'

But there was finality in the air, and they both knew it.

She lingered for a week, tender and considerate. In bed she continued to delight him, but there was a wistful, almost ceremonial air about the lovemaking; the last rites. One day she was gone, leaving a wry note:

'Thanks for everything, Nigel. Forgive me for doing it this way, but I'm bad at farewells. Good luck with the trial, come and see the show. And give her my regards. Yours, Theresa.'

Not 'love', and for that he was grateful. They'd parted on civil terms, could meet again without hostility; his record stood. He heated something from a tin, played himself some Beethoven, and thought of Grace Yardley. The case was shaping much as he'd expected. Fortesque, mole-like, burrowed among the documents and held amiable meetings with the prosecutors. From one of these he'd returned grimmer than ever.

'They're cock-a-hoop,' he reported, sniffing an inhaler, 'and wondering what possessed you. I wonder myself, often. You haven't a prayer, they're saying; holding sweepstakes on the length of sentence.'

'Does that mean they know more about the gun?' Nigel

asked anxiously, and Fortesque grinned, all dentures and deviousness.

'What gun?'

'I see. Let's hope it stays that way.'

'I've bet on acquittal, myself,' Fortesque confided. 'There's no fool like an old fool.' And he coughed lugubriously.

In fact, Nigel was reasonably content with general progress. Gradually, he'd won entry to Grace's background – her work, her family, her struggle for Caroline. More and more, he could sympathise with Evans; an extraordinary woman.

Caroline's father had ceased to interest him. More than likely, he would remain anonymous. Even if the prosecution unearthed him, anything he said would be fifteen years out of date and worse than useless in court. The gun, however, continued to haunt Nigel. Grace had forbidden it as a topic, closed off a narrow but crucial portion of her life. He thought he understood; having made her stand on truth, she refused to lie. Only Evans was likely to confound her, and at worst there'd be prior warning.

Very well, it was time to build a strategy, time for what she disdainfully called 'rehearsals' – and another clash of wills.

In February, Beddoes took leave and it snowed. Hardly Alpine, mind, a mere inch of feathery chill. Maybe back home the mountains looked pretty, but the weather boffins had spoken and the city was prepared. Salt and grit lay ready on the main roads. Drifting flakes settled and melted into a lethal slush which numbed the feet, scarred the paintwork and bumped up the traffic casualty toll.

Hassled by Smythe and denied Beddoes's wit, Evans discovered new depths of frustration. The flood of words from McKay's inquisitors slowed to a trickle and dried up completely. Froze, more likely. The Army connection, as expected, dissolved at the first touch of his hunter's breath.

'IRA?' brayed an irate major. 'Poppycock, man. Still using bows 'n' arrows then!'

'Vital evidence in a murder case, mind.' Evans warned, not to be intimidated. 'Else I'd not ask.'

'Forget it, old boy,' the major advised. 'Too long ago. It's history now, like Cromwell.'

'Just thought you'd like to handle it yourself, see, not to have the busies in.'

'Point, Inspector. I'll turn the MPs loose on it, let you know, all right?'

Lot of good that would do. Tear-arsing round in jeeps and clobbering tiddly squaddies, all their brains in their truncheons. Military Police, duw duw.

Every other lead quickly petered out, driving him to despair and informers. An unlovely and feckless breed, a necessary evil, really. Ninety per cent useless if not actually misleading. Fairy tales, peddled in hoarse whispers behind grubby hands. Trading on leftovers from the underworld feast, they hawked their crumbs to the highest bidder. Lovely lads. Yet every copper had one who reported to him alone and whose name he would never reveal. Because once or twice a lifetime, they might happen on pure gold and a high-rolling hood might fall. So Evans paged the snouts and waited. He was waiting still.

Returning to the nick after another futile and freezing foray, Evans endured more sarcasm from Smythe and a pitying glance from Warner. Retreating to his office, he fortified his tea from the hipflask and watched the clock; until Beddoes, smooth in sheepskin and cavalry twill, sidled through and closed the door.

'Managin all right without me, uncle?'

'Absolutely ripping, thanks,' snapped Evans, la-di-da. Then, reverting, 'What are you doing out of bed? Wrong time of the month, is it?'

'Give over. I'm 'ere to save you, mate.'

'Darro, don't say she's Sally Army.'

'Caught a whisper,' Beddoes said, warming his backside at the radiator. 'One of me grasses came through.'

Evans put his cup down carefully. 'Had a messy day, see. If you're having me on, I'll ...'

'Straight up, sir, honest.' He glanced at his watch. 'The

149

Lord Nelson, over on the posh side. Know it?'

'I'll find it.'

'Plain clothes, the snout said, so wear yer best chapel suit.'

'All right, Fauntleroy, get on with it.'

''Alf-seven in the jug 'n' bottle. Big guy, deerstalker, carnation in 'is buttonhole. Bookie. You can't miss 'im.'

'Know me, does he?'

'Of you, 'e says.'

'Any form?'

'Plenty, but it'll keep. You better scarper, you got an hour.'

'Roy? ... Thanks.'

'Yeah. Mind 'ow you go. Roads are bloody murder.'

Salt clogged the wipers and the de-mister was on the blink. On this glassy surface, people drove like lunatics or little old ladies. Evans picked his way, shoulders tight with concentration. Nice night for a run, really.

The Lord Nelson straddled a corner where suburbia gave way to the domain of the genuinely rich. Striped curtains, leaded windows and acres of car park, Jag and Daimler country. Just seeing it made his throat ache for a pint of Brains in a proper pub. The bar was crowded with camelhair, furs and cigar smoke. Genteel vowels and braying laughter. Noisy buggers, the toffs, he'd noticed before. He worked out the geography and shouldered through, apologising to no one.

His man sat alone on a plush wall bench and nursed a colourless drink. No smell; vodka, then. A broad fleshy face, pepper and salt moustache, strong, hairless hands and hard, dark eyes. The deerstalker hid his hair – balding, probably; the suit patterned but nicely cut, and the carnation, yellow, very bold. Evans sneaked a glance at the time; 7.32, close enough. The big man looked him up and down. In deep Belgravia cockney, he drawled, 'You the filth?'

Evans fashioned an easy grin and lapsed into softest Welsh.

'Now then, boyo, let's not spoil a lovely friendship. Bin insulted by experts, I have.'

'Yeah, I bet. What's your poison?'

150

Evans beamed, his simpleton approach.

'Normally it's 'alf o' bitter, see, but I'd 'ate to get you a bad name. Scotch, then, a double.'

The big man's lips drew firmly together. Angry and menacing and not bothering to hide it. He punched a bellpush; when the girl came, he gave the order like a command.

'What's up then, boyo?' enquired Evans artlessly. 'Something to tell me, is it?'

'Just wait,' snapped his host. 'Never mind the amenities.'

The drinks arrived, no money changed hands, and Evans sipped luxuriously.

'Lovely, that. Hits the spot. Cheers.'

The big man rumbled, took a short swallow and said brusquely, 'Little bird told me you was "making enquiries".' He made the stock phrase sound obscene. 'Something about a shooter.'

Evans nodded casually.

'Aye. Nothing urgent, mind.'

'Balls. No one drags 'emselves out in this weather for fun.'

Evans made his voice more businesslike.

'Right then. Say your piece.'

A decisive shake of the head.

'Not here, cock. Big race comes later.'

Evans, peering at a hunting print on the wall, suggested, 'Could always get comfy down the station, mind.'

The big man laughed, a sharp bark totally devoid of humour.

'Pull the other one, it's got bells. There's four blokes in the bar'll swear I never left, and that girl just went blind.' Off hand, he added, 'Gotta big stake in this place.'

Evans shrugged easily.

'Well, you're making the running, then.'

'Too right, cock, and don't you forget it.' He twirled his glass, poked at the lemon and sucked his finger.

'Walk in the country suit you, week tomorrow, say around two-ish?'

He leaned forward, baring his teeth. 'Don't care to be seen with the filth, see. Bad for business.'

'The feeling's mutual, boyo, absolutely.'

151

There might have been a twinkle in the dark eyes, quickly doused. 'That's nice. Common interests.' Concisely, he described a route and fixed a rendezvous.

'Just you 'n' me, OK? No gatecrashers, a private party.'

'Going away then, are you? I mean, a week?'

The big man laid a finger beside his nose.

'No questions. Course, if you don't fancy it ...'

'I'll be there.' Evans said, draining his glass. 'Nice crack, that.'

Next morning, Beddoes outlined the form.

'Name of Hunter, Bert. Dockside lad, in school with me old man.'

'Nice to have friends, mind.'

'Part of me charm. Bit of a tearaway, old Bert, but sharp, a good 'ead for figures. Used to make book in the third form. 'Ad a wild patch, ran with the gangs and took a fall. Three to five on GBH. Model prisoner, out in two years. Told 'em 'e wouldn't be back, the quizzine wasn't to his taste. He was right on both counts.'

'Oh aye. Humourist, is he?'

'There's not many'll laugh at him, not to 'is face, anyway. Got in with the Brighton mobs, worked his way up, an enforcer, 'andy with 'is mits. Branched out on 'is own just before the Gamin Act. Suddenly 'e was legit, Simon-pure. Onward and upward ever since.'

'He's on the pig's back now, no doubting it.'

'Yeah. They say 'e's still got fingers in pies, but from a distance. Diversification, he calls it. Moves with the moguls, likes the jargon. Married an ex-stripper, two kids in a snooty school. Solid citizen, untouchable.'

'Local boy makes good, then. Warms your heart, doesn't it. So where's the link? Apart from your Dad, I mean.'

Beddoes shook his sleek head.

'Don't ask. A grass got lucky. I told you.'

'Fair enough. Who followed up, you?'

Beddoes gazed at the ceiling, whistling tunelessly.

'Weather 'asn't bin up to much, 'as it?'

'OK, bach. Wise monkeys, is it?'

152

'Brass ones, more like. Look, I'm on 'oliday. I'm off to put me feet up.'

'Get your leg over, you mean.'

''Oo, me?'

Left alone, Evans set to rummaging. Not that he doubted Beddoes, mind. Only, the files sometimes threw up tit-bits. He had time; he wanted to know his man.

Starting from the present and working back, he checked out contacts, memorised the children's names, filled up a mental dossier. Beddoes had covered most of it; bent fruit machines, protection, prostitution. Only hints, though. Hunter used the best legal talents and his associates were tight-mouthed to a man. Just once a case had taken shape, only to fall apart in a sudden dearth of witnesses. Hunter played in the premier league these days, probably at least half straight.

Next, he considered the timing. The 'country walk' was due only two days before the trial opened. Should he warn Buxton? Warn him of what? Sure, there'd be a story, real or imagined, but Hunter would be the last man to stand and be counted. Without corroboration, he could hardly go to court; so why raise a hare? Where ignorance is bliss ...

The same applied to Smythe. The Super had made it crystal clear – 'Don't waste my time, man.' Even if Hunter was selling a true bill, there'd be work to do, pieces to put together, people to interview. In his present frame of mind, Smythe was best avoided altogether. Evans would prepare as fully as he could; and go solo.

For only the second time in his career, Nigel intended to use all three of his challenges during jury selection. He knew exactly what he wanted – upper middle-class parents, mothers preferably, with teenage daughters of their own. People who would identify with Grace Yardley and think, there but for fortune ... Throughout these proceedings, the senior prosecuting counsel, a short, round, deceptively jovial man named Wilshaw, would eye him indulgently. Enjoy yourself, my learned friend, it won't make a scrap of difference.

Fortesque, leaning on a cane and bemoaning the effects of frost on lumbago, delivered a synopsis of the prosecution case.

153

'They've got her cold. Police witnesses, ballistics, the why, the who and the where. Dotting the i's and crossing the t's. It's unassailable, naturally.'

'We know that already.'

'Us and half the population. The line seems to be, We're not vindictive, we sympathise; but if she's misguided enough to plead not guilty, put us to all this trouble, we demand due penalty. Got an answer for them, young Buxton?'

'I'm working on it.'

The work he spoke of had been hard; he was not nearly as confident as he pretended. Grace had submitted to 'rehearsals' unwillingly. Her scruples had proved well-nigh unshakeable, her resistance to questions still caused him concern. In court, her fastidious delivery and precise language could harm her cause. Her self-possession could be taken for coldness, her composure for callousness. She might yet prove her own worst enemy.

Long interviews in her room had fostered a curious intimacy. In many ways, he knew her very well; the light on her hair, the changing depths of her eyes. Once, when he'd protested at her secrecy, she'd taken his hand and begged, 'Please don't be annoyed with me, I'm depending on you,' and the brief contact stirred him.

Sometimes, after a particularly gruelling session, she would stretch voluptuously, a wholly natural movement, a hint of intriguing sensuality. Perhaps, he reasoned, in the aftermath of Theresa, he might be somewhat vulnerable himself. Dangerous thoughts, to be concealed at all costs; but then it was a dangerous case.

Throughout all this, he played on her maternal instincts, knowing the prosecution would seek to establish revenge as motive. This was the only point he could hope to attack – yet the crucial stratagem could not be 'rehearsed'. If spontaneously produced in court, her confidence in her own innocence might just sway the jury. It was treacherous ground; but he had to walk there.

Just once, he had acknowledged an alternative. A display of verbal and emotional pyrotechnics, an appearance of defence without substance. He could do it, and in a way that only the most perceptive of his colleagues would recognise. Stanmore, for one. The majority would give credit for a brave attempt; a favoured few would privately applaud his shrewdness. A safe option harming no one – except the client.

In the final analysis, he was committed to her; as he told Theresa, for better or for worse. Grimly, he realised it might well turn out for worse.

Chapter Fifteen

The ultimate rarity, a perfect English winter's day; crisp and clear and bitterly cold, a blue sky and a low, full sun. Evans, locking his car and stamping his feet, surveyed the meeting-place critically. Hunter had chosen well. A chalk hill at the edge of the Downs, away from main roads and sprinkled with small spinneys. In summer, a site for picnickers, dog-walkers and outdoor lovers; at this time of year in mid-week, as isolated as anyone could wish.

Even so, Hunter had taken extra precautions. They must approach from different directions, park in separate lay-bys and meet, by chance, on an open slope. More like paranoia than security, but Evans hadn't argued. Thrusting his hands deep in his pockets, he set off upwards.

It was very peaceful. The grass underfoot lay flat and icy, the trees stood bare and metallic, patches of unthawed snow cushioned the hollows. Within minutes, exertion had warmed him. Only his face felt the bite. Somewhere, a lone and opti-mistic blackbird called, and the air smelt faintly of cattle. He could've been back home, it only lacked for sheep. Come on, Bert, he thought, let's be having you.

Movement below caught his eye; a big, quiet car. It drew up some distance from his own and a figure got out, foreshort-ened by the angle. The expensive clunk of the door carried clearly. Mercedes, Evans noted – he's come a long way from St Louis. The tune echoed in his head as Hunter trudged towards him.

Gannex top coat, paisley scarf and the hat; houndstooth tweeds and solid brogues. Add binoculars and a shooting stick and you have your actual country squire. The cold had heightened his colour and put a gleam in his eye. He came straight up, looking neither right nor left, his breath condensing in small plumes.

'You wired for sound?' he demanded curtly.

Evans shook his head. 'Private, you said.'

'How do I know?'

'Have to take my word, boyo. Be damned if I'll strip up here.'

Hunter stared hard for a moment, then nodded.

'Yeah. Bit parky, innit. Let's walk.'

Evans fell into step beside him. He moved purposefully, a man secure in wealth and self-esteem.

'Where to start?' he muttered and Evans advised, 'Try the beginning, I would.'

Hunter halted and swung to face him, aggressive.

'I'll talk and you listen, right? You got any nasty little fuzz plans, you forget 'em fast. I'm legit these days, see.'

'All ears, I am, Bert.'

'Done your homework, have you? That's a good boy.'

Evans assumed a bumpkin's grin. 'I can manage the short words, thanks.'

Hunter struck out again, breathing easily. Fit, then.

'I'm doing you a favour, OK? Respectable citizen passing on information.' He paused, a hint of reluctance in his voice. 'There's just one small problem.'

Evans grinned again.

'Funny. There always is.'

'Yeah well, don't hold your breath. I can handle it.'

'Oh sure.'

Hunter smacked sheepskin gloves together abruptly. 'Coulda knocked me down with a feather. Didn't believe it, had to look real hard. Know the bit in the street, where they panned right in? Head and shoulders and her holding that bloody great shooter? Fancy camerawork, that.'

'Didn't watch it too closely myself. Not my favourite viewing, see.'

A quick, tight, sideways smile.

'Wasn't your day, was it? Still, nobody's perfect.'

'You were saying?'

'Grace. I only knew her first name.' Hunter stopped again,

the same warning in his eyes. 'I got friends, see, from the old days, haven't seen the light. Small time, mostly, not worth your notice. A man's not answerable for his friends, right?'

'You told me already.'

'Bears repeating. So OK, once in a while they drop in, bit of advice for old time's sake. This feller – no names – runs a few girls through dockland. Slags,' he added disgustedly, 'no class. Still, we *were* mates.' He paused, took out a cigar, went through the sniffing ritual and lit up with a gold Colibri. He tilted his head and sent out a blue aromatic cloud.

'Nice leaf, this. Fancy one?'

Evans, outwardly patient, said, 'Gave 'em up when I was ten. Saving for roller skates, I was.'

'Maybe you'll get 'em one day. This mate had aggro, some rich bird musclin in on his racket, pinching customers. Pulled her in, came the heavy and she froze him solid. Take me to your leader, she says, I don't deal with scum. You gone soft, I told him, show her the razor, she'll be nice. Birds don't care for razors,' he confided, stating a fact. 'Looked at me like I'd farted in church, this mate. You ain't seen 'er guv, he says, I wouldn't dare. Do us a favour, he says, you tell 'er.' He had the accents and the voices, he was enjoying the act. Evans waited, tense and hiding it.

Hunter drew on the cigar and gave off more smoke. 'Well, what the hell. I'm soft, me. Anything for a mate.'

'I'm touched.'

'In the head, mate, like all coppers. Where was I? Yeah. So one day I'm sat in the office sussin out the lay-offs and she walks in, cool as you please. Little blonde piece.'

Evans stopped dead. 'Blonde? Grace?'

Half a pace on, Hunter snapped, 'Just wait, cock. I'll do it my way, d'you mind. Gonna stand there all day?'

Walking again, Evans muttered, 'Be my guest.'

'Blonde, like I said, OK?' His profile softened, took on a faraway look.

'Been around a bit in my time, I have, seen the lot. High-class tarts, strippers, models, even the odd starlet.' He grinned suddenly. 'Very odd indeed, some of 'em. Anyway, this Grace beat the band.' He slowed, stopped, and faced Evans, his eyes bright with the memory.

'She had this dress, bit of cleavage, split to mid-thigh, must've been painted on. Not a stitch underneath, you could see. Never seen a body like it. Not big, just absobloodylutely perfect. But it wasn't that so much. Plenty of good meat about if you know where to go. No, she had a look in her eye and a way of moving you couldn't mistake. Oozed out of her, it did, pure animal sex. No wonder the slags were getting the heave-ho. Had me sweating just standing there, and me a regular family man. Don't look like that, it's true.'

Evans nodded, not trusting his voice.

'I tell you, my missus turned a few heads; still does, bless her frilly knickers. This bird was something else again. You all right, cock? Looking a bit peaky.'

'I'll survive.'

'Want to walk some more?'

'Aye.'

Hunter moved slowly, reliving the scene.

'"I'm surprised at you, Mr Hunter," she says, her voice like velvet. "You ought to be more careful. What if I'm a police-woman in disguise?" "I'd join tomorrow," says I, and we have a good giggle. "What can I do for you, gorgeous?" "I want a gun," she says, just like that. Well, I waffled a bit, told the tale, but she wasn't having it. "Come, Mr Hunter, we both know you can do it." Eating out of her hand, I was. "It'll cost you," I says. That far gone I didn't even ask why she wanted it. "I'll pay, Mr Hunter, cash or kind, or both." "Kind?" I says, not believing it. "A night to remember when you're old." She did something with the dress, gave me a flash.' He stood still once more, a curious, fixed look on his face. 'Know the muscle right up on the inside of a nice thigh? Gets me going, that does, really turns me on. Anyway, to cut a long story short, I got her the shooter. And d'you know what? I took cash.'

Evans's mouth felt like parchment. Reflex rescued him, a tribute to constant sparring with Beddoes.

'You're a true gentleman, Bert, a credit to the profession.'

'I kid you not, mate. When it came to the crunch she lay

there like a side of mutton. It was weird, believe me. Spooky. Wouldn't even take her wig off.'

Fighting horror, Evans mustered his wits. 'So that's your small problem, then. The gun.'

Hunter flung away the long-dead cigar, a violent jerk of the arm.

'Hold your horses, copper. I'm in Doncaster today, ask anyone.' Which explained the delay, and the paranoia. Alibis. Evans managed a soothing tone.

'Just prompting, bach. Carry on, you.' Another suspicious frown. They had reached a spinney. Hunter tore down a thin branch and snapped it into pieces, crack, crack, like matchwood.

'I got it off a bloke in a dark alley. Now that's straight, all I'll ever say. Never saw him, never spoke to him, handed the cash and took delivery. A mate fixed it.'

'No names, for old times' sake?'

'You're learning.'

Evans was putting one foot in front of the other, his mind all over the place. The ring of truth, mind, but he had to test it.

'Fancy yourself on the box, do you?' he taunted.

'Watcha mean?'

'David Kossof, bedtime stories. Clean it up a bit, the kids'll love it.'

The dangerous anger erupted, loud in the frosted stillness.

'You thick fuzz git! Think I've got nothing better to do than freeze the family jewels off, you oughta be back on the beat!'

Evans harnessed the rage which had ridden him for the past hour. 'Watch your lip, boyo. Just the two of us, remember?'

For a fleeting instant, he thought he might have to act, relishing the prospect. Slowly, Hunter relaxed, took half a step backwards.

'What the hell. Do one busy, you have to do them all.' He moved on, head down, kicking at the grass. Evans, purged and thinking again, couldn't fathom it. Hunter was hardly the type to fear confrontation, physical or otherwise. Striding out, he pressed home the attack.

'I'm gullible, boyo, I believe you. Different in court, mind. Honest big-time hood gets religion and grasses to the filth.

160

Inadmissable evidence, see. Give me the big laugh, they would.'

For the first time, Hunter looked unsure of himself.

'Yeah, that's what Solly said.'

'Solly?'

'Tame lawman, rentagob.'

'Done some homework yourself, have you?'

Hunter dredged up a sickly smile.

'Listen, cock, how about a deal? Queen's evidence and anonymity for the witness.'

'Oh aye? Mice and pumpkins and we all live happy ever after.'

Hunter sniffed dolefully.

'Solly said that, too.'

'You pay him; you want to listen.'

'So what's the bottom line?'

'If you want it to stick, stand in court and say it. 'S on you, boyo.'

The silence extended. They puffed steam softly, upright and motionless like horses asleep. A voice in Evans's brain warned, this'll finish her, she doesn't deserve it, whatever; tell him to forget it, stick to the nags and buy a Rolls. Yet if Hunter persisted, he'd have to go along, self-preservation and bloody duty. Hunter shifted from one foot to the other, flapping his arms.

'Christ, it's cold.'

'Aye.' He held his breath. 'You coming in?'

A long, heavy sigh.

'Porridge at my age. Solly said it could happen. Six months, he reckons, with luck.'

Evans went very carefully now.

'Look, there's bits of this I don't much care for. If we edit, I might be able to swing something. No promises, mind.'

The hope in Hunter's eyes was pitiful to see.

'You wouldn't con me? It's the kids, see. Me 'n' Doris can hack it, we've been there before. But the kids, Jesus, they'll be shattered.'

'Just the gun and the money, that's all you have to say. Doris wouldn't like the other anyway.'

Even in this extreme, Hunter managed a knowing grin.
'Doris loves the other, cock. But I see what you mean.'
'I'll put in a word, then, try for the Mr X treatment.'
Unconsciously, they'd been edging down the hill. The sun
had set, the wind had risen, farm lights twinkled below. Evans,
perished, talked softly, preserving the fragile truce.
'Follow me in, bach. A quick statement, helping with
enquiries see.' Hunter plodded beside him, wordless and
hunched against the cold. At the car, Evans asked his final
question.
'Why are you doing it, Bert? After what Solly said?'
Hunter drew himself up, a flash of the old arrogance.
'Jesus, it's obvious, innit? I'm a family man, I got respon-
sibilities. A weirdo like her loose and we're all up there to be
shot at!' He was breathing heavily, his eyes angry. 'What this
country needs, cock, is law and bloody order!'

Evans kept his word; discreet and low key. It took an hour and
he typed the statement himself, expurgated. Hunter signed,
gave a private number, refused tea, and left tight-lipped and
very subdued.
'I'll try,' Evans reassured him, but he didn't look convinced.
It was after seven, Smythe would be long gone. Evans slipped
the statement, original and duplicate, into the file and locked it
in his desk. He thought of calling Buxton; not now, boyo, it's
always too soon for bad news. In spite of what he'd heard, he
would continue to shield her. Couldn't help himself, really.
Slipping into his raincoat and glancing round the drab office,
he felt an immense weariness and distaste. That's what comes
of ferreting, bach.
The sense of betrayal held him through a meagre supper and
a long, empty evening. He simply couldn't imagine Grace
Yardley coming on like the siren in a fifth-rate movie.
Hunter's story seemed wild; yet clearly he'd been describing
a very real experience. For fourteen years, she'd devoted
herself to Caroline, needing no male on the scene. Now she
had two very different men jumping through hoops; briefly,
he wondered how Buxton was faring. Her many images
mingled in his brain: cool and sultry, chic and sleazy, frank and

deceitful. Will the real Grace Yardley please stand up? Preferably, the one he could continue to admire, for he still couldn't forsake her.

The more he thought, the less he understood. The case bulged with improbables, an entire cast acting out of character. Buxton the career man playing knight-errant, Hunter the poacher turned gamekeeper, Grace the suburban matron turned whore. And Evans the enforcement raising her sleeve. He took the mysteries to bed, drifting into their complexities – and sleep.

He woke as to an alarm, sharp and alert. Sodium light tinted the window, he could see frost ferns through the curtains. The small-hour lull which comes to every city, when noise and motion cease. The word on his mind was consistency; a complete departure from his earlier thoughts.

From the first, he'd taken the case as his own, accepted the responsibility, the challenge, the triumphs and the disasters. Done his duty; consistent, see. At the same time, he'd heeded his instincts. He would do as much for any woman in her position. Common humanity. Only this time, the two couldn't be reconciled and he'd been fooled. Fair enough, he wouldn't have it any other way. Because Inspector Evans, policeman, must co-exist with Huw, ex-husband of Eirwen, member of the human race. Better a fool than a robot. Policemen see people in one dimension, he's a villain, she's a tart, they're a gang. Have to, really, or you can't function. People are consistent, but only by their own lights. Therefore, Bert Hunter, bookie, could also be a doting parent, and Grace Yardley, doting parent, might also be a whore. You couldn't call it betrayal, then; duw, had she been consistent! At last it made a kind of sense. He could speak for the prosecution while supporting the defence, use Hunter's evidence while wishing him dumb. And in so doing, rid himself of Grace Yardley's spell. Maybe.

Chapter Sixteen

Sometime in the pre-dawn hours, the frost had relented. Into milder air, the river had thrown up a dense mist, and Smythe's large windows overlooked a sinuous murk; at 9.15 he still needed the striplights. As Evans entered, the Superintendent lowered the phone, a small ping signalling the opening of hostilities. Smythe's face looked raw and vengeful.

'Ah, Evans, a happy coincidence. That was the Pillock, crowing. He had a nice sense of history – still smarting from Flodden, I imagine. The Flower of Scotland. Not a pleasant experience.'

Evans, nursing the file and Hunter's statement, muttered something inane.

'Your sympathy overwhelms me, Inspector. You'd do well, however, to save some for yourself. McKay, in his charming way, offered consolation. My officers, he suggested, being used to misdemeanours and operating in suburbia, are not privy to his more wordly sources. Those accustomed to apprehending shoplifters and returning lost cats must not be expected to cope with murder. He has a pithy turn of phrase.'

In this mood, Smythe tolerated no interruptions. Puzzled and apprehensive, Evans waited while he stood up and marched to his usual station.

'You've blown it, Evans. Despite my indulgence, despite the access I fought for, McKay's clan beat you to the post. They know about the gun.'

Evans felt old and tired. Good job Smythe's back was turned. The words seemed to come from a great distance.

'Not the whole story; even the Pillock concedes that. Enough, though. She took to the streets, apparently.' The distaste in his voice was caustic. 'She'll be seen as a liar and a whore, as well as a murderess.' He turned, thin-lipped and very bitter.

'So much for obsessions. Too high-minded for informers these days, I suppose.'

'Of course not, sir!' Evans indicated the file. 'Matter of fact ...'

'No excuses, man! Whatever you hold, McKay can trump.'

'Sure of that are you, sir?'

Smythe's gaze was contemptuous.

'Napoleon Charlesworth. Would that be a name to you, Inspector?'

'Never heard of him.'

'Then the Pillock reigns.'

'Down at Central,' Evans murmured, 'he's called the Laird.'

Smythe smiled grimly.

'Really? How very entertaining. Hardly the scoop of the year, though. Mr Charlesworth is Caribbean, it seems, bookies' runner turned pimp. He has a stable of fillies in dockland. Mr Charlesworth also sings, when pressed. Miss Yardley infringed his territorial rights and solicited his clients, he says. When he objected, she claimed protection; *your* protection. McKay was very thrilled.'

'Come on, sir, surely you don't believe ...'

'McKay's granite conscience allows a certain latitude, he informs me. Bargaining, for instance, so long as justice is served, the noo. In return for immunities rendered, Charlesworth will deliver an abridged solo in court. Whatever his faults, the Pillock is a loyal policeman; on this one issue, we agreed to close ranks. Your account, Inspector, is overdrawn.'

Evans, adrift and struggling, mumbled, 'What about the gun, then? Charlesworth gave her that, did he?'

'It doesn't signify. Let her cling to mystery, if she likes. It can only make things easier.'

'Not with you, sir. Sorry.'

Smythe came heavily back to his desk, sighing with exaggerated patience.

'Central says she did the rounds, picking up the dregs. Somewhere alone the line, she got lucky - my lily-white body for your gun. An offer *no one* could refuse, correct? Let her

165

deny it; the jury will see her as she is – hardly the respectable grieving mother.'

Evans tried once more.

'Look, sir, the prosecution could be making a mistake. She's been consistent, see ...'

Smythe's open hand crashed on to the desk.

'Enough! After the shambles of the past few months you can sit there and ramble about mistakes? Good God, man, the entire damn force is laughing at you! It's finished, Evans. You will give evidence, such as it is, close the file and forget the wholly bloody mess.'

His head down, the file resting on his knees, Evans asked, 'Is that an order, sir?'

'Very perceptive. Damn right it is! When the dust has settled, I'll be taking a long hard look at your future.'

Back on duty and restless with curiosity, Beddoes asked, ''Ow was it with Bert? 'Ave a nice chat?'

'Oh lovely. Near froze to death.'

'Give over. Bet 'e gave you a winner.'

'Turned out a non-starter.' For some ill-defined reason, Evans was feeling secretive. Beddoes shrugged.

'Well, bookies. Wat'cher expect?'

'Less every day, bach.'

Hovering near the radiator, Beddoes gave him a charitable grin.

'Smythe still leanin?'

'Leaning? Came down like a ton of bricks. Central got there first, see. They've rumbled her.'

'What, the Pillock? Must be 'is lucky year. Thick Scotch git.'

Evans, aping Beddoes's own mannerism, tilted his palm to and fro.

'Win some, lose some.'

'That's the ticket, uncle. *Non-carborundum*. Age an' virtue will triumph in the end.'

'Latin, is it? Want to learn the Queen's English, you do.'

'BBC Wales callin.'

'Leave it now, boyo. There's hard thinking to do.'

Beddoes sniffed, acting offended.

'You're gettin moody, mate. Worse than a bleeding bird about the place. You oughta get married, or something.'

'Piss off, Roy!'

Left alone, Evans fingered Hunter's statement. No one else had seen it, he realised. Well that was Smythe's fault. Losing his touch, the Super, allowing the Pillock to rile him like that. Let him cool off, show him the evidence, recover some lost ground. Common sense, really. But was it? Grace Yardley's cause was already lost; Bert Hunter's lay here on the desk; and perhaps, at last, it was time to look out for himself for a change.

Indirectly, McKay had given him the idea. Under the Caledonian sarcasm there lurked a sound principle; knowledge is power, whatever its source. Smythe had rubbed it in – *too high-minded for informers, I suppose.* Funny, two top coppers pushing him towards a clear dereliction. Hunter's statement was important, should be used; and neither of them wanted to know. Fair enough; he could find a use for it himself. He hesitated a moment, conscious of the step he was about to take; for the first time in his career, off the straight and narrow. But, in the long run, for the good of the force. There's pompous, mind. He tucked the statement into his pocket, locked the file away and went out.

Mid-morning, no one much about. A pair of muffled matrons chatted, their prams double-parked on the pavement. Miraculously, the corner phone box hadn't been vandalised. He slipped inside and dialled.

A female voice, hard but refined.

'Doris Hunter. Who's calling?'

Evans, inspired, mumbled, 'Napoleon Charlesworth. Your husband in?'

A beat, a curt 'Wait,' and Hunter came on, the aggression boiling over.

'Listen, you gormless spook, 'ow many times've I told you not – '

Evans cut him off. 'We went walkies the other day, remember? Little heart to heart.'

A sharp intake of breath, a long, cautious pause.

'The filth?'

167

'Himself.'

'Where're you calling from?'

'Phone box. Secure your end?'

'As Ford Knox, cock. Speak.'

There was tension in the voice, a hint of apprehension. Evans had turned, leaning against the directories, keeping an eye. A woman passed, elderly, laden and hobbling. Arthritis, then, a bugger in the cold.

Quietly, he said, 'Few questions for you.'

'We oughta meet.'

Evans smiled to himself.

'Bad for business, remember?'

'Yeah, yeah, smartarse.'

'Look, Bert, you answer straight, maybe we can deal.'

'No names, cock. What d'you take me for, a mug?'

'A parent.'

A longer silence this time, a perceptibly softer tone. Evans cleared the glass, still on watch.

'Ask away.'

'You're legit these days, you said. Sure of that, are you? No involvement?'

'I'm clean, cock. Ask anyone.'

'Take Charlesworth, now. No rake-off from there?'

'Do me a favour! I told you, we used to be mates. Listen, that Gamin Act's a cracker. Don't need to be bent, the arithmetic and the mugs do it for you.'

He sounded sincere, slightly amazed at his own good fortune.

'Besides, I got kids to bring up, a position to maintain.'

'Oh sure. So how d'you get the gun?'

A breathy sigh. Evans could imagine the big head wagging.

'Yeah, well, anyone can have an off day. That Grace ...'

'Yes,' said Evans, feelingly. 'Tell me about the feller.'

'What feller?'

'Who sold you the gun.'

'Never saw him, cock. Set up by a middleman. It was dark, I gone deaf, dumb and blind.'

'Did he have an Irish accent?'

''Ow in hell ... Listen, I was home in bed, ask the missus.

Cock?' A note of genuine fear. 'Those are some very rough boys.'

'Aye, well you can relax. Walk away, go and pay school fees.'

'Whadaya mean?' Hunter sounded deeply suspicious.

'Just what I said. Your mate Charlesworth's got in first; don't need you, see.'

'Oh yeah? What about Grace, what about the statement?'

'Steady on,' cautioned Evans mildly, 'I ask the questions, mind.'

'Very funny. You ought to be on the stage.'

Evans unfolded the duplicate, a nice crackle in the confined space.

'You listening, Bert? I'm tearing it up, right?' He tore the paper, folded, tore again.

Silence. Then, 'How do I know it's the original?'

'You don't. How do I know you're clean?'

The phone spluttered in his ear. Hunter was actually laughing.

'Know what, cock? You ever want to leave that outfit, I could fix you up. You got talent.'

'Just so we trust each other, see.'

'Yeah, like foxes. Listen, you on the level, no court, no hassle?'

'Aye.'

Hunter's voice thickened, he seemed to have difficulty with the words.

'I owe you, cock. I won't forget, it's one of my rules. Anything I can do, right?'

Evans allowed the shortest of pauses.

'I might take you up on that one of these days.'

'Welcome. I mean it, Inspector.'

He strolled back to the office, the original snug in his pocket, the day seeming milder and brighter. He didn't feel particularly guilty, and the prospect of Bert Hunter, supersnout, intrigued him. Nicely placed source, that, good as anything the Pillock could manage. When the day came for Smythe to 'take a long hard look at your future', Evans could produce some insurance. If you can't be good, be prepared.

*　　*　　*

Grace Yardley ran the brush through her hair, a simple, half-forgotten pleasure. The mirror told her she had survived; a hint of colour replaced the dreadful gauntness. When Morris had fallen at her feet, she'd thought it was over. She didn't care what happened, prison seemed a fair reward for what she'd done to Evans and to herself. Darkness possessed her, she dwelt in a land of brittle, hard-eyed whores and a spidery negro who filled her with revulsion. The kick of the gun in her hand, the sound of agony, the stench of blood and cordite. Through it all, a haunting image of Caroline's smile, of joy forever lost. Each session with the interrogators thrust her deeper into the nightmare. She had slept little, eaten less, and tried not to think at all.

Then, gradually, came the realisation that she'd done what she must in the only way she could. She'd been true to herself, need apologise to no one for seeking forgetfulness and life once more. In time, she would remember Caroline with pleasure, not pain; first she must escape this mean and dreary place.

Sometimes she thought of Evans and the debt she owed; not because she'd used him, but because he'd shown her who and what she was. She attracted men whether she wanted to or not. This knowledge, and a compliant body, had carried her through the terrible nights of her quest; the rasping chins, the reeking breath, the frenzied groping. Even Hunter, of the greedy eyes and hard hands, had bowed to her will. Such conquests gave her neither pleasure nor conceit – only self-awareness and a vague, distant hope.

She laid the brush aside, stood and stretched luxuriously. If she ever got out, she would walk more often. When Caroline was younger ... she shied from the thought, turning to more immediate issues. Nigel Buxton. Alone among the men she'd met, he refused to be dominated. Over the past weeks, he'd worn her down, steadily imposing his own will on the shape of the defence. More than she had ever intended, she was in his hands, and she found the knowledge curiously reassuring. For the first time in her life, she chose not to stand alone.

Around her, the prison lay dim and silent. From a great distance, she heard the sound of drunken singing, quickly cut off. She laid out her clothes for the morning – Buxton had helped her choose – and prepared for bed. She would carry into court peace of mind, self-assurance, and a valediction; Caroline and the others had been avenged. On these terms, she could take her place among the living. If they would have her.

Between them, Grace and Theresa had created an unusual vacuum in Nigel's life. Tonight he was glad of it. This, he supposed, was why fighters retired to isolated camps; to be alone, to concentrate, to gird physically and mentally for the contest ahead. No distractions.

He'd done the best he could. Gradually, in the face of quiet but steely resistance, he'd whittled away most of Grace's reservations. At times he'd been brutal; more so, he hoped, than the prosecution would dare. Patiently, he'd armed her against the loaded question and the verbal trap, readying her for the ordeal and nudging her always in the direction he was determined to take. She seemed more poised now, less guarded, less obsessed with privacy.

There remained one formidable technical problem. Unable to call Evans for the defence, he was tempted to dispense with witnesses altogether. He could then legitimately present an unsworn statement from Grace, sparing her the trauma of cross-examination. If, on the other hand, they proceeded as planned and her total rejection of guilt emerged under *Wilshaw*'s questioning, the effect would be devastating.

The uncertainty haunted him, but was not the only source of disquiet. He had spent too much time in her company, learning to admire her not only as a person but also as a woman. In the claustrophobic intimacy of prison, he'd watched her draw back from the edge and bloom. Her beauty was of a kind which repaid close study, and he'd done plenty of that. At this eleventh hour, he sensed the approach of Evans's sin – personal involvement. And unless his instincts served him false, she was neither unaware of, nor displeased by, his dilemma. Women were his grail and ambition was his spur; the two came together all too smoothly on this case.

Win or lose, he could expect support from fringe elements, the dewy-eyed liberals and those who like to see egg on establishment faces. With these as friends, who needed opponents? If Stanmore and his like expected a bravura performance, all show and no substance, they would soon be disillusioned. He did not propose to lose by default. The root of his anxiety, buried deep beneath these superficialities, could be stated in a single sentence. In freeing Grace Yardley, he might forestall his own ambitions.

As a young barrister, Nigel had discovered a foolproof remedy for pre-trial butterflies. Often unable to eat and no fit company for man or beast, he would take himself to some mindless amusement – a dog-track, a bingo hall, a Kung-fu movie. Alone in a crowd, he would surrender wholly to the odds or the numbers or the flickering screen; and return home calm and restored. It was the best idea he'd had all evening.

Evans's numbed conscience had woken outraged, and he spent the evening talking it down. Charlesworth's evidence was quite enough, thank you, Hunter had shown willing, crossed the floor, really, why rub it in? If he took the stand, his mates would cold-shoulder him, he'd be useless as a snout. Anyway, the Super had spoken, given an outright order, and coppers obey orders, don't they. What's done is done, boyo, too late for second thoughts. Damn her in court, wish her the best and walk away.

There was one thing he could do; had to, really. But when he rang Buxton to warn of the prosecution's new knowledge, he heard only the long beep of an unmanned line. Briefly and mutinously, he considered the ultimate folly – call the prison, talk to Grace herself. Even now, he couldn't quite swallow Central's assessment and Smythe's condemnation of her, there had to be more to it. And anyway, he didn't fancy being her Judas. No use, bach, she'll be abed by this time. He fell into a clammy and oppressive sleep and dreams of bloodied maniacs, childish corpses, a hanging judge and a lily-white body. Waking much too early, he cut himself shaving, spilled fried egg on his dress uniform, paid the earth for a daffodil buttonhole, and went unwillingly to court.

Chapter Seventeen

Grace's obsessive privacy and Nigel's own growing isolation had rendered the junior largely superfluous. Luckily, Erskine seemed content to liaise with Fortesque and occupy a back seat. So he should, Nigel assured himself, he's getting a fat fee. The three were making their way through the court-house chatting casually, a pleasant frisson of anticipation between them. On this mild St David's Day, pale sunlight softened the austerity; a hint of spring in the air. Then, from a corner of his eye, Nigel detected urgent movement. Evans, in uniform, beckoning. Nigel excused himself and dropped back.

Evans approached, decidedly shifty.

'News, sir. The prosecution have something on the gun.' Nigel felt blood draining from his face.

'What? You promised to let me know!'

Evans, staring down at his boots, mumbled something, and Nigel's fears broke loose. Viciously, he whispered, 'The prosecution put you up to it! You're paying her back!'

'Steady on, sir,' Evans cautioned. 'Nothing to do with me, mind. The Pillock's lot.'

'The *who?*'

The Inspector's embarrassment was painful to watch.

'Sorry, sir, Superintendent McKay of Central. I tried to tell you last night; no reply.'

Evans looked thoroughly miserable, and Nigel reined himself in.

'I was out. My turn to apologise. A bit wound up, you see.' Bitterly, he added, 'The timing's just perfect.'

'Aye. Look, I can't talk here.'

'Of course not. I'm sure you did what you could. I'll see the prosecutor; thanks.'

He was already moving when Evans said, 'Sir? It's nasty, see. Very nasty indeed.'

Someone was approaching, another uniform. Evans raised his voice to social level.

'Nice to see you again, Mr Buxton, sir. Good luck in court. You'll need it, mind.' And went on his way, innocent as dawn.

Shaken badly, Nigel sought out Wilshaw. The prosecutor, toad-like in his robes, stood chatting to his team. Sunshine glinted on his spectacles; he looked cheerful and animated. Seeing Nigel, he came forward, hand extended.

'Buxton, day to you. May the best man win and all that rot.' A surprisingly strong grip, a clear, open gaze.

'Indeed,' said Nigel, very dry. 'I hear you'll be presenting stuff we haven't seen.'

'I was about to mention it. They contacted you, then. Good.'

He sounded genuinely relieved; Nigel had his doubts. Coldly, he asked, 'Not pulling a fast one, by any chance? Getting one in before the bell?' Wilshaw's geniality fell away sharply.

'I resent that suggestion, old boy. We only heard ourselves last evening; I've been trying to contact you ever since.' Seeing Nigel's expression, he added, 'I've read the statement. Wouldn't be in your shoes for a knighthood. Very brave of you, my view.'

He meant rash, and Nigel knew it. Forcefully, he said, 'We'll demand an adjournment, of course.'

'That is your right. I shouldn't fuss, though. The witness won't be on for a day or two. We're all in the same boat, d'you see, no need for panic.'

'Nevertheless, I'm going to the CJ right now.'

'In that case, old boy, I'll join you.'

'You're very kind. I appreciate it.'

If Stanmore noticed the coldness they brought to his chambers, he gave no sign.

'Gentlemen. Ready for the fray, I trust?' Wilshaw seized the initiative; smart move, Nigel acknowledged, he's playing the magnanimous victor already.

'Actually, sir, there's a development.'

174

Stanmore frowned and Nigel took up the story. When he'd finished, Stanmore remarked, 'Hmph. Can't say I'm over-joyed. Everybody geared up, so to speak. Still, we don't have any choice, I suppose.'

Relieved, Nigel murmured, 'I thought it best to come at once, sir, before jury selection.'

Stanmore's eye narrowed.

'The point had not escaped me, m'boy.'

Very conscious of the atmosphere of a second false step taken and past recall, Nigel soldiered on. 'If you'd be so kind, sir, I'd like to consult my client. Examine the implications, seek further instructions.'

'Yes, yes. Take as long as you like. Up to lunchtime anyway.'

Nigel forced a chuckle at this testy joke. Into the momentary ease, Stanmore tossed another small grenade.

'She might like to reconsider her plea.'

It would be very easy, Nigel reflected, leaving, to imagine a conspiracy here. And forced the thought down.

Graciously, Wilshaw offered copies of the statement. Nigel thanked him tersely, rounded up Erskine and Fortesque and retired to a musty room set aside for the defence. There, in utter disbelief, he read Charlesworth's evidence, while Erskine sat like a mouse and Fortesque even forgot to cough. Pushing the document aside, Nigel rested an elbow on the table, pinching the bridge of his nose between thumb and forefinger.

'Well, young Buxton,' challenged Fortesque, in an I-told-you-so voice, 'where do we go from here?'

Unmoving, Nigel muttered, 'Run it through for me, would you? Just to be clear.'

Deliberately, Fortesque applied the inhaler to one nostril, then to the other. The reek of medication overpowered the dust. He sniffed, closed his eyes, cleared his throat, and began.

'They haven't nailed the transaction. Better if they had, for us. Cash changing hands, d'you see, something everyone understands. As it is – well, it's character assassination, pure, simple and total.'

'Not so pure,' murmured Erskine, and Nigel nodded appreciation. Fortesque shook his head.

175

'Makes no difference. We have presumed,' he continued, including Erskine and making his scepticism very obvious, 'that you were determined on some sort of *moral* approach. Dodgy at the best of times, now quite hopeless. A fallen angel, with a vengeance.' He sniggered at his own morbid pun, descending into a lengthy bout of coughing. Erskine offered comfort and he recovered strongly.

'Quite all right, young man, I'm used to it.' Proving the point, his voice took on depth and firmness.

'She must be prevailed upon to plead. If she doesn't, we'll be crucified legally, morally and in public.' Erskine nodded vigorously. Now it's unanimous, Nigel thought; Yardley and Buxton versus the rest.

'One man's word,' he mused, 'puts her on the street. The prosecution will say she did it for the gun. An inference, at best. Suppose she denies it?'

Fortesque sniffed again; for effect, not need.

'We'd be better placed to answer that if we knew the woman at all. I must say she's been very foolish. However, denial or not, the damage will be mortal. You must tell her so.'

Wearily, Nigel raised an eyebrow.

'Erskine?'

'Oh, I agree. Totally.' A tart little sting there, too. Nigel sighed for the demise of three month's work.

'Then I'd better go.'

Sunlight played on her hair, gave a peach-like tint to her skin. Fleetingly, she looked as Fortesque had described her – angelic; one glance at him was enough. Her shoulders drooped, her eyes closed, and she sank gently on to her chair.

'They told me there was a delay. You've heard about the gun.'

He shook his head, thrust his hands forward in despair.

'Why in God's name didn't you tell me? What on earth possessed you ...?'

He trailed off, lost for words. She looked up at him, her self-possession intact. 'What exactly are they saying?' Something in her tone arrested him, a hint of reserves as yet untapped.

176

Dully, he said, 'A man named Charlesworth went to the police.'

'Charlesworth?'

'A West Indian. A - procurer.'

'Come, Mr Buxton, I'm not that naive. He's a black pimp.' No coyness, a flat statement of fact. She sat intent and disciplined, not at all discomforted. 'What did he tell them, this honest and upright citizen?'

Nettled, Nigel snapped, 'His exact words were, "She pulled my mugs, marn."'

'Well, that's true enough.'

He rounded on her, at last prepared to be really angry.

'For months I've guided you, aiming at a viable defence. I've assumed you sane, sensible, and, in a moral sense, innocent. Perhaps I'm to blame, knowing what happened to Evans. Very well, I congratulate you. I've seldom been so wrong about anyone.'

Her eyes were dark, almost smoky. Very quietly, she said, 'Tell me what changed your assessment.'

Incredulous, he muttered, '*You're* demanding an explanation?'

'Yes. Don't I deserve one?'

'I'm by no means sure! However. You took to the streets, you bedded the scum of the city until you found what you wanted. A murder weapon.' Staring at her, he felt a prickle behind his eyes; he could have wept for the loss and the waste of such perfection. Heavily he said, 'Obsession. That is the kindest explanation I can find, and it leaves me a single course of action. I shall go to the judge and change the plea.'

Instantly she was up and pacing, sinuous and feline.

'You will do nothing of the sort!' She faced him, hands on hips, eyes blazing; breathtaking.

'I will say this once, for you alone. Yes, I lied to you. Yes, I lured men away from pitiful whores; weak men, drunken men. Yes, I let them kiss me, I endured their embraces before I could escape. I did not, *could* not, sleep with them. I bought the gun, Mr Buxton, from a man who will *not* go to the police; I paid, God knows, I paid; but not the way you seem to believe.' She

177

paused. Then, very soft, the hurt open and bleeding, 'How could you?'

She sat down, her anger spent. In a tone which beseeched understanding she said, 'How does a single, respectable woman obtain a gun, quickly and without attracting attention? I'll tell you. She uses the only weapon she owns; herself. She has to make contact with the criminal world, but she doesn't know where to begin. So, she must draw attention, starting at the bottom, on the streets. She goes from whore to pimp to crooked businessman until she reaches someone who can give her what she wants. And she pays, Mr Buxton, in ways you couldn't begin to imagine.' Her head had fallen forward; through the sunlit hair which shrouded her face, he could see the dampness on her cheeks. He felt nothing more than a sense of awe. He *had* misjudged her; something worth saving. Always it could be reduced to that. Just then, he would have done anything she asked.

Even as he groped for the words, she rallied. Lifting her head, brushing her cheeks, she said, 'Remember, I have done nothing, *nothing*, I am ashamed of. They may think what they like of me as a woman, as long as they judge me as a mother. It's all I ever asked and all you ever promised. I will not change my plea!'

'Grace, you've been discredited. They won't believe a single word you say!'

'That is their problem and your challenge. *You* know the truth.'

'You must deny the inference the prosecution will draw from Charlesworth's statement.' He collected himself, saw how he must persuade her. 'If you don't, the jury will see you in exactly the way which caused you such pain a moment ago. They may even doubt your sanity.'

For the first time, she hesitated, uncertain.

'All right. If you can bring it out just as I've said it, I'll deny it. What do you call it, cross-examination?'

'One can't cross-examine one's own witness.'

A pitying glance.

'This is hardly the time for technicalities.'

'You're mistaken. First, we need an adjournment, time to

178

study Charlesworth and his evidence in detail. A week would help, a fortnight would be better. Please, for once, hear me out! Second, I should ask for your instructions in writing. No competent lawyer will believe me!'

She actually smiled, wide and warm.

'Poor Mr Buxton. Of course I'll write it down if it helps.' Her face altered again, pure and stern. 'But there will be no adjournment.'

'Now look here …'

'I'm sorry. If I stay in this room any longer, my sanity really will be in doubt. The trial must go on, now.' Another change; he couldn't keep pace with her moods.

'I'm on trial for murder, not illegal arms dealing. What does it matter how I got the gun?' Appealing, vulnerable, brave, beautiful. He couldn't fathom her any more.

'What can I do with you?' he wondered aloud. 'You ask the impossible and make it sound easy.'

Astonishingly, she touched his hand.

'Think of it this way. The harder the struggle, the sweeter the victory.' Well, she should know.

Over a brief and scrambled snack lunch, Nigel broke the glad tidings and set the team to work. Fortesque grumbled to himself, belching eucalyptus like an infirm dragon. From time to time he glanced at Nigel as if observing a hitherto undiscovered species. Erskine, willing but neutral, was given the jury list and instructions to mark off anyone who might conceivably prove unsympathetic. Meanwhile, Nigel, clawing his way towards some kind of balance, pored over Charlesworth's statement. At two, they put on wigs and gowns and bland faces and went into court.

Swearing proceeded, as Nigel had anticipated, slowly. Wilshaw, exuding a kind of benign scorn, sat silent and unmoving as the challenges followed one upon another. Stanmore made little secret of his growing impatience, but Nigel was not to be deterred. True, the prosecution was scoring points without saying a word; but the bout had hardly begun. Finally, at ten to five, Stanmore said sarcastically, 'I presume, Mr Buxton, you are now satisfied, and will have no objection to an adjournment. Tomorrow, I hope, we can begin.'

179

Reason warned Nigel to make himself scarce, find an oasis somewhere and give his full attention to the new evidence; without conscious will, he found himself treading the familiar prison corridor outside Grace's room.

She had changed into casual clothes, and her face lit as he entered. A sudden, inexplicable sense of domesticity took him; she'd be like this to come home to.

'Hello,' she said easily, 'I didn't expect you again today.'

'Thought I'd put you in the picture.'

She sat down, one of her neat, feminine movements. 'That's nice.'

As she listened attentively, he found himself giving the inside details – Stanmore's disapproval, Wilshaw's patronage, Fortesque's infuriating cold. Ruefully, she admitted, 'A wasted day, and all my fault.'

'Since you mention it, yes.' Anger and frustration had left him. He spoke casually, as to a friend.

'It would have been far more sensible to tell me, you know.'

She bowed her head, genuinely penitent.

'I couldn't imagine Charlesworth going to the police, or being believed. A known criminal – he is so obviously unreliable.'

'You're feeding on myths. The police are fascists, unintelligent clods, overblown traffic wardens. A few may be; many are quite the opposite. Honour among thieves; arrant nonsense. They'll queue up to make mischief, curry favour, even clear the way for their own advancement. Put the two together the truths, not the myths – add a known fact, such as your gun, and the police can be very thorough and tenacious. I warned you once; formidable.'

She made the connection instantly.

'Was it Evans who found me out?'

'No.'

'Then he's still in trouble?'

'I would imagine so. It can't have done him much good, someone else coming up with the story. But he did warn me, this morning.'

'Oh.' Another of her soft, eloquent sounds.

'Yes. A man of his word, our Inspector.'

Night had fallen, much colder now. He felt no great desire to move, enjoying a quite unexpected closeness; comrades in adversity. As though sensing the thought, she asked, 'How much have I lost?' She was watching him steadily, demanding an honest reply. He shrugged, sighing.

'Doubtless, Charlesworth will hurt us. Just how much remains to be seen. Factually, we're no worse off, they're still guessing. Morally, we're weaker.' He paused. 'I suppose you wouldn't care to tell me the rest of it?'

Her eyes clouded, her face closed.

'I don't see how it could help. I'm sorry.' Her head came up and she added tartly, 'I didn't sleep with anyone, if that's what's worrying you.'

'But you would have, if necessary?'

'Probably.'

He stood up, turning towards the door.

'Better not say so in court.'

She was following quite close behind.

'See you tomorrow, Nigel.' Amazed, he swung around. She stood, eyes wide, a hand raised to her mouth.

'I'm sorry. I wasn't thinking.'

'Don't be ridiculous. It's my name. Though,' he added, in a weak attempt at humour, 'we haven't been formally introduced.'

Suddenly mischievous, she held out her hand.

'How do you do? My name's Grace Yardley.'

And he carried away with him a whiff of her perfume, an image of her smile, and the warmth of her touch.

Just before four, Beddoes bustled into the office and gave Evans a military salute.

'Yekki Dar, or whatever. 'Appy St David's. All dressed up an' nowhere to go?'

'Adjournment,' Evans grunted.

'Courtesy of the Pillock?'

'Not really. Charlesworth.'

Beddoes did a little flourish, showing off. 'Given name, Napoleon; occupation, immoral. He's a spook.'

'Busy little busy, you are. Want to watch your mouth, though. Us minorities can be sensitive, see.'

'Me 'eart bleeds. Listen, I've been pokin' about, 'ad words with Nappy's slags.'

'Nappy?'

'Nice, innit. 'E's full of shit, they say.' Beddoes's smile thinned. 'Not this time. Our Miss Yardley was there three nights till they got narked and 'ollered for the spook. Beg pardon; our beloved and equal brother.'

'More particular about relatives, I am.'

'Not with friends though.' A rather embarrassed silence. 'Sorry, sort of slipped out.'

'Oh sure.'

Beddoes hastened on.

'Wearing a blonde wig, but they fingered her anyhow.'

'I know,' Evans muttered tiredly, thinking of Hunter. Beddoes's eyebrows went very high.

'Do you now? Didn't see it in the statement, meself.' He smiled, inviting confidences. Evans gazed at the ceiling.

'Well, if you don't want to tell me ...'

'Ignorance is bliss, boyo, believe me. Contagious just now, I am.'

'Who says so?'

'Smythe, for one. That's why I'm playing it cagey.'

Beddoes gave him a burlesque wink.

'Nod's as good as, uncle. I got things to do, anyway.'

'Give her my love, mind.'

Evans went home to too much whisky, too much of his own company, and more ominous dreams.

Chapter Eighteen

From a long-ago and otherwise forgettable party, Nigel recalled a single moment of wisdom; a fleetingly popular radio commentator revealing trade secrets. Modish, self-important and slightly tipsy, employing the Merseyside dialect of the time, he had commandeered the limelight and asked, 'Know how many people I'm talking to when the old red light comes on?'

Answers were bandied; ten million, twenty million, fifty million. Suspecting a catch, Nigel held still.

'Just one. Little old lady in a council flat, peering at the rain and fiddling with her deaf aid. I'm brightening her life, y'know, cheering her up. The personal touch; it never fails.'

It worked on juries, too. From his place on the bench, Nigel surveyed twelve faces, choosing a target. He remembered her from yesterday, a Mrs Davidson. The right age to have children of her own; tall, trim and auburn haired, a woman who might glance at the dock and think – it could be me. His eye went naturally to her; easily the most attractive of the group.

Without effort, he gave a superficial level of his mind to Wilshaw's opening while thinking himself into Mrs Davidson's head. He wanted to view this setting through fresh eyes, to gauge its effect on her. March sunlight through high windows, glinting on dust motes and varnished panels. A vaulted ceiling to catch sound, tiled floors which rang underfoot, wig and robe reflected in polished wood. A scene of order, he decided; tiered benches, the gallery filling rank by rank; prisoner, judge and jury in their assigned boxes, counsel opposed in line and face to face. A dignified atmosphere, archaic speech and studied decorum. To him, a workaday environment, its impact cushioned by time and familiarity. A newcomer would feel the full effect; a weighty air which, if not guaranteeing truth, must render falsehood more transparent. Mrs Davidson seemed properly impressed, sitting severely and hanging on every word. Wilshaw speaks well, he noted. Good diction. A noise from behind intruded; Fortesque's eternal cold.

For a while, the dock stood spotlit. Grace Yardley's hair had grown, framing her face. She looked serene, young, and very innocent. Sometimes Mrs Davidson glanced at her, puzzled and sympathetic, and Nigel relaxed, his instincts vindicated. A satisfactory choice.

Wilshaw, concluding, was clear, confident, and mercifully brief. 'Milud, I confess myself astonished at the defendant's plea. Seldom have I undertaken a more straightforward case. I will not, therefore, waste time, yours, mine and the court's. The prosecution will show that the accused was present at the material time and place; that in obtaining a weapon well beforehand, she demonstrated her intent; that the fatal bullets issued from the gun she held and that she was seen to fire them; and that she had a compelling motive for her action.' He looked up from his notes, his spectacles flashing. 'In short, we shall prove her guilty as charged of wilful, malicious and premeditated murder.' He moved briskly back to his place, squat, robed, wigged and goggled. Toad, Nigel thought, of Toad Hall. During the hiatus, feet were shuffled, noses blown, throats cleared. Fortesque coughed relentlessly, like a dog barking at night.

A parade of policemen began, large pale men, members of Morris's escort. One after another, in similar voices and almost identical words, they described a death in December. Nigel let the first three go unchallenged. The fourth, a sergeant, he detained.

'You remember these incidents clearly?'
'Yes sir.'
'You have related them in your own words?'
'Yes sir.'
'You have not consulted or collaborated with your colleagues?'

184

The smallest of hesitations.

'No sir.'

'Remarkable. I can only congratulate the police on achieving such consistency of thought and expression.' Sitting down, he was conscious of Wilshaw's supercilious smile. A trivial blow, doubtless, but it was never too soon to plant a seed of disbelief, never too early to attack. Mrs Davidson was watching him too, intelligent and pretty. She has the Irish colouring, he observed; let's hope she's heard of the Terrible Beauty.

Next came the medical expert, a man noted for verbal diarrhoea and impenetrable jargon. The court, a captive audience, grew restless under his pleasantly modulated voice, and Fortesque snuffled loudly, as though the attention of any doctor would do. Skilfully, Wilshaw cut through the verbiage to his basic premise; the fatal wounds were caused by two bullets fired at point-blank range.

Over lunch, restored by food and a stiff whisky, Fortesque condemned the medical profession at large.

'Quacks, all of them,' he declared, from long experience. 'Disciples of the capsule cult.' Erskine nodded agreement and said nothing, the court mute.

Wilshaw reopened with a showman's flair. Producing the gun like a conjuror, he laid it on the bench and announced, 'Exhibit A, milud.'

The court woke. The preliminaries were over, the full gravity of the situation had suddenly emerged. The gun lay gleaming dully in diffused light; cold, ugly and lethal, the focus for every eye, a silent witness to a bloody deed. Watching Mrs Davidson, Nigel charted the course of her thoughts. Her gaze shifted to the dock, lingered on its occupant, and returned to the exhibit. The green eyes narrowed, a minute shake of the auburn hair. How could this woman have handled this weapon? As if seeing the doubt, Wilshaw called the fingerprint man.

A technician, this; quiet, concise and definite. In a soft West Country burr, he stated his conclusion. The defendant had fired the killing shots. Under Nigel's cross-examination, e remained firm and unhurried.

'There were other prints on the gun?'

'Oh surely, sir. The policeman, you see, the one she passed it to.'

'Then how can you be sure Miss Yardley actually fired the shots?'

'Palm prints, sir, on the butt and the barrel, were identified as those of the policeman. There was only one trace on the trigger, a forefinger; hers.'

Another knowing glance from the prosecutor, an audible wheezing sigh from Fortesque. Stanmore jotted something in his notes, the press scribbled frantically. Wilshaw, polishing his spectacles, turned to ballistics.

Another expert, more abstruse phrases. Persistently, like a pauper at a carcass, Wilshaw extracted the meat. The tests were positive and conclusive. The fatal bullets had come from Exhibit A. For another long, intent moment, Mrs Davidson and her colleagues stared at the gun. Round one to Wilshaw, Nigel conceded, as the judge moved adjournment.

In her room that evening, Grace was subdued and distant, the closeness of yesterday a fading memory.

'He made it sound so cold,' she complained, 'so calculated.'

'And it wasn't?'

A spark of real anger. 'You, of all people, should know it wasn't!'

He smiled gently. 'There we are, then. Nothing to be ashamed of, remember?'

But she wouldn't unbend, and he left quite soon.

When Evans strode to the witness box next morning, there was a quiet buzz of anticipation. The tabloids had speculated freely on his relationship with the defendant; Nigel sensed the licking of salacious lips. Immaculate and outwardly impassive, Evans intoned the oath without a glance at the card; Grace was watching him with a curious expression, half sympathy, half apprehension. Wilshaw was very crisp.

'Inspector, how long have you known the accused?'

Evans consulted his notebook.

'I went to her house on 11 September last missing person report, I was.'

'You had never met her before?'

186

'No.'

'Since then, though, you've had a good deal of her company?'

'In a professional capacity, sir, yes.'

The next part, Nigel guessed, had been rehearsed. Wilshaw was at pains to scotch the rumours, to establish Evans as an objective witness. The press, hungry for sensation, waited in vain. Gradually, the tone of the questions changed. Wilshaw more insistent, Evans more guarded.

'It was you, Inspector, who followed up the disappearance, broke the news of her daughter's death, trapped the murderer, and stood by Miss Yardley during Morris's trial; was it not?'

'Yes.'

'And during that time you came to know her well?'

'Objection,' said Nigel. 'Council is leading his own witness, milud.' Stanmore upheld him, and Wilshaw rephrased the question.

'Inspector Evans, how well did you know the accused?'

Evans hesitated, clearly unhappy with the implications, but powerless to avoid them. At the press bench, pencils were poised to strike. Finally, Evans muttered, 'As well as anyone, really.' An answer which clearly gave Wilshaw quiet satisfaction.

'On the afternoon in question, was her behaviour in any way unusual?'

'Perfectly normal, I'd say.' Evans was on safer ground, and it showed.

'You didn't find it suspicious, her insistence on being there?'

'Not at all.'

'Why?'

'She wanted to see it through. That's the way she is, mind. Determined.' In his eagerness to protect her, Evans had said too much and Wilshaw pounced.

'Indeed,' he said, very dry, and allowed the inference to penetrate. 'You accompanied her into the street, right up to the vehicle, for the same reason?'

'Yes.'

'Even though, on a bitter afternoon, she was wearing only a sleeveless dress?'

'Yes.'

Another deadly pause, stressing the unlikelihood. Consulting his notes, Wilshaw murmured, 'Curious. You were standing next to her; yet according to your statement, you didn't see the fatal incident.'

An old hand, Evans said nothing; but didn't escape.

'Why not?'

Nigel watched the Inspector weigh the virtues of an evasion; and reject them. Heavily, he said, 'I was distracted.'

'By whom?' A movement in the dock caught Nigel's eye. Grace was leaning forward, gripping the rail, her posture imploring Evans to answer. Staring downwards, his voice low and agonised, Evans said, 'By the defendant.'

Wilshaw pursued him pitilessly.

'She deliberately deceived you, then?' Grounds for objection, Nigel knew, but Wilshaw would force the admission anyway; an interruption now would merely lend undue emphasis. Nice touch; a classic, when-did-you-stop-beating-your-wife question.

Evans merely nodded, and the judge ordered, 'Give your answer clearly, please.'

Evans threw the word down, flat and bitter: 'Yes.' And Grace Yardley eased back in her seat.

With perfunctory nods to the judge, half a dozen reporters scrambled for the door. Evening headlines on their way, Nigel thought, 'Inspector distracted' or 'Top cop duped', according to your journalistic taste. Gradually, the court subsided, the tension ebbed. Wilshaw sat down, pleased and not troubling to hide it. Fortesque's symptoms erupted afresh, and Stanmore shot him an irritated glare. Nigel rose unhurriedly and sauntered to the witness box. Time for recovery and repair, time to fashion Evans's reprieve.

'Tell us, please, exactly where you were when sentence was passed on Morris.'

A tight suspicious frown.

'In the courtroom. Beside the defendant.'

'You had been called as a witness?'

'Yes. I had every right, mind.'

Nigel hastened on, conscious of the inaccuracy.

188

'How did Miss Yardley react?'

'She didn't, really. Not so you'd notice.'

'Did she say anything to you?'

Nigel saw the dawn of realisation, the sudden flare of hope in the pale blue eyes.

'Matter of fact, she did – "At least I can be certain."' He paused, glanced quickly at the dock, and added, 'Words to that effect, anyway.'

'At least I can be certain,' Nigel repeated, staring straight at Mrs Davidson.

'The shooting happened how long, approximately, after these words were spoken?'

'Fifteen minutes. Twenty at the outside.'

'During those fifteen minutes, would it have been possible for her to approach Morris?'

'He'd been taken inside. They were getting him ready, see. No.'

Mrs Davidson looked puzzled, and the judge was frowning ominously. Nigel moved on.

'Now, Inspector, I want you to think carefully. After the shooting, did Miss Yardley look excited or elated?'

Playing up nicely, Evans paused, considered, shook his head.

'Can't say she did. Just tired and cold, and sort of – relieved.'

'Thank you. No more questions.' Wilshaw was up at once, hostile and sarcastic.

'Are you a psychiatrist, Inspector?'

'No, sir.'

'You have studied psychology, perhaps?'

'Not directly, no. I've seen the books, mind, most policemen ...'

'Thank you. You are not, I take it, a thought reader?'

'Unfortunately, no.' Evans's rueful delivery won him some sympathetic smiles.

'So, when you presume to instruct us on the state of the accused's mind, you are merely expressing a personal supposition, are you not?'

Looking up into the hush, Nigel saw the faintest of grins on Evans's face.

189

'Knew her as well as anyone, see. But only an opinion, yes.'

Oh well done, Nigel thought. Mrs Davidson will remember *that*.

Today, Fortesque insisted on what he called 'a proper lunch', and led them to a nearby curryhouse. There, while Nigel toyed with boardlike steak and undercooked chips, Fortesque and Erskine addressed themselves to the hottest masala on the menu.

'Spent some time in India,' Fortesque explained, sneezing heartily and mopping sweat.

Erskine swigged from a tankard and murmured diffidently, 'Charlesworth's next. Quite fancy a crack at him myself, having done the donkey-work, so to speak.'

'Sorry old boy,' Nigel said at once. 'Best if I handle it. Things could get sticky later, I'd rather take full responsibility. Carry the can alone.'

'Your privilege, of course.' Erskine didn't sound very pleased. Fortesque, following the exchange intently, asked, 'Something up your sleeve, young Buxton?'

'Nice day, isn't it?'

Sitting in a fuggy police canteen, eyeing the larger portion of an unappetising and uneaten meal, Evans stirred his coffee and thought about thirty pieces of silver. OK, Buxton had pulled a bit back, but not nearly enough. A fleabite, really. She'd go down for sure, not least because of Evans's own testimony. Sod the Pillock and all his disciples.

The place was nearly empty when Beddoes breezed in, plonked a loaded plate on the table beside him, and set to with every sign of enjoyment.

''Eard you 'ad a rough time,' he said, through a mouthful of gluey pie.

'Bad enough.'

'Forget it, mate,' Beddoes advised. 'Storm in a teacup. It was you who nicked Morris, right?'

'You're only as good as your last game, mind.'

'Christ,' muttered Beddoes, in mock dismay. 'City'll be for the big drop, then.'

'Really upsets me, that does. Puts me off my grub.'

'You oughta tell their manager. He'd be thrilled.' Beddoes gave him a speculative glance. 'Listen, I've got something on. Whisper of a bank job next week, could be a lulu. I'm checking it out right now. Comin?'

Evans smiled wanly.

'Therapy, is it, cheering up the invalid? Nice of you, Roy, but I'm committed, see. Back to court, I am.'

Beddoes frowned, a subtle warning.

'Dodgy, innit? If Smythe 'ears, I mean?'

'Close the file, he said, and that's what I'm doing. If he asks, you can tell him.'

As he left, Beddoes was tucking into steam pud.

Napoleon Charlesworth, he reckoned, was the kind of spook who gives 'em all a bad name. Evans wasn't racist, mind. Just prejudiced against pimps, black, white or khaki. Tall, thin and gangly, clad in multicoloured shirt and purple jeans, Charlesworth had a mobile face, huge eyes and a third-rate comedian's line of patter. He was totally out of place in the witness box, a man who'd come to a DJ party in fancy dress. Even the judge looked askance.

Under Wilshaw's expert prompting, he broadcast his conversion.

'Ah is saved, marn,' he claimed dramatically. 'The Lawd tole me, give up thy evil ways, and ah done it. Working on the buses now,' he added, abruptly prosaic. 'Ah turned my back on crime.'

Believe that, Evans thought, and you'll believe anything. The Pillock's home for fallen immigrants, come 'n' join us. Duw duw.

'We talkin about things past,' Charlesworth insisted. 'You folks gotta understand.'

Patient and persistent, Wilshaw ignored the frills and drew out the pattern.

'My girls was delicate flowers,' Charlesworth declared, in another outburst of fervour, 'goin about a dangerous business. They in trouble, they run to Daddy fo help 'n' protection. She a stranger, they say, she *interferin*.' He spread his long arms, measuring the size of his plight.

191

'Times like that, a marn has to do something.'

'And what did you do, Mr Charlesworth?' Wilshaw enquired, all interest.

'Don't you fret, honeychiles, I tole them, she just a *transient*. Give her some days, she be long gone.' Charlesworth's speech was an exotic blend of West Indian sing-song, American slang and cockney idiom. A clown, Evans decided, but shifty and vicious with it.

'But she didn't go?' murmured Wilshaw. Charlesworth heaved a sigh, clasped his large-knuckled, heavily ringed fingers together. Enforcer's hands, thought Evans, tools of the trade.

'You got it. So, ah invited her, fo' a friendly word, like.'

Evans glanced at Grace. She sat bolt upright, feet braced, back pressed against the chair as if putting as much space as she could between herself and the witness. Her face was a study in revulsion.

'Advised her, Mr Wilshaw, sah, that's what I done. Lady, ah says – could tell she was a lady in her pretty wig an' all – you in badlands. This where the city dross hang out.' His eyes rolled, his face turned tragic. 'Why, some dudes out there even carries *guns!*'

Buxton was on his feet, appealing to the judge. 'Milud, this is rambling, speculative and irrelevant.'

Stanmore fixed the witness with a steely eye.

'You'd oblige me, Mr Charlesworth, by confining yourself to direct answers.'

'Sorry, marn.'

'And you will address me as milud!'

'Yes*sah*, milud.' Stanmore ordered the comment struck off. Useful that, thought Evans. He's said it now, the jury's heard. Clever little bugger, Wilshaw.

The barrister ploughed on.

'Did the accused take your advice?'

From the dock, the smallest of sounds, a Grace Yardley special. Wordless and still, she managed to convey her loathing and contempt to everyone. Stanmore glared at her, but there wasn't much he could do. Nice one, girl. Charlesworth, oblivious, maintained the act. His face turned mournful, the long arms dangled.

'People is kinda stubborn, jus' won't be tole.' He brightened again, a sly smile. 'By 'm' by she moved on. Found what she wanted, I reckon.' Buxton rose as if to intervene; and sunk back again. Fair enough. Can't argue with intangibles.

Winding up, Wilshaw wanted to know why a man who had reason to shun the police would volunteer information.

'Saw the lady on TV, sah. That her, ah thought, wig or no wig. Ah saw my duty clear, bein a 'sponsible citizen.'

Dear God, all he needs is angel voices in the background, Evans thought. Hope Buxton gives him stick. I would.

But defence counsel merely rose, pointed out the time, and suggested adjournment. Evans shook his head ruefully. That's why he's a barrister and you're a cop. Wants to let him sweat overnight, see. Smythe was right – we catch 'em, they cook 'em.

At their ritual evening meeting, Grace threw a rare tantrum.

'How *dare* they allow that man into court! A habitual criminal, a congenital liar. He's evil and depraved – I know!'

'He'll be unmasked tomorrow, never fear.' Nigel paused, trying to soften the blow. 'You *did* go there, after all. Be assured Wilshaw will have witnesses to say so.'

Her occasional petulance broke through, the heritage of the only child.

'I'm quite prepared to admit it. There's no need for this – farce! It's like the Black and White Minstrels.'

He had to smile. She was becoming more open, less inclined to guard feelings and small prejudices. A hopeful sign, the jury would respond better to a human than an iceberg. Gently, he asked, 'Was Charlesworth very – unpleasant?'

A grimace of graphic distaste.

'I told you, he's evil. Striding about, rolling his eyes and threatening like some vodoo demon. Those women were terrified.'

'And you weren't?'

'Of course I was! But I wasn't going to let him know it.'

'He didn't give you the gun?'

A short, sharp gesture of utter dismissal.

'He wouldn't know where to begin. Evil, but totally insignificant.'

'So I'm not due for surprises tomorrow?'

One of her quicksilver changes of mood. Suddenly she was tender, making amends.

'Poor Nigel. You still don't trust me.'

'You haven't made it easy. Look, old thing, the prosecution bat first. At this stage, they're always out in front. Relax; our turn is coming.'

A tired, strained smile, without much force.

'I'll try.'

Chapter Nineteen

Obviously, Erskine had burned midnight oil; and also revealed a rather uncanny access to high-level sources. His brief on Napoleon Charlesworth was a miniature classic; thorough, factual and devastating. Compiled in record time and crammed with hard evidence, it armed Nigel for a full-scale attack; worth every penny of the fee.

Some kind soul, it seemed, had enlightened the witness on sartorial standards in the courtroom. Today he wore a suit, a drunken tailor's extravagance in electric blue polyester. A snowy shirt and a scarlet tie completed the ensemble. On this grey March morning, Charlesworth glowed like a neon advertisement for patriotism. Mrs Davidson, Nigel noted, couldn't keep a straight face, and Stanmore looked distinctly affronted. Good. Every little helps.

He opened with an innocuous, almost friendly enquiry.

'How long have you been "saved", Mr Charlesworth?'

'Oh, months, marn,' replied Charlesworth, airy and relieved.

'How many months?'

A fluid, boneless lift of the shoulders, the physical ease of his race.

'Ah don't see that it matters.'

'Then,' said Nigel equably, 'with milud's permission, I'll explain.' He waited, received the nod, and continued:

'You have said the defendant interfered with your – operations. You had not yet "turned your back on crime". Shortly afterwards, you reported her, doing your duty as a responsible citizen. If we are to believe you, Mr Charlesworth, we must assume your salvation occurred during this brief interim.'

Charlesworth nodded eagerly.

'Sure thing. You right, sah.'

195

'Curious,' said Nigel, in a perplexed tone. 'The record shows that your business in dockland flourished for some time *after* Miss Yardley was arrested. But I'm sure you can account for the apparent contradiction?'

Charlesworth fidgeted. He looked sullen and menacing; Grace's revulsion was suddenly understandable. Finally he growled, 'Ah has bad trouble with my memory.'

'Most unfortunate,' Nigel consoled him. 'Perhaps I can help you recover it. You began work for the City Transport Authority precisely six weeks ago?'

'Yeah.'

'Up to that time, despite being in Britain some nine years, you had paid no social security, and had no visible means of support. Let us into the secret, Mr Charlesworth; what did you live on?'

'Ah got rich friends.' A glower, an undertone of real threat.

'How nice for you; though not, I fear, a satisfactory answer. You have already insisted that you are saved. Very well, tell us from what?' Nigel put steel into his voice. 'You lived on immoral earnings, didn't you?'

Suddenly, Charlesworth was grinning, sly and mocking.

'Dunno why you pickin at me, Mr Buxton sah. Ah never shot no one. My sins are behind me, forgive and forget, right?'

Nigel could tolerate a laugh at his own expense; he'd set the fuse. Conversationally, he asked, 'Is that what the police said when you agreed to testify?'

Wilshaw polished his spectacles, totally absorbed in the task. Knows a fair question when he hears one, Nigel thought. Mrs Davidson was sitting intent, she and eleven others. The court waited, taut and still. Even Fortesque, handkerchief halfway to his nose, forebore to sniff.

Charlesworth did his best. Big-eyed and soulful, shoulders raised, pink palms upturned, he looked almost innocent.

'Ah was persuaded, marn, shown the error of my ways. Sure, we talked turkey, we all grown-ups. Kept my word, sah, ah swears it.'

'I'm waiting, Mr Charlesworth.'

A sigh, a roll of the eyes, a heavenward glance.

'OK, you got me. An agreement between gentlemen.'

Nigel needed it on record, clear and uncontested.

'Give evidence or face criminal charges yourself?'

'Yessah.'

'Thank you. Your witness.'

Ever the pragmatist – least said, soonest healed – Wilshaw ignored the issue of Napoleon's conversion entirely, using his re-examination to underscore the crucial, unarguable fact. Grace Yardley had been in dockland, soliciting. Well, Nigel reflected, she smiled once this morning, and at least the evening editions will have a choice of headlines.

Wilshaw devoted the afternoon to corroboration, a procession of dull-eyed, hard-bitten women who'd witnessed Grace Yardley at work in various sordid quarters. Nigel raised doubts about their character and credibility, but he was going through the motions, falling back over indefensible ground. Out of sheer persistence, he won a minor success. A Miss Yolanda Smith, bleached, flighty and unreliable, remarked, 'I will say one thing for her. She told ole Nappy where to get off, and not before time, neither!'

For the rest, Erskine might have been carved from stone, Fortesque's cough punctuated every other sentence, and Grace had done a disappearing act; absent in all but body. Resting his case on the stroke of four, Wilshaw adopted a satisfied, almost ceremonious air. Foregone conclusions. And well he might, Nigel admitted, to a sniff from Fortesque and a sardonic 'Amen' from his junior.

Grace's withdrawal extended into the evening; he was becoming weary of monologues. He prescribed sleep and mental diversion and took away her faint, ironic smile for consolation.

At a prearranged Saturday meeting, he lifted a few veils for Fortesque, drawing the old man into closer confidence. Red-eyed and wheezy, Fortesque heard him out, his face growing longer by the minute.

'That's not a defence, it's a surrender,' he snorted at last, and sneezed mightily.

'Spell it out for me,' Nigel invited, and the solicitor counted on his chalky fingers.

'One, you're depending on showmanship, the right word at

197

the right time, maybe. Totally unsound, Perry Mason country.'

Thank you, Theresa Da Silva, thought Nigel; aloud he said, 'Go on.'

'Two, you're sailing awfully close to the professional wind, cocking a snook at centuries of precedent.'

'I know.'

'Three, the jury might well go for manslaughter, and you've still lost.'

'Risk nothing, gain nothing.'

'And four, Stanmore could shut you down, just like that.' He snapped his fingers forcefully, a surprisingly solid noise. 'Chuck the jury and convict on evidence. It's been done before, and survived appeal.'

'Not this time. He simply wouldn't dare. The whole world watching, half the population saw the act, and one man decides?'

'That's politics. I'm talking law.'

'In this case they can't be separated. That's the whole point, d'you see. A *public* issue.'

Fortesque, wincing, tended his nose.

'Going bald-headed for this one, aren't you. Win at any cost?'

Quietly, Nigel said, 'You mustn't feel bound, old boy, if you're really anti.'

A sudden unlikely smile, one of his ghoulish chuckles.

'I'll stick. Always wanted to see *hara-kiri* first hand ...'

Nigel took one look at the blustery Sunday rain outside and retired to bed with the papers. He worked his way through the supplements, Sport and Travel, the Arts, who was doing what to whom; saving the news for last. Nobody actually came out and said it, the press barons still paid lip service to *sub judice*. But the trial took up a lion's share of space, and the content could be reduced to a single query. How long will she get? He smiled to himself. Couldn't be better.

Grace was at her worst that evening, elusive, edgy and waspish by turns, impossible to pin down.

'Since you've forbidden rehearsals,' he said eventually, 'I'm restricted to words of advice.'

'Go ahead.' She sounded wholly disinterested. Patiently, he outlined what he wanted.

She was pacing distractedly, miles away.

'For heaven's sake!' he muttered, standing up.

Instantly, she became anxious and conciliatory. 'Please don't go. I'm listening, honestly. It's just – I can't wait to get it over, to get out of here.'

'Then you *must* listen!'

She nodded, sighed, settled.

'Yes. I'm sorry.'

Standing over her, speaking quietly but firmly, he primed her for the coming ordeal.

'Wilshaw's competent and very determined. Like most of us, he believes the first question in a cross-examination is decisive. He will do his utmost to set you off-balance and keep you that way. Be prepared. And be yourself. Don't try to hide your feelings. The majority of people function on emotion, and juries are people.'

'Yes sir, no sir, three bags full.' The spark of mischief warmed him. Peering sideways under long lashes, she didn't look a day over seventeen.

'The details are important,' he insisted, and waited while the whimsy faded.

'This trial turns on two issues; *when* you decided to kill Morris, and *why*. Everything else is window-dressing. Remember that day with Evans; anything you saw, heard, thought and felt. When you've got it straight, ask yourself why you've never known a twinge of remorse. And when you've done *that*, put it out of mind and get some rest. Clear?'

She nodded, a swirl of dark hair around the small, serious face.

'Nigel? Wish me luck?'

'Gladly. You're going to need it.'

An intermittent gale drove rain against the building like grapeshot. The silver of condensation made mirrors of the windows; nothing outside existed. This morning, Evans thought, the world revolves within these walls. He wasn't the only one. The air hummed; the Arms Park just before kick-off.

Buxton called the defendant. In tense and total silence, she moved from the dock to the witness box. She managed it beautifully, poised and elegant in a grey suit which matched her eyes, and black patent heels for the extra height. The centre of attraction, in every sense. She read the oath, her voice only slightly unsteady, and Buxton let her stand there a moment while he studied the jury. Tactics, realised Evans. Look well at what you would destroy.

Approaching her with a reassuring smile, Buxton asked quietly, 'Did you love your daughter, Miss Yardley?'

A sharp, gulping breath, the colour bled from her face. Wasn't ready for it, Evans thought furiously. Whose side are you on, anyway? Then, as her distress settled over the entire court, he understood. First and last a mother, cruel to be kind. Shakily, her control adrift, she mumbled, 'Very much.' She rallied, spoke more strongly. 'For fourteen years, she was my life.'

Buxton nudged her onward, pursuing the thread. An appearance of calm returned, private memories reluctantly revealed, a sense of aching loss. Wilshaw objected, citing irrelevance, and was curtly overruled. Save your breath, boyo, this time is hers alone. Even as the thought formed, Buxton enlarged it. Not merely Grace, but Grace and Caroline together, taking on the world and winning. Risky stuff, mind, a hair's-breadth from bleeding-heart melodrama; but Buxton skirted the pitfalls, steering a course of poignant understatement. Evans, who knew the story and more besides, was deeply moved.

Judging the atmosphere nicely, Buxton changed pace and style, jumping forward to the day Morris was sentenced, giving emotion a rest. The press, idly bored for an hour or more, sat up and took notice. Briefly, Buxton tested her memory, the date, the weather, the name of the judge. She answered readily, accurate and alert.

'Now, Miss Yardley,' said Buxton, 'please tell the court how you felt when sentence was passed.'

'I was appalled.' She sounded it, too.

200

'Why? The outcome, surely, was not unexpected?'

She leaned forward, resting her fine hands on the rail, the attitude of appeal Evans knew so well.

'The technicalities had been explained to me. I thought I understood. Then he was absolved, not punished. I went there to put an end, you see. It seemed so ...' Her face tight in the search for precision, she found the perfect word, '...unjust.'

The judge stirred, frowning ominously, and Wilshaw smiled. Buxton, undeterred, said, 'Do you recall what you said to Inspector Evans at the time?'

'I said, now it's certain – or something very much like it.' She looked frank and untroubled, nothing whatever to hide. If you asked them now, Evans thought, the jury'd acquit in ten minutes flat.

Next, Buxton took her into the December street. She described the cold and what had seemed an endless delay.

'How long was it, actually?'

'Fifteen minutes or so.' It hadn't occurred to her to try to approach Morris, she hadn't thought it possible.

'Did you feel anger or hatred?'

'No.'

'What did you think about?'

She drew herself up, speaking directly to the judge.

'Only – it would be better for everyone with Morris dead.'

A resigned, almost wistful tone. The tension eased, the suspense was past. Evans frowned, trying to fathom Buxton's intentions. Old Fortesque looked grim, too; him and his damn cough.

Buxton turned his attention to vice.

'Miss Yardley, did you sleep with any of Mr Charlesworth's customers – in dockland?'

'Of course not!' A spontaneous reaction, utterly convincing. Evans was glad. Never believed it, really.

'But you did meet Mr Charlesworth?'

'I was – persuaded – to join him for what he called a business chat.' She made the phrase sound very incongruous.

'Persuaded?'

'Threatened.'

Predictably, Wilshaw intervened. Without much sympathy,

Stanmore demanded, 'In what way were you threatened?'

She bowed her head, the flush of acute embarrassment suffusing her cheeks.

'Physically, milud. The language and the proposal were obscene, unrepeatable. I'm sorry.' Grudgingly, Stanmore relented, and Buxton resumed the floor.

'Miss Yardley, why did you go to dockland in the first place?'

Her head came up, the familiar air of defiance.

'I couldn't think of anywhere else. To get a gun, I mean.'

Cat among the pigeons, muttered Evans to himself, as the reporters hurried out; what the hell's he playing at? Buxton waited impassively for order. In mild, unbelieving tones he said, 'You didn't consider Morris better dead until after the verdict, yet you were looking for the weapon a week earlier. In so doing, you exposed yourself to very real moral and physical dangers. Are you asking the court to accept that you took such risks on the off-chance of needing a gun?'

He's pinching Wilshaw's questions, Evans realised, spiking his guns. Lovely. Her head high, her expression pure and proud, she declared, 'I'm telling the court the exact truth.'

During the lunchtime recess, Fortesque's symptoms and the weather relented.

'A competent performance, young Buxton,' he grunted, filleting a grilled trout. 'You brought her out rather nicely.'

Nigel nodded, well pleased.

'Yes. Mrs Davidson was with her all the way.'

Fortesque gave him a knowing grin.

'The red-head in the jury-box? Some day, my boy, that wandering eye will be your downfall.'

Encouraged by this freedom, Erskine ventured a rare unsolicited opinion. 'Don't get carried away. Wilshaw's out for blood.' And so it proved.

Sticking to chronology and facts, Wilshaw mounted a sustained and brutal attack. Under his aggressive stare, Grace grew sullen and petulant. You are an odious little man, she implied, unworthy of attention or civility. A sound approach, Nigel had to concede, exposing her latent arrogance and

202

playing to the prosecution's strength. Evans looked fearsome, his big fists bunched, his pale eyes anguished; Mrs Davidson was clearly having second thoughts.

Twice, Nigel objected to bullying, but won only respites, not reprieves. Relentlessly, Wilshaw listed her sins for the official record; issuing a false statement, soliciting, illegal possession of a firearm, enlisting and deceiving Evans, wanting Morris dead. Damning enough as it stood, but Wilshaw went further, showing her in the dimmest possible light. Liar, he was saying, whore, shrewd and calculating killer. And she abetted him, careless and contemptuous. Nigel's premonition came to pass; her own worst enemy. As the day faded and the rain sluiced down again, Wilshaw threw her a direct challenge.

'Miss Yardley, you have already admitted to a range of criminal acts. Will you persist in denying murder?'

She made a small, dismissive gesture.

'Certainly.'

'Milud,' Wilshaw said, 'I'm far from finished with this witness. May we adjourn?'

Pointless to object, Nigel knew. Let Wilshaw have his highspot. In her present mood, the less said the better, and tomorrow's another day.

Later, in her room, she protested angrily. 'It's ridiculous! He's treating me like a common criminal.'

'Which, in his eyes, you are.'

'Then he's a fool!

'That he most definitely isn't, and you'd do well to remember it.'

Suddenly she was weeping, distraught and inconsolable, her despair echoing in the small space. 'I'm so tired,' she sobbed. 'And so frightened. Will it never end?'

Nigel offered ham-fisted comfort; he wasn't good at tears. 'It's nearly over,' he promised, and as she quietened, added, 'Are you up to a bit of theatre?'

She dried her eyes, suspicious and faintly curious.

'What do you mean?'

'Can you carry on tomorrow where you left off today?'

'I wouldn't call that theatre; anyway, why should I?'

'He'll go for motive, I'm sure. Are you ready for him?'

'Of course. It was because ...'

'Don't tell me now. Lead him on, make him think you're weary and disgusted with the whole affair.'

'I am.' She hesitated, her eyes dark with doubt. 'Nigel, is it *right*, what you're suggesting?'

They should see her now, he thought, and then judge her honesty. Warmly, setting himself to persuade, he told her.

'You're on oath, Grace, bound to the truth. It has to be demonstrated, though, not merely spoken, and that makes us all actors, like it or not. Wilshaw, you may be sure, is priming his questions, going for maximum effect. Our resources are limited; we must exploit them as best we can.'

'Well – if you say so.' She sounded very unsure.

'Very well,' he conceded. 'If it bothers you, scrap it. He'll sense your doubts, and that could be disastrous. Just be sure of your reasons. When the time comes, tell them straight and true. It's still our best hope.'

She's looking rough this morning, Evans thought; dull-eyed, ashen, jumpy as a cat. Had a bad night, no doubt, just as Wilshaw intended. The prosecutor faced her, deceptively mild, and the mutter of conversation subsided.

'Miss Yardley, you've had time for mature consideration of my last question. Do you wish to proceed?' He was goading her again, and she didn't disappoint him.

'Of course I do!'

Wilshaw squared his shoulders and waded in. If she had nothing to hide, why had she lied to the police? Privacy, she said, it was none of their business. Wilshaw let that hang, savouring the absurdity and the grim faces of the jury. Surely, he insisted, twenty minutes between sentencing and shooting had been sufficient to regain balance and recognise the consequences? She wasn't unbalanced, she retorted, and the consequences didn't concern her. Evans despaired for her. The to-hell-with-you attitude won't help, for God's sake steady down. If she hadn't slept around, Wilshaw wanted to know, how had she obtained the gun? Had she stolen it, perhaps? Bought it, she snapped icily, from a contact she'd made. Which

204

rendered the purchase immoral as well as illegal, Wilshaw observed at once. She gave him a single withering glance.

'Your words, Mr Wilshaw, not mine.'

Too clever by half, girl. Evans sensed the weight of opinion swinging inexorably away from her. He'd lost all objectivity now, it was worse than his father's funeral.

Apparently satisfied at last, Wilshaw moved towards his seat. Halfway there he stopped, as if struck by a random afterthought. Swinging on his heel, his gown billowing, he cried, 'Why did you kill Edward Morris?' It was a crucial question, demanding a considered response; and she dismissed it with the rest.

'That should be obvious, even to you.'

'Milud?'

'The defendant will answer,' commanded Stanmore, stern and implacable. Briefly, and in Evans's view, suicidally, she included the judge in her disdain.

'He murdered Caroline and got away with it. He made a mockery of the law, of justice, of everything I'd always cherished!'

There's plenty who'd agree, mind, but not to stand up and say it. St Joan, thought Evans wildly, and they're burning her. Wilshaw only nodded, suddenly and uncharacteristically gentle.

'This I can understand. You have sworn, and I believe you, that you loved your daughter very much. You thought Morris would be better dead; you thought he deserved it. Am I right?'

She stood motionless, frowning slightly. Sensible, mind, waiting for the objection. Buxton, oblivious, pored over his notes, a gold pen poised and glinting.

'Come, Miss Yardley,' prompted Wilshaw, 'admit it. Any parent would think the same.'

Watch it, girl, he said think, not do. And where the hell's Buxton? Buxton was writing. It's a fix, cried a voice in Evans's mind, he's taking a dive; and Wilshaw, unchallenged, delivered his righteous accusation.

'It was vengeance, pure and simple! You killed to avenge Caroline, didn't you?'

A moment of utter stillness, every eye on the dock. Grace Yardley stirred, her face clearing. Awake at last, thought Evans, too bloody late. In a voice of infinite sadness, she said, 'No, Mr Wilshaw. My daughter was already dead. Nothing I did could bring her back.'

Wilshaw shook his head in disbelief, a flicker of light on his glasses.

'Then why take the law into your own hands? Why kill Morris?'

There were tears in her eyes now, but she spoke evenly, as to an obtuse child.

'So that it couldn't happen again. So no one else would suffer as she did; and as I do.'

The words hung, the hush extended, the court sat in thrall. Dead God, she's got a chance, Evans realised, and saw the knowledge reflected fleetingly and triumphantly in Buxton's face. Frustrated, Wilshaw lashed out, savage and sarcastic – Do you seriously expect the court ... A killing lapse, and the atmosphere hardened against him. The cross-examination faltered and failed under her blinding serenity. Without rising, Buxton set the seal on her victory.

'No re-examination, milud. The defence rests.'

Chapter Twenty

I'll probably never know, Nigel mused, how much she acted and how much she truly felt. He doubted if she knew herself. At the end, though, her sincerity had been absolute, disarming Wilshaw, moving Mrs Davidson to tears, recapturing the sympathy of the court. Wilshaw's dramatic adjournment had misfired, too, for now the timing worked against him. He must make his summation in the wake of a serious set-back, and without the breathing space of a re-examination. So far, the luck she'd wished for had held; but Stanmore might yet destroy her.

Wilshaw rose and waited for silence, looking squat, impatient and disgruntled. Still kicking himself, thought Nigel; good, let him feel the pressure for a change.

Once launched, the prosecutor steadied, taking refuge on the safest of ground. He reiterated his opening submission, emphasising that the act had been openly admitted by the defence.

'It shouldn't be necessary for me to say more. The burden of proof has been lifted. Since, however, my learned friend has raised certain issues, I am bound to comment on them. It has been suggested that until a relatively short time before she killed Morris, the accused had not made up her mind to do so; that, in fact, she obeyed a sudden impulse. This is at best a doubtful argument. In this case, it has no validity whatever.'

He adjusted his robes, stared hard at the jury, and continued:

'During the period in question, Miss Yardley was, in the words of every witness, calm and in full possession of herself. She was also in the constant company of a senior policeman who, had she even hinted at her intentions, would surely have intervened. She did not. Indeed, she made sure his attention was diverted at the vital moment; the clearest evidence of calculation and premeditation. So much for impulse.'

We'll see about that, Nigel thought, and winced as Fortesque sneezed yet again.

'The second issue,' Wilshaw announced, 'concerns motive. The accused has denied vengeance,' he gave Grace a disparaging glance, 'though whether you choose to accept such noble altruism is for you to decide.' His tone made his own opinion very clear; but did not, Nigel noticed with satisfaction, endear him to Mrs Davidson.

'Even if you incline towards charity and accept Miss Yardley's explanation, the defence profits nothing. No amount of rationalising can excuse or justify a private citizen acting as jury and judge; but the accused went a good deal further, assuming a function long since abolished by law. She became self-appointed public executioner.'

A slight shrug, what more is there to say? But he said it anyway, flat and final.

'Members of the jury, I submit that the accused stands proven beyond any conceivable doubt of cold and premeditated murder.'

Sound and predictable and, to Nigel, largely irrelevant. He had listened with one eye for the judge and the other for the clock: time and Stanmore's reactions were crucial to the second phase of his strategy. He intended to make his submission at once, to run on into the lunch recess, and oblige Stanmore to sum up this afternoon. The slightest delay might prove disastrous.

Just this once, he thought, it would be nice to amble over and lean on the jury-box and talk to them like a Dutch aunt. Now see here, y'all – the ideal presentation for what he had in mind. But he was already contemplating dangerous unorthodoxy; appearances, at least, must be maintained. From the dock, Grace watched him expectantly, composed and confident, preserving the faith. If only you knew, old thing. On his feet, ne was conscious of intent faces in the gallery, of Evans's anxious gaze, of Fortesque's throaty breathing.

Sauntering towards the jury, his eyes on Mrs Davidson, he admitted blandly, 'Grace Yardley killed Edward Morris, a fact the defence cannot and does not contest. Whether, in so doing, she committed murder is for you and you alone to decide.' A quick nod of the auburn head, a flicker of green-eyed relief. Terms of reference understood. Nigel adopted an easy conversational tone.

'Television has made this case unique in legal history. My learned friend calls the issue straightforward; it is anything but. He sets great store by facts and precedents; the facts are not in dispute and no precedent exists.' Out of the corner of his eye, he saw Stanmore stiffen and glare; better to watch Mrs Davidson.

'Let us now examine facts; not those upon which my learned friend has dwelt, but those of direct relevance to the issues before you. Driven by a compulsion she has so clearly explained, my client took to the streets of dockland, a totally hostile and alien environment. The physical and moral hazards she faced must be obvious to you all. Can you honestly imagine her resorting to such an extreme out of any but the direst necessity? Not surprisingly, she concealed her move-ments. Would any of you willingly confess to visiting Mr Charlesworth in his late but recent professional capacity?'

On Mrs Davidson's pretty, freckled face, the answer was written clear, and Evans looked grimly approving. So far so good.

'My client claims, and a reliable witness supports her, that until a few minutes before she acted, she had not finally decided to kill Morris. My learned friend contends that she ought to have used the intervening moments to discuss her newfound resolve with a senior policeman. Need I comment on the absurdity of this suggestion? She might as well have asked him for a weapon in the first place.'

In the dock, Grace smiled faintly. I wonder if she did, he thought, Wilshaw should have asked. Then, 'This much I will concede: if there had been a delay measured in hours rather than minutes, we might not be here today. I would beg you, therefore, to consider the definition of impulse, to ponder how long an impulse can be said to last. If, for example, you are impelled to buy a new dress, do you not sometimes weigh the decision for a week and then buy the dress anyway?'

209

A wry grin of acknowledgement from the lady juror; point taken. Nigel lowered his voice and slowed the delivery. Now, every word must count.

'We come to a vital issue; *why* did she do it? The prosecution spared no effort to establish vengeance as motive – an apparently plausible assumption. In the face of such tragedy, it is a reaction most parents would understand; and in their heart of hearts, condone. Yet she denied it: and her poignant authority reduced my learned friend to unworthy sneers. Remember it well. It was a moment of incontestable truth.'

Wilshaw polished his spectacles, the scepticism naked on his face, and Stanmore frowned a warning. Let them think what they like: I'm talking to Mrs Davidson.

'The term "malice aforethought" has an illustrious pedigree. It is not much used these days in legal circles, where phrases such as "premeditation" and "criminal intent" are often preferred. Nevertheless, I submit that in order to prove murder, the prosecution *is* required to demonstrate malice, especially to jurors not versed in abstruse legal jargon. Had vengeance been established, malice could be assumed. Revenge, after all, is an enactment of malice.' He paused, wanting their full attention; and got it. 'You all heard my client's reason for her action; no one else must suffer. Does that sound malicious to you?'

Nigel moved slowly back to his bench, conscious of Stanmore's censuring gaze. The legal arguments were finished, he would give the court a moment's respite. He laid his notes aside, waiting while the whispers died and Fortesque controlled his snuffles. Still at a leisurely pace, he crossed the floor and stood beside the dock, focusing once more on Mrs Davidson. With a casual, almost negligent gesture, letting words alone convey drama, he said softly, 'Before you sits a mother. Motherhood demands love and sacrifice; money, time and labour. How much greater are the sacrifices of a single parent?

'My client spoke, briefly and in some embarrassment, of her love for her daughter. No one who heard could doubt her sincerity. A daughter she brought up alone, to the very brink of womanhood, there to be raped and killed and tossed aside by a man she had never even met.' A small movement beside him; Grace Yardley, head bowed, hair hiding her face, trembling. He shifted aside, letting them look. Quietly, insistently, he continued, 'For a month, she endured agonies of uncertainty we hardly dare imagine. In grief and horror, she sat through a trial not unlike this one, every dreadful detail made public. And finally, she watched this same man, found guilty, taken into care; and knew that at some future time he might well walk free.'

Beside him, Grace Yardley glanced up, under control again, the tearmarks damp. She looked weary, very pale – and unashamed. Someone in the gallery began to applaud, and the usher shouted urgently. The disturbance bubbled and subsided, and Fortesque coughed, short and loose. Coldly and deliberately, Nigel set out to provoke the judge.

'My client sits in the dock, charged with the most hideous of crimes. Over the past days, you have had ample opportunity to assess her character. Ask yourselves, if you will, does she look, speak or behave like a liar, a prostitute and a murderess? This, remember, is what the prosecution would have you believe. You may have noticed that the witnesses presented by my learned friend, with the exception of a few policemen, have all been habitual criminals themselves, reformed or otherwise, whose credibility has been at best doubtful, at worst non-existent. Yet even they have expressed, however grudgingly, an admiration for the defendant. And why shouldn't they? Miss Yardley's courage and integrity have survived the most rigorous of examinations in the most adverse of conditions; not least in this courtroom.'

Stanmore, he saw, was simmering nicely; no doubt he would regard these as blatantly American tactics. Erskine's face wore a curious expression, part envy, part distaste, part sympathy. And Mrs Davidson was still listening intently. He drew himself up, extended both arms in appeal.

'Members of the jury, I believe that the case before you transcends legality in the strictest sense.'

Stanmore stirred, and Nigel hurried on, forestalling him.

'Milud, who is wiser and more experienced than I, will doubtless instruct you on the legal options open to you, and direct you as to the decisions you must take. When you have

211

heard him, I beseech you to ask yourselves three questions. Did Grace Yardley commit murder? Does she deserve to be treated as a common criminal? And will you, as parents, sleep more easily because of what she did?' A cool, thoughtful stare from Mrs Davidson, a furious, contemptuous glance from the judge, a grateful, rather tremulous smile from Grace. Now, it depended on Stanmore's self-control and a quirk of human nature ...

Strange, Nigel reflected, how quickly we become creatures of habit. Since the trial opened, the lunchtime meeting had become as much a ritual as the evening visit to Grace's room. There was some familiar element missing today, and it took him until the main course to identify it; no sniffles, no medicinal smell.

'Why, Fortesque,' he exclaimed, 'your cold's better!'

Fortesque sniffed experimentally and conceded.

'A bit. No thanks to my doctor, I assure you. Nature takes her course.'

'You should be grateful for small mercies,' murmured Erskine drily, and Fortesque shot him a prickly glance.

'Wait till you're my age, m'boy. You won't find it so amusing.' Then, sawing away at a large steak, he added, 'If it was your intention, young Buxton, to upset the CJ, I must say you managed very well. I've seldom seen him so cross.'

Erskine nodded. 'You *were* rather flashy, old boy. Not a lot of substance, was there?'

Nigel shrugged, showing less concern than he felt.

'Let's leave that for the jury to decide, shall we?'

Fortesque paid the bill and rose creakily to his feet, clutching his back.

'What's the matter now?' asked Nigel impatiently. Fortesque grimaced, pained and morose.

'Lumbago.'

Evans had come to terms with the courts years ago. You trotted along and said your piece, did your best to put Chummy away. Panto stuff, really, with the defending mouthpiece cast as villain. You won some and lost some, and went back to work. Nothing personal. This was different. He was rooting for the defence, mind, a new and uneasy feeling, almost a betrayal. Involved too, like watching Wales play. You suffered with them at every unkind bounce.

The gallery was packed, the press bench overflowed. The jury filed in, slow and self-important; that nice-looking redhead reminded him of Grace. How does she do it, he wondered, alone in the dock, calm as you please, her future in the balance? Counsel came next. Buxton tall and distinguished; Wilshaw blocky, determined and ugly. St George and the dragon, and a damsel in distress. Steady on, boyo, this is real.

Movement beside him, a familiar voice in his ear.

'Shove up, will you?' Beddoes.

'What the hell 're you doing here?'

'Playin hooky, uncle, just like you. Greatest show on earth, this, all the papers say so, 'ow could I stay away?'

'Keep a cool head, then. We're into injury time.'

Beddoes's eyebrows rose indignantly, a sharp retort on the tip of his tongue; and Stanmore's entry upstaged him.

The judge stalked in, his colour high, his face grim.

''Ere, what's up with his nibs?' Beddoes wanted to know.

'Disagreed with something he ate?'

'Something he heard, more likely,' said Evans. 'Shut up and listen.'

Stanmore planted himself, glared out over the courtroom, and in a voice laden with acid, began:

'During this trial, almost every accepted principle and procedure of our legal system has been flouted. The police have been tardy in obtaining and producing vital evidence, and have engaged in the kind of sordid barter which typifies their transatlantic colleagues. The prosecution neglected their obligations to the defence, and paraded a list of known criminals as witnesses. On more than one occasion, the defence has attempted to convert this court of law into a theatre. A pitiful and degrading exhibition which could give rise to many misapprehensions, perhaps even pervert the course of justice. I will not permit that to happen.'

'Means it, doesn't he?' whispered Beddoes, and Evans shushed him fiercely. Stanmore, still smouldering, focused on the jury.

213

'The basic fact, demonstrated by the prosecution and conceded by the defence, is this. The accused killed the man Morris. Except in very special circumstances, none of which apply here, the killing of another human being constitutes a very serious crime. You must not forget this, neither must you concern yourselves with punishment. You may decide *only* the precise nature and degree of the crime committed.' He glared down, stern and commanding.

'Twenty to one on conviction,' Beddoes muttered and Evans couldn't argue.

'I have been surprised,' the judge continued, in the same hectoring tone, 'at the weight given by both senior counsels to the issue of impulse. Such a defence presupposes a degree of mental abnormality; that, for a brief interval, the impulse was ungovernable and the accused was not then responsible for her actions.'

'She doesn't look potty to me,' Beddoes observed, and Evans nodded glumly.

'Far from it, boyo.'

With a disdainful glance for Buxton, Stanmore went on:

'Defence counsel has made no such inference. Indeed, he has stressed the stability and constancy of his client's mind. Nevertheless, I am bound to draw your attention to this possibility. If you decide the accused's action, in itself, is sufficient evidence of impulse, only one course is open to you. You must find her guilty of manslaughter, not murder, by virtue of diminished responsibility.'

Beddoes was watching Grace Yardley.

'Smart bird,' he said appreciatively, 'better than 'er pictures. But she doesn't fancy that a bit.'

'Course not,' Evans hissed. 'Puts her in the same class as Morris, see.' She was looking very nervy now, and his heart went out to her. Stanmore wasn't finished yet, not by a long chalk.

'The issue of motive, too,' said the judge, still lecturing severely, 'must be seen in proper perspective. Where there are no witnesses to the crime itself, the establishment of a credible motive can make a substantial contribution to the prosecution's case. Here, however, we are concerned with a known and admitted act; the precise motivation is of little significance. If you are satisfied that, being of sound mind and having laid careful plans, the accused killed Morris, then she committed murder. Her reasons for doing so can have no bearing whatever on your judgement.'

He's crucifying her, Evans thought, one nail at a time; while Beddoes deeply absorbed, murmured, 'Ole fart's really layin it on, comin the heavy. Gettin some dirty looks from the jury, too. 'Oo upset 'im, then?'

'Hard to say. Buxton, maybe.'

Beddoes gave him a bright, quizzical stare.

'Funny. 'E looks pretty perky.'

Throughout Stanmore's remarks, Fortesque had shifted restlessly on his bench, groaning and cursing under his breath. Now, as the judge paused for a sip of water, he touched Nigel's shoulder and wheezed, 'He's knocked your castle down. She's for the cooler.'

Nigel whispered, 'O ye of little faith,' and Stanmore was off again, speaking forcefully.

'It is your sacred duty to reach a decision in keeping with the laws of the land and based on the evidence you have heard. You will please note the operative word – evidence. Inferences and surmises must be discarded. Senior counsel for the defence, I regret to say, based his closing submission on emotionalism and the somewhat stony legal ground I have already covered. The latter you may consider; the former must be set aside. Remember, mercy is not yours to command; that is the prerogative of the court.'

Go on, Nigel urged him silently, tell them only the judge can dispense mercy. Give us grounds for appeal. Stanmore met his eye, mocking and sardonic, well aware of the danger.

'Remember also that no matter how persuasively expressed, the concept of a trial which "transcends mere legality" is an open invitation to anarchy, *carte blanche* for anyone with a real or imagined grievance to take matters into his – or her – own hands. In which extreme,' he added with heavy irony, 'no one, parent or otherwise, will sleep easy in his bed.'

Grace was staring at him in incredulous horror, as though

215

seeing, for the first time, a version of truth she couldn't bear to face. Control yourself, old thing. It's not what he says, it's the way he's saying it.

Stanmore sat very straight, imposing himself upon the jury. Thin lips, hard eyes, the voice of a schoolmaster instructing the feeble-minded.

'Only two options are open to you. You may decide that for a few vital moments, the accused ceased to be responsible, in which case you may pronounce her guilty of manslaughter; or you may find her guilty as charged.' With a final, imperious tilt of the head, he added, 'After due consideration of all the evidence presented, I am bound to direct you that acquittal is not only morally unacceptable, but legally impossible.'

And, as the tension splintered and the hubbub started, Nigel glimpsed what he had been waiting for throughout the afternoon: a brief bright spark of rebellion in green Irish eyes.

The jury had been out for forty minutes, still an hour to opening time. Evans sat in a café he didn't like, stirring coffee he didn't fancy, awaiting a verdict he didn't want to hear.

'Daft, really,' he complained to Beddoes. 'Putting her through the hoop. Better off pleading guilty, I'd say.'

'Hindsight,' grunted Beddoes. 'I'm good at it meself.'

'Oh sure. What I mean is, if the Pillock can bargain with the likes of Charlesworth, how come Buxton wouldn't plead? Save time and trouble, hold out for a suspended sentence?'

Beddoes nodded slowly.

'Bothers me, too.' He gulped some coffee, grimaced and surveyed the grotty wallpaper distastefully. 'Smart place, innit. Wonder 'oo did the daycor?' Puzzled and thoughtful, he added, 'At the end there, when 'is nibs gave the thumbs down, you'd expect Buxton to worry, right? Well, he didn't. Eyeballing that red-head, 'e was, not a care in the world. 'Ow does that square?'

Evans gave him a pitying glance.

'*You're* asking *me*? Come on, boyo, lawyers play Mummies and Daddies too.'

For once, Beddoes refused the bait.

216

'I dunno. Look, there's gotta be more to it, somethin 'e knows and we don't.'

'You're dreaming. She'll go down for sure. It's only a matter of where and how long. Lawyers!' He glanced at his watch. 'I'm going back. Won't take 'em long, mind.'

'Pity. Coupla pints'd do me a treat right now.'

'We'll have them after, then.'

'You're on.'

She'd met him at the door, grave and reproachful.

'You should have told me, Nigel.'

He checked, genuinely surprised.

'Told you what?'

'Acquittal is legally impossible.'

He hesitated only fractionally; a hope he dared not reveal.

'I'm sorry. I thought you realised. After all those law books, I mean.'

'Those were for Morris, not me. How long will they be?'

'The longer the better. Shall we sit down?'

Another of her endearing, girlish reactions, another apology. Astonishingly, in tension and confinement, they managed twenty minutes of quiet conversation.

Eventually, her patience gave out.

'What will happen to me, Nigel?'

'It depends on the verdict.'

She shook her head, near to tears.

'Please. You don't have to humour me any more.'

He kept his voice calm and level.

'If you're convicted, I'll appeal, of course. Stanmore was very severe, he left them no choice.'

'But he was within his rights?'

'That's for the Appeal Court to decide.'

She glanced around the small, mean room, and her despair moved him profoundly.

'How long will that take?'

He swallowed hard.

'Several months.'

The faintest of sounds, the purest of agony. Then, slowly her head came up, her eyes widened. Far away, a bell

217

clamoured insistently. He glanced at his watch; one hour thirty-six minutes.

'The longer the better, you said.'

He nodded, very wound up himself.

'Yes. We'd better go down.' And, in a doomed attempt at bravado, 'See you in court.'

Even then, she managed a warm, weak, smile.

'Thank you, Nigel. Thank you for trying.'

He'd been here, waiting, many times before; always edgy, always concerned. It was his livelihood, after all. But never like this, never when it really mattered, deeply and personally. Everything seemed brighter, sharper, happening in slow motion. The court was packed, already hushed and expectant. Presently, she was ushered in, her head high, her carriage still flawless. She sat neatly and weightlessly, legs crossed, hands folded in her lap; she might have been waiting for a friend. Next came Stanmore, moving firmly and confidently. He looked impassive now, his anger a thing of the past. And every eye turned to the twelve empty seats.

The jury filed in, solemn and expressionless, looking straight ahead. Nigel shifted ostentatiously, clearing his throat, trying to catch Mrs Davidson's eye; and failing. Not good. It took an age, but at last they settled, upright and blank. No empty seats now, just empty faces. Not a hint of what was to come. In an atmosphere vibrant with tension, the usher begun the ritual.

'Foreman of the jury, please rise.'

A slight, nondescript man in a grey, nondescript suit, sallow and balding. Feverishly, Nigel cast about his memory for the name. Smith, of course; what else. Why in God's name had he been elected? Evenly, Stanmore asked, 'Have you reached a verdict?'

'Yes, milud.' A steady eye, a strong voice. *That's* why.

'Is your verdict unanimous?'

'Yes, milud.' Not once had Smith so much as glanced at the dock, a sure pointer to conviction. Nigel relaxed, resigned to defeat. Madness to rely on Mrs Davidson against the weight of history and Stanmore.

'Do you find the accused guilty; or not guilty?'

218

Nigel watched dully as the foreman took a breath and faced Stanmore squarely.

'We find the defendant ...' Nigel glanced up, suddenly alerted ... *defendant?*

'Not guilty, milud.'

Across the courtroom, Grace Yardley stood smiling radiantly at him, her tears falling unnoticed on the rail of the dock.

Chapter Twenty-One

'We must hope,' concluded the tart editorial in a 'quality' paper, 'that the aberration of a perverse and gullible jury will set no precedent. While few would question Miss Yardley's claim to mercy, glib advocacy and a pretty face must never again be permitted to get away with murder.'

A lone voice, overwhelmed by the popular media which installed Grace as a heroine and Nigel as her champion; and he dismissed it, dwelling instead on those final, euphoric court-room scenes. Stanmore's face, outraged and unbelieving; Mrs Davidson's broad smile of satisfaction; the outbreak of jubilation in the gallery. There, heedless of his uniform, Evans gave the prize-fighter's salute, fists clenched above his head; even Wilshaw managed a handshake and a curt nod of acknowledgement. Fortesque, his discomfort temporarily forgotten, wagged his grey head and murmured, 'Amazing. You ought to join the Magic Circle.'

Only Erskine remained aloof. 'The conmen's union,' he declared frostily, 'would seem more appropriate.'

Later, laughing and light-headed, Grace Yardley tossed clothes into a suitcase.

'My last night here,' she cried. 'Somehow, I always knew you'd do it.'

And lifting her face, she offered a chaste, grateful kiss. Stepping back, her grey eyes wide and serious, she added, 'Give me a little time. Then I'll thank you properly.'

Coming from any other woman, a promise to quicken the blood; but he could set no great store by it. He still couldn't fathom her, couldn't predict her moods. In spite of everything, she remained a lovely, tantalising and intensely private enigma.

Ignoring the accumulation of briefs on his desk, he took

220

time off, walking in the park, feeding the ducks, basking in the spring sunshine. He had to unwind, to dispel the aura of personal involvement, before he could consider purely legal issues again. And be ready for Stanmore's summons, which came a week later.

Stanmore was old school, and favoured the ultra-conservative. Half-panelled walls, sombre colours, heavy drapery and massive furniture. On this grey April morning, it was a setting of gloomy dignity, designed to impose and intimidate.

'See,' he breathed, as Nigel entered, 'the conquering hero comes.' Grim and sardonic, not a smile in sight.

'Forgive me for not joining the general adulation,' he continued, without a trace of regret, 'I reserve that for genuine achievement.'

'She *was* acquitted, sir,' Nigel pointed out reasonably, and Stanmore's anger took flame.

'Against my express direction! If you expect me to applaud such monstrous perversity, you are sadly mistaken, m'boy.' Controlling himself with a visible effort, he added, 'I will concede that you manipulated me along with everyone else. Subtle timing, brilliant showmanship. If that gives you pleasure, you're welcome. Pure theatre, Buxton, a contrived conflict of personalities and emotions devoid of any claim to legality.' Assuming an expression of intense disgust, Stanmore flung Nigel's own words in his face.

'"Does she look like a murderess? Does she deserve to be punished? A trial which transcends the law." All you needed was a barrel-organ and a monkey! You were after charity, man, not justice!'

A beam of watery sunlight stole between the curtains, glinting on dust-specks and falling on a single print. A stag at bay; very appropriate.

'Look sir,' Nigel said persuasively, 'I can understand how it might have looked, but I couldn't see any alternative. First duty to the client; even you must grant me that.'

'Exactly! The honourable course was perfectly clear – plead and invoke mercy. She would have escaped very lightly, no one wanted her victimised. You took appalling and quite unwarranted risks; duty to the client indeed!'

Then, abruptly, his anger appeared to dissolve. He studied Nigel across the desk, shrewd and assessing.

'You say you understand how it looked; I wonder if you do.'

Nigel waited, hearing the muted rumble of traffic from somewhere outside. In this mood, the CJ seemed much more formidable.

'It has been suggested, d'you see,' Stanmore murmured, 'that the whole farrago was engineered with a single aim in view; the greater glorification of Nigel Buxton, QC.'

'I hope you can substantiate that, Sir George!'

Stanmore smiled, faint and ominous.

'Of course I can't; neither will the rumour go beyond these chambers.' He glanced around, taking obvious pleasure from the ornate room.

'On balance,' he explained, 'my advisers consider your conduct reprehensible, but not quite beyond the pale. An enquiry would merely prolong the affair, focus public attention where it is least desired. The vulgar demonstrations in court were quite sufficient to make the point. The sooner this case is decently buried the better.' He raised his eyebrows quizzically. 'No doubt you counted on that?'

'It did occur to me,' Nigel admitted equably; and Stanmore pounced.

'You have no cause for complacency! Erskine is a good deal less sanguine!'

'Erskine?'

'An ambition to match your own, Buxton. He had hoped, with every justification, to take a part in an important trial. Instead, he was treated like the humblest clerk, reduced to a mere spectator. He regards it as a public humiliation; in his own words, playing skivvy to the silk. With difficulty, I persuaded him not to make an outcry.'

'Very generous of you, I'm sure.'

'Take care, m'boy. You're already here on sufferance.'

'Sir George, I told Erskine at the start – my risks, my responsibility. He should thank his lucky stars! As for his – suggestions – they hardly do him credit!'

'Be that as it may,' replied Stanmore, in a tone which boded ill for Mr Erskine, 'he has let them be known in a number of influential circles. At this moment you are the villain of the piece, and I am subject to considerable pressure.'

Briefly, he unbent, the sun soothing the hardness from his face. Leaning forward, speaking man to man, he said, 'You *were* over-zealous, anyone could see your commitment went beyond the merely professional. Can't you give me some explanation, something personal, perhaps, which they could understand?'

He was invoking his own past, inviting an indiscretion. We were all young once, he was implying, fair game for a well-turned ankle. The petticoat pitfall; well, he should know.

It was a tempting proposal, an easy and obvious excuse. Give them something to chuckle about over their port; and something to hold over him, now and later.

Firmly, meeting Stanmore's eye, Nigel said, 'I can't oblige you, sir. It simply isn't true.' The musty air was still and quiet. Stanmore sighed and leaned back, retreating to the shadows. His voice emerged, weary and tinged with disdain.

'The tycoons of this world, Buxton, have a standard remedy for such corporate ailments. They call it, I believe, kicking an embarrassment upstairs.'

About to protest this assessment, Nigel took in the complete statement; and waited.

'I'm offering a judicial appointment, m'boy.'

An instant of incredulous delight, the prize within reach. But Stanmore, reading his expression, was already hurrying on.

'Don't jump to conclusions. The appointment is in Hong Kong.'

The sheer unexpectedness stunned him, left him literally breathless.

'But I never asked ... It wasn't my intention to ...' He shook his head, bereft of words.

'Nevertheless,' Stanmore declared strongly, 'it is a proposal you would be ill advised to reject without very careful thought.'

As a semblance of balance returned and the implications

223

took form, Nigel had to admire the old man's cunning. A grey fox in a gloomy den.

Superficially, a promotion, the reward for spectacular success. Declining it would brand him, Nigel, an ingrate, and uppity with it; he was still very young to be a judge. Those in the know – Stanmore's cronies, Erskine and his highly placed friends – would read the message clearly; win or lose, you cross the CJ at your peril. And even this charge Stanmore could deny. Judicial posts in the colonies and ex-colonies were reserved for has-beens, out to pasture and beefing up their pensions; and young pretenders too impatient to wait for dead men's shoes. Stanmore would consign Nigel to the latter category, thus silencing the inquisitive.

I should've known, Nigel thought. Powerful old men are never beaten; even the appearance of victory must be bought at a price.

'Suppose I decline,' he muttered. 'Make a few – suggestions – to *my* friends?'

'What friends?' Stanmore asked, quite gently. 'The soft-liners, the social scientists, the liberal press? You must be realistic, m'boy.' Stanmore shifted, the light catching his expression. He looked old, and cold and inviolate.

'You're drumming me out, then,' said Nigel, aware of the tremor in his own voice.

'My dear chap,' protested Stanmore, 'no one would dream of such a thing.'

Slyly, he went on, 'After your recent triumph, any number of people will be clamouring for your services.' He gave the word 'people' a contemptuous ring; he meant hard-case, lost-cause criminals in search of a miracle. 'Enough, certainly to keep you busy, in the public eye; and very decently off, I imagine.'

A master of the unvoiced threat, Stanmore. He was saying, with perfect clarity, you can bid goodbye to ever presiding over a High Court in England. Saying it, meaning it, and having the power to enforce it. *What* a price! The taste of defeat like bile in his throat, Nigel asked, 'And if I go? If I'm a good boy?'

Suddenly, Stanmore was smiling, genial and expansive. 'A

fascinating place, m'boy, a real test for law-givers. Three cultures, some of the loveliest women in the world. I envy you, really.' He made it sound like a travelogue – *and as the sun sets slowly over Kowloon.* Why don't *you* go, you bloody old fraud.

Aloud, Nigel said, 'Go east, young man, is that it?'

'It's not for ever, d'you see', Stanmore consoled him. 'Two-year contracts, renewable by mutual consent. A solid performance to reassure the doubters, those who question your motives.' He paused, almost avuncular. 'After that, who knows? I haven't forgotten the acolytes; neither should you.'

'The return of the prodigal?' Stanmore's face tightened.

'I make no promises.' Another telling pause, then, 'I mentioned this once before; you'd do well to remember. Marriage does wonders for a man, publicly and privately. Leaves less ground for speculation, d'you see.'

He was brisk now, and dismissive.

'The offer stands for ten days. Let me know, won't you.'

Coming home from the Falklands must've been a bit like this, Evans reckoned. Two weeks of life or death, then back to blanco and square-bashing. Wanted a bit of getting used to. He tackled it by degrees, closing the file, gathering the threads, relying on Beddoes for the latest gen. Humdrum, but he'd live with it; enough excitement, thank you very much. Before long, he must see Grace. There was something she had to know, a few questions he had to ask. But Smythe beat him to the punch; he'd been expecting it, really.

Beddoes delivered the message; and a warning.

'The Super is desirous of your company, uncle. Like, now. Walk soft, OK? 'E's a bit jumpy, Gloria says.'

'Gloria?'

'His secretary. You know, the one with the boobs.'

'Oh aye. Friend of yours?'

Beddoes grinned.

'Off 'n' on.'

'I'll bet. You ought to slow down. Could be fatal, over-doing it.'

Beddoes rolled his eyes.

'Whadda way to go!'

A beautiful April morning, mild and clear and bright. Seven-a-side sunshine. From Smythe's window, for once, you *could* see across the river, and beyond. Perversely, the Super sat at his desk, his back to the view. Perhaps he's a bad-weather man, Evans reflected; looks a bit stormy.

'Well, well, Inspector Evans. Sure you can spare the time?'

'Not a lot on at the moment actually, sir.'

'*Actually*, Inspector, that's hardly news. For at least six months.'

'Closing the file, sir, like you said.'

Smythe was handling the paperweight, dead iridesence through the perspex.

'Must've been comforting. She made a fool of everyone else, it seems.'

Playing along, Evans grunted, 'Cleverer than me, mind, most of them.'

'Not the most demanding of criteria, these days.'

Done with sparring, Smythe set the butterfly down and hunched forward aggressively.

'The Pillock doesn't share your opinion of the lovely Miss Yardley. His witnesses came unstuck, he took some stick from the judge.' Clearly, these mishaps caused Smythe little grief. 'Highland pride has been injured, you understand, the clans must be avenged. More likely, I suspect, excuses must be found. Anyway, McKay has hinted that you might, after all, have stumbled on information you chose to conceal. He made much, the Commissioner says, of your televised indiscretion.' Smythe shook his head, a moment of genuine sympathy. 'He really is insufferable.'

Evans sat very still, cold despite the sun on his face. Charlesworth might sell his mother for five pence, but Hunter wouldn't crack, not in a million years. The Pillock was guessing then, had to be. Close to home, though. Choosing words carefully, he said, 'I found nothing for the prosecutor, sir. Not for lack of trying, mind. I had every reason.'

Smythe nodded.

'More or less what I told the Commissioner. Even so, there

226

was a bargain and you failed to deliver. The time has come for the reckoning I promised.'

From an adjoining room came the faint sounds of a type-writer, clack and ping. A helicopter drifted along the horizon, slow and noiseless as a distant bee. Smythe looked weary and embarrassed, doing his duty, not liking it.

'The annual reshuffle is upon us. Not, I'm afraid, the usual formality. McKay claims he needs reinforcements of your rank. In the traffic section.' A swift, defensive glance. 'You are both Celts, after all, both Non-conformists. No doubt you will discover common ground.'

'Oh sure,' Evans snapped. 'In the chapel cemetery. Eventually.'

At last, Smythe did get up and trail to the window. Nothing he saw, apparently, gave him pleasure.

'Oddly enough,' he admitted, 'I don't like it any more than you. I'm stymied, though. Your Miss Yardley has drawn blood, and the Commissioner's hunting scapegoats.'

'Aye,' said Evans, sour and low. 'Well, I'd best be on my way.' He paused, squinting at Smythe's trim figure against the blue brightness. 'One thing you should know, before I go. About the Irish connection, see.'

Smythe didn't bother to turn, just a wag of head.

'Come, Inspector, Smythe's folly, the station joke? You'll have to do better than that.'

Jesi Mawr, thought Evans, I'll need to show him the statement. Urgently, he said, 'Remember the markings, sir, on her gun? Not evidence, but suggestive?'

'You're flogging a dead horse.'

Evans swallowed, breathing fast. 'That gun came from someone Charlesworth knew; someone higher up.'

Smythe rounded on him; livid. 'McKay was right, you *did* withhold information. It's not traffic for you, Evans, it's the bloody lock-up!'

'Go easy, sir. Nothing for the prosecutor, and that's God's truth.'

'Two minutes, Evans. After that I'll book you for obs-truction and sweat you dry!'

'No need, sir. I'm on your side.'

227

'Ah, something new, at last!' But his curiosity was stirring, he just couldn't resist it. Strike while the iron's hot, boyo.

'Look, sir, the army'll not admit it, but they know, same as us, where that gun went. There's more, mind. Given time, a lot more.' Keeping it quick, naming no one, he outlined Hunter's part in the affair. Smythe listened, doubtful but intent, drumming his fingers lightly against the glass.

'He owes me personally, see. Not the force, not a replacement; me. He's in the big league now, untouchable. Wherever we meet, there's an alibi you couldn't crack with gelly. I want to use him, sir, not just for the gun. There's gold in him, mind; I can smell it.'

Slowly, Smythe came back and sat down, never taking his eyes off Evans's face.

'Let me get this straight. An anonymous source, information on trust. A vague link, maybe, into arms deals and the IRA. A gambling boss who's going straight. He's going to talk to an inspector? This is how I buy off the Commissioner?'

'I won't name him, sir, now or ever. He's leery of the hard men. It's only a hope, nothing more. But it's not the sort of thing they do, in traffic. And I'd hate to hand it to the Pillock.'

'Me too,' breathed Smythe. 'Go and catch a villain, or something; justify your existence. I've got to think.'

He phoned Grace that evening. No time to lose, now. At first she sounded pleased, a chance to thank him. When he asked to see her, her tone altered; skittish and elusive. She hadn't changed, then.

'It's not what you think,' he explained. 'Business, really, things we need to discuss.' She was sorting herself out, settling down. Couldn't it wait? For some reason, he had a feeling she wasn't alone. He was edgy himself, waiting for Smythe, and he got quite shirty.

'It's vital, girl, for both of us. I could come anyway, you know.' And still she baulked.

'Listen, I know about the gun, where you got it and who from. Also how. Now, when do we meet?'

He heard her indrawn breath, sensed her sudden tension.

228

Finally, she snapped, 'Tomorrow, here, at seven,' and hung up.

She *had* changed, he saw it at once. Nothing to put your finger on, she was just – alive. But as cool and reserved as he'd ever known her. The room looked the same; might've been back in September, when it all started. She offered tea, the ritual gesture, giving nothing; and he accepted, anything to break the ice. But she wouldn't have it. She prowled; beautiful and somehow menacing. He was seeing it now, the hardness, the central, implacable will which had driven her for so long. For a wild, passing moment, he actually thought she might be setting herself for a crack at *him*.

Finally, sullen and resentful, she muttered, 'You'd better tell me what you want.' She stood near the window, hunched and defensive. And suddenly, he understood. She was seeing someone, she was afraid he'd try some kind of emotional blackmail. That's what it's done to her, he thought, in anger and sorrow, made her expect the worst.

'Look,' he said gently. 'It's me, Evans. Still looking out for you, I am.'

Her eyes softened, but she wasn't convinced, not yet.

'I know most of it,' he reminded her, 'I was there, start to finish, more or less. A couple of questions, then.'

She nodded, resigned and apologetic.

'I suppose I owe you that much, at least. I'm sorry. I thought ...'

'Doesn't matter what you thought, and you owe me nothing. But still.'

He finished his tea, set the cup aside. She gazed at him, waiting; the beginnings of trust? Enough for him, anyway.

'Hunter told me the whole story,' he said. 'Never mind why: he did. How you reached him through Charlesworth, what you promised and what you actually paid; and what you didn't.'

Her head came up, the old defiant pride.

'Is it true?' he asked, and she nodded.

'Every word. You heard what I said in court; my only weapon.'

'Fair enough. We're at the heart of it now, mind. No more evasions. It's very important.'

'It's over,' she said quietly, 'I don't need to hide anything.' She hesitated. 'Not from you, anyway.'

For the first time, he was reading her, picking up every shade of meaning. Just as well, really. She sat down, her usual composure returning.

'Last question. Did Hunter give you any idea where the gun came from? A name, a place, anything at all? Think about it, girl; I need to know.' She obeyed, her grey eyes smoky with concentration. The silence extended, in no way uncomfortable. At last her eyes cleared, she faced him steadily.

'No.'

'And you contacted no one else, just the whores, a few drunks, Charlesworth and Hunter? No one else knew what you were after?'

'You said last question. But the answer's still no. Inspector, I didn't want *anyone* to know.'

As clear a truth as he'd ever heard.

'All right, Grace. I won't tell anyone, ever, and I'll see that Hunter doesn't, either.'

She smiled then, warm and tearful, dazzling.

'I never thought you would. But thank you, anyway.'

It would be nice to take her hand for the next bit. Just for reassurance, mind. Carefully, he said, 'They'll hound you, Grace, as long as you stay here. Like it or not, you're a star. TV, the papers, mark my words, some clown will even want to buy the movie rights. There's something about the gun, too, something we have to follow up. Sounds crazy, I know, melodramatic. But you could be in danger, one day. Some nasties in this lot, somewhere; very nasty indeed.'

No tears now, a real smile, one you'd go a long way to see.

'I'm saying this: you ought to get away, change your name.'

'Funny,' she murmured. 'That's exactly what I have in mind.'

It wasn't intuition, he'd never been more certain of anything.

'In love then, are you?'

Instantly, she was gone again, her eyes dark and withdrawn,

her body tight and defensive. Slowly, very slowly, she relaxed, gave him a steady, direct stare.

'I loved my daughter, Inspector. Briefly, and in a very different way, I loved her father, too. How many chances do we get, I wonder? I'm afraid of love; I don't know if I'm capable any more. For the moment, I'll settle for comfort and security and someone who'll cherish me. Is that very selfish?'

A moment of complete intimacy, the appeal against which he'd always been helpless.

'No more than you deserve, I'd say. Decent type, is he?'

'Ever the policeman, Inspector.' She was laughing at him gently, not to hurt. He grinned shamefacedly.

'Bad habits. No offence.'

'You can relax. He's quite distinguished, in his way, and he's going to work abroad.' She looked away, shy and excited. 'He doesn't know it yet, but I'm going with him.' Essentially she'd never change, he thought, yet she changed by the minute. Quite a handful, mind, a woman for all seasons.

She stood up, slim and straight, her eyes bright with pleasure and regret.

'I'll never be able to repay you; sorry is such a silly word.' She offered her hand and he took it firmly, the very last contact. It didn't hurt much, really.

'I won't forget, Inspector. Ever.'

Gruffly, he said, 'Good luck, Grace. Mind how you go.'

A week of suspense, the weather in and out and Smythe in his eyrie, brooding. A week of coming to terms, of forgetting something which could never have been, whatever. A week of driving past the man on point duty and smiling, just in case. Traffic section, there's nice. He managed quite well, really. She'd given him something; one day, maybe he'd grasp what it was. Self-knowledge? Something worthwhile, anyway.

City played their last league match, floodlit, Thursday night. On Friday, Beddoes trooped in, soaked, the face of tragedy.

'Bleedin clowns,' he raged, 'only needed a win to stay up. One–nil and three minutes to go, and the soddin fullback slots a lovely back-'eader. Past 'is own keeper!'

'It's in the paper, boyo. 'Ard lines. Second Division's better, they say. Less pressure.'

'Cobblers!' snapped Beddoes, in deep disgust. 'Bunch of cloggers and 'as-bins. Kick 'n' rush.'

'Always pop over and watch United.'

'Do me a favour! Me Dad'll kill me. Bloody heresy, that is.' Still desolate, Beddoes hunched over the newspaper.

Wonder if the traffic lads get duty at Twickers, thought Evans.

'Hey,' said Beddoes, 'your mate Buxton's done all right. Made 'im a judge, it says 'ere.'

'Read the small print,' Evans advised. 'He's off to Hong Kong. Upset the CJ, didn't he.'

'That's a punishment?' Beddoes asked in wonder. 'Crumpet capital of the world, mate. Tell you what, I wouldn't mind a sentence like that.'

'Go blind, you would.'

'No problem. Have to feel my way, wouldn't I.'

Out of nowhere, Evans made a connection. *Distinguished in his field, going abroad soon.* Could she mean Buxton ...? How long would *that* last ...? Not your business, boyo; not any more. He doesn't know it yet, she'd said. Well, he'd know by now, poor dab. *Lucky* dab.

Outside, the rain came on again, and he stared at the familiar, faded paintwork. A bit like that Sunday, really. Any minute, the phone'll ring and ... The phone rang. Beddoes grabbed it, grunted, sat to attention. He listened head cocked, eyeing Evans curiously. Finally, he said, 'Yessir,' and replaced the receiver gently.

"Ere,' he said accusingly. 'What've you been up to? Smythe, no less, with a funny little message for you. Ready?'

Evans held his breath.

'Tell the Inspector, he says, Scotch is off, he'll 'ave to settle for Irish. Make any sense?'

'Oh sure,' Evans said, grinning.